THAT'S AMORE

Praise for Georgia Beers

Whisk Me Away

Whisk Me Away "was exactly what I hoped for…and then some. From the first bite (err, chapter), I was hooked by the irresistible setup: two rival pastry chefs with sizzling tension, creative drive, and just enough baggage to make the stakes feel real. Regan's passion and persistence clashed so beautifully with Ava's cool confidence, and watching them go from frosty to fiery was a total delight. This isn't just your average "rivals forced to work together" trope. There's heart here, real emotional growth wrapped in buttery layers of tension, vulnerability, and personal redemption (and growth)…If you're into slow-burn sapphic romances with snark, sweetness, and soul, this one's worth devouring."—*Brian's Book Blog*

Can't Buy Me Love

"Everything about the story and the characters was exciting and I adored every minute. It had everything from the magical moments of instant attraction to the misunderstandings that cause all the drama that every great romance needs…A great story, lots of humorous moments, some heartfelt ones, and lots of cute getting to know one another ones as well. I really, really enjoyed the story and will definitely be reading it again."—*LesbiReviewed*

Aubrey McFadden Is Never Getting Married

"Georgia Beers has become a household name in the world of LGBTQ+ romance novels, and her latest work, *Aubrey McFadden Is Never Getting Married*, proves she is worthy of the attention. With its captivating characters, engaging plot, and impactful themes, this book is a pure delight to read. Its enemies-to-lovers narrative tugs at the heart, making one hope for resolution and forgiveness between its leading ladies. Aubrey and Monica's push-and-pull dynamic is complicated and knotty, but Beers keeps it fun with her quick wit and sense of humor. The crafty banter ensures that readers have a good time."—*Women Using Words*

Playing with Matches

"*Playing with Matches* is a delightful exploration of small town life, family drama, and true love…Liz and Cori are charming characters with undeniable chemistry, and their sweet and tender small town, 'fake-dating' love story is sure to capture the attention of readers. Their journey reminds readers of the importance of love, forgiveness, family, and community, making this feel-good romance a true triumph."
—*Women Using Words*

Peaches and Cream

"*Peaches and Cream* is a fresh, new spin on the classic rom-com *You've Got Mail*—except it's even better because it's all about ice cream!… [A] delicious, melt-in-your-mouth scoop of goodness. Bursting with tasty characters in a scrumptious story world, *Peaches and Cream* is simply irresistible."—*Women Using Words*

Lambda Literary Award Winner *Dance with Me*

"I admit I inherited my two left feet from my father's side of the family. Dancing is not something I enjoy, so why choose a book with dancing as the central focus and romance as the payoff? Easy. Because it's Georgia Beers, and she will let me enjoy being awkward alongside her main character. I think this is what makes her special to me as an author. While her characters might be beautiful in their own ways, I can relate to their challenges, fears and dreams. Comfort reads every time."
—*Late Night Lesbian Reads*

Camp Lost and Found

"I really like when Beers writes about winter and snow and hot chocolate. She makes heartache feel cosy and surmountable. *Camp Lost and Found* made me smile a lot, laugh at times, tear up more often than I care to share. If you're looking for a heartwarming story to keep the cold weather at bay, I'd recommend you give it a chance."—*Jude in the Stars*

Cherry on Top

"*Cherry on Top* is another wonderful story from one of the greatest writers in sapphic fiction...This is more than a romance with two incredibly charming and wonderful characters. It is a reminder that you shouldn't have to compromise who you are to fit into a box that society wants to put you into. Georgia Beers once again creates a couple with wonderful chemistry who will warm your heart."—*Sapphic Book Review*

The Secret Poet

"[O]ne of the author's best works and one of the best romances I've read recently...I was so invested in [Morgan and Zoe] I read the book in one sitting."—*Melina Bickard, Librarian, Waterloo Library (UK)*

On the Rocks

"This book made me so happy! And kept me awake way too late." —*Jude in the Stars*

Hopeless Romantic

"Thank you, Georgia Beers, for this unabashed paean to the pleasure of escaping into romantic comedies...If you want to have a big smile plastered on your face as you read a romance novel, do not hesitate to pick up this one!"—*The Rainbow Bookworm*

Flavor of the Month

"Beers whips up a sweet lesbian romance...brimming with mouthwatering descriptions of foodie indulgences...Both women are well-intentioned and endearing, and it's easy to root for their inevitable reconciliation. But once the couple rediscover their natural ease with one another, Beers throws a challenging emotional hurdle in their path, forcing them to fight through tragedy to earn their happy ending." —*Publishers Weekly*

Fear of Falling

"Enough tension and drama for us to wonder if this can work out—and enough heat to keep the pages turning. I will definitely recommend this to others—Georgia Beers continues to go from strength to strength."
—*Evan Blood, Bookseller (Angus & Robertson, Australia)*

One Walk in Winter

"A sweet story to pair with the holidays. There are plenty of 'moment's in this book that make the heart soar. Just what I like in a romance. Situations where sparks fly, hearts fill, and tears fall. This book shined with cute fairy trails and swoon-worthy Christmas gifts...REALLY nice and cozy if read in between Thanksgiving and Christmas. Covered in blankets. By a fire."—*Bookvark*

The Do-Over

"You can count on Beers to give you a quality well-paced book each and every time."—*The Romantic Reader Blog*

"*The Do-Over* is a shining example of the brilliance of Georgia Beers as a contemporary romance author."—*Rainbow Reflections*

The Shape of You

The Shape of You "catches you right in the feels and does not let go. It is a must for every person out there who has struggled with self-esteem, questioned their judgment, and settled for a less than perfect but safe lover. If you've ever been convinced you have to trade passion for emotional safety, this book is for you."—*Writing While Distracted*

"I know I always say this about Georgia Beers's books, but there is no one that writes first kisses like her. They are hot, steamy and all too much!"—*Les Rêveur*

Calendar Girl

"A sweet, sweet romcom of a story…*Calendar Girl* is a nice read, which you may find yourself returning to when you want a hot-chocolate-and-warm-comfort-hug in your life."—*Best Lesbian Erotica*

Blend

"You know a book is good, first, when you don't want to put it down. Second, you know it's damn good when you're reading it and thinking, I'm totally going to read this one again. Great read and absolutely a 5-star romance."—*The Romantic Reader Blog*

"This is a lovely romantic story with relatable characters that have depth and chemistry. A charming easy story that kept me reading until the end. Very enjoyable."—*Kat Adams, Bookseller, QBD (Australia)*

Right Here, Right Now

"[A] successful and entertaining queer romance novel. The main characters are appealing, and the situations they deal with are realistic and well-managed. I would recommend this book to anyone who enjoys a good queer romance novel, and particularly one grounded in real world situations."—*Books at the End of the Alphabet*

"[A]n engaging odd-couple romance. Beers creates a romance of gentle humor that allows no-nonsense Lacey to relax and easygoing Alicia to find a trusting heart."—*RT Book Reviews*

Lambda Literary Award Winner *Fresh Tracks*

"[T]he focus switches each chapter to a different character, allowing for a measured pace and deep, sincere exploration of each protagonist's thoughts. Beers gives a welcome expansion to the romance genre with her clear, sympathetic writing."—*Curve magazine*

Lambda Literary Award Finalist *Finding Home*

"Georgia Beers has proven in her popular novels such as *Too Close to Touch* and *Fresh Tracks* that she has a special way of building romance with suspense that puts the reader on the edge of their seat. *Finding Home*, though more character driven than suspense, will equally keep the reader engaged at each page turn with its sweet romance."—*Lambda Literary Review*

Mine

"Beers does a fine job of capturing the essence of grief in an authentic way. *Mine* is touching, life-affirming, and sweet."—*Lesbian News Book Review*

Too Close to Touch

"This is such a well-written book. The pacing is perfect, the romance is great, the character work strong, and damn, but is the sex writing ever fantastic."—*The Lesbian Review*

"In her third novel, Georgia Beers delivers an immensely satisfying story. Beers knows how to generate sexual tension so taut it could be cut with a knife...Beers weaves a tale of yearning, love, lust, and conflict resolution. She has constructed a believable plot, with strong characters in a charming setting."—*Just About Write*

By the Author

Romances

Turning the Page

Thy Neighbor's Wife

Too Close to Touch

Fresh Tracks

Mine

Finding Home

Starting from Scratch

96 Hours

Slices of Life

Snow Globe

Olive Oil & White Bread

Zero Visibility

A Little Bit of Spice

What Matters Most

Right Here, Right Now

Blend

The Shape of You

Calendar Girl

The Do-Over

Fear of Falling

One Walk in Winter

Flavor of the Month

Hopeless Romantic

16 Steps to Forever

The Secret Poet

Cherry on Top

Camp Lost and Found

Dance with Me

Peaches and Cream

Playing with Matches

Aubrey McFadden
Is Never Getting Married

Can't Buy Me Love

This Christmas

Whisk Me Away

That's Amore

The Puppy Love Romances

Rescued Heart

Run to You

Dare to Stay

The Swizzle Stick Romances

Shaken or Stirred

On the Rocks

With a Twist

Visit us at www.boldstrokesbooks.com

THAT'S AMORE

by
Georgia Beers

2025

THAT'S AMORE

ISBN 13: 978-1-63679-841-7

THIS TRADE PAPERBACK ORIGINAL IS PUBLISHED BY
BOLD STROKES BOOKS, INC.
P.O. BOX 249
VALLEY FALLS, NY 12185

FIRST EDITION: AUGUST 2025

CREDITS
EDITORS: LYNDA SANDOVAL AND STACIA SEAMAN
PRODUCTION DESIGN: STACIA SEAMAN
COVER DESIGN BY INKSPIRAL DESIGN

Acknowledgments

Here's a thing about me you might not know: I do not have an adventurous spirit. I'm not sure why. Maybe because, as a kid, I moved a lot. I changed schools a ton (including for my senior year of high school). Maybe that feeling of never quite being settled is why I now love to be home. I'm fine taking short trips around the country for conferences or book events, but I don't have that pull to go overseas, to visit other countries like so many folks I know. I just don't. I want to be home in my space with my stuff and my animals. It's where I'm happiest and most comfortable.

However.

Not long ago, I was coaxed into taking a cruise with several members of my family. We'd fly into Rome, Italy, stay there for a few days, then board a cruise ship that would take us to several other stops in Italy, as well as Greece and Malta. I actually don't mind cruising (mostly because all my stuff stays in the same place) and the trip was pretty amazing, but my favorite part was definitely those first four days in Rome. I loved everything about it—the food, the architecture, the food, the history, the people, the food—and the second I was on the plane home, I knew I wanted to set a novel there. (To be clear, no, I did not start a whirlwind affair with a sexy Italian woman while I was there, but I did go on a food tour led by a sexy Italian woman that sparked the idea for this book. Marta, wherever you are, thank you for the inspiration. This one's for you.)

Now for the somewhat repetitive, but always necessary gratitude:

The state of the US has been so many things recently, none of them good. Families and friends have been divided (mine included) and there's a real fear around being anything but straight, white, and male. It's stressful for me (as I'm sure it is for many of my fellow Americans) to wake up each morning bracing for whatever bad news is coming today. People are worried about money, which means a decline in the sale of luxury items. That includes books. So, if you're reading this, I thank you from the bottom of my heart for trusting me to deliver something worth you spending your hard-earned, hard-saved money. I'll do everything I can not to let you down.

Thank you to my amazing editor, Lynda Sandoval, for keeping my spirits up and making me laugh, while at the same time, making me look like the best writer I can possibly be. I've learned so much from her over the years, and I look forward to continuing to do so. Also, the eagle eyes of my copy editor, Stacia Seaman, have saved me more than once, and I am eternally grateful for her ability to catch things the rest of us miss. I don't know what I'd do without this awesome duo!

As always, thank you to everyone at Bold Strokes Books who keep things running smoothly behind the scenes. I've said it before, but we now seem to be in a world where most of the recognition on socials and from reviewers is going to the Indies or the Big Publishers, and as an author at a small press, it's become alarmingly easy to be overlooked or even forgotten. I'm hoping that changes and the pendulum swings back the other way, but in the meantime, BSB keeps me focused and takes good care of me. I appreciate that more than anybody there knows.

And last, but never least, to my crazy, chaotic, unconventional family. I never in a million years expected to be a Gigi, but here I am, with four toddlers who live two doors down and who make me feel more loved than I ever thought possible. They climb on me like I'm a jungle gym, they sneeze directly into my eyeballs, they cover me with soggy peanut butter and squished strawberries, and they give the best hugs in the world. I am so very grateful for them.

To everybody who has ever felt unlovable, unchosen, unvalued.

You're not. You're not. You're not.

CHAPTER ONE

I need more suet.

It's the thought that runs most prominently through my head as I sit at my desk, looking out the big picture window of my office and into my backyard. Certainly a better thought than "What the fuck should I write?" which has been the mantra for the past several weeks and will absolutely take over my brain if I don't work hard to focus on the birds.

Honestly, the amount of money I spend on birdseed and suet and peanuts in the shells for the squirrels (squirrels gotta eat, too!) and little dried out corn cobs is insane. I am single-handedly keeping the birdseed company in business.

I sit back in my very comfortable desk chair, pushing it back enough so my feet don't touch the ground, and blow out a huge breath. I'm doing that a lot lately. The sighing. The pathetic sighing. I sound like a leaky steam pipe half the time because all I can think of now is what if I'm tapped out?

Oh, God, what if I actually *am* tapped out?

No more ideas. No more meet-cutes. No more dark moments. No more happily ever afters. Maybe I have a limit. A finite number of stories within me, and I've used them all up. Maybe it's time to look for a new career. I could probably get a job bagging groceries. Or maybe as the person that sprays down cars before they head into the car wash. I always thought it would be fun to use that water gun thingie. And I bet spraying off bird poop or caked-on mud is very satisfying...

"Oh my God, stop. Just stop."

Reggie lifts his little head from his dog bed and gives me a look with his beady, marble-sized Chihuahua eyes. He's as tired of my pathetic whining as I am, I'm sure. If he could roll those buggy eyes, I bet he would.

I gesture to my keyboard and say to him, "Listen, you're welcome to give it a shot. Maybe you should start pulling your weight around here, you know? I don't see you doing anything to contribute to the mortgage."

He continues to look at me for a good five seconds, then puts his head back down and closes his eyes with a sigh that says he is a very put-upon dog.

"Uh-huh. That's what I thought."

The cardinal couple is back. She pecks at the ground while he sits on the feeder and knocks seed down to her. Now, that's true love. One squirrel chases another away, and I raise my voice and tell them there's enough for all of them, as if they not only hear me but understand. My gaze wanders back to my computer monitor and its antagonizing goddamn blinking cursor and the field of white on the screen. It does say, "Chapter One," so I've actually written two words today.

Not bad for a day's work.

A groan of irritation rumbles up from my throat just as my phone buzzes on my desk. A glance at it tells me it's my agent. Great. I seriously consider not answering it, but he's not only my agent, he's kinda my really good friend. A text pops up on my screen.

Birds'll wait...answer the damn phone.

Shit. I hate that he knows me so well.

"I'll have you know the birds are far more entertaining than anything on my computer screen right now," I say by way of greeting.

"Why would you tell me that? I don't want to hear that." Scott's teasing, but then his voice goes slightly soft. "Still struggling?" And is that sympathy I detect? I'm not sure, but it's not what I expect from him. He's usually a slave driver, a drill sergeant, and a badass all rolled into one—which really is what you want in an agent. But he can also be a teddy bear, which is a good quality in a friend, and he knows that I've never had this kind of problem before. He doesn't take it lightly, and I appreciate that more than he knows.

"A little, yeah." That's a lie. It's not a little. It's a lot. It's huge. I have a block the size of Montana, and I have no idea how to get past it.

"Well, I have an idea." Scott's voice rises a little in tone, as if he can barely contain his excitement, and I'm already worried.

"Okay." I draw the word out so it has about five syllables, unsure where this is going. Plus, I love it when people who don't write give me writing advice. So awesome.

"So, I was talking to Devon last night." Devon is Scott's husband, a super sweet guy who owns a moving company.

"He's too good for you." My standard line when Devon is introduced into the conversation.

"Tell me about it," Scott says, his standard reply. "But I was telling him about your struggle."

"Oh, good." I try to keep the sarcasm out of my voice. I fail.

"No, hear me out. His sister got back from her honeymoon last month and can't stop talking about it, how romantic it was, that it was the most romantic place she'd ever been. And I got to thinking, what better way to inspire some romance? Going to a romantic spot, so... how would you feel about a change of venue? For a few weeks or even a few months. Could that unstick you?"

"A change of—like, go someplace else and try to write?"

"Exactly."

"Where was this most romantic place?" I brace myself, expecting him to tell me I need to go off into a cabin in the forest or isolate myself by some obscure lake on a mountain. Neither of which sounds terrible, mind you, but I'm already pretty isolated at my own house, and it hasn't helped.

"Rome." He's practically giddy. I can hear it in his voice.

"Rome? *Rome* Rome? As in *Italy* Rome? That Rome?"

"Exactly that Rome, yes."

Okay, so not isolated. Not close, either, not by a long shot. "Ugh. I don't know, Scott."

"Come on, Lils, all that history? The art? The *food*? I mean, think of the wine, for Christ's sake." We both chuckle at that, and he goes on, but his voice does that softening thing again, and it occurs to me that he might actually be worried about me. "Don't you think you could find some inspiration there?"

I hate to let him down, as my agent and as my friend. And I am kind of stuck as to how I can break this block. "Lemme think about it?"

His relief is almost palpable. "Absolutely. In the meantime, I'll send you some of the info Devon's sister gave me. Places to visit, restaurants to check out. I even have a place for you to stay."

"You've done some work on this already, I see." I want to be mildly insulted, but I'm actually not. I'm not surprised either. Scott is good at his job because he's always prepared. Like I said: He excels at badassery.

We hang up after I promise I *will* actually think about it, that I'm not just killing time before saying no. Using my toes, I spin my chair around so my back is to my desk, and I take a good look around my office.

It's a sizable space because I live in a sizable house. There are four framed movie posters hanging on the walls—four of my books have been made into screenplays. There are awards on one shelf, polished and shiny, some glass, others brass or gold-plated, various writing awards. Not bad for a romance writer. We don't get a ton of credit, since we're rarely considered "literary." Which is bullshit, but don't get me started. That's another topic for another day. I've got photos of Reggie everywhere, because he's adorable, and also because I'm a childless, crazy dog mom who loves her pet more than life itself. My desk is large, my laptop state of the art. My chair is leather, ergonomic, and expensive. I had shelves built on two walls and over and around the doorway, and they're stocked with books. It's my favorite room in the house, truth be told. I love the huge windows, especially in the winter, when I can sit at my desk and watch the snow fall as I write. It's peaceful and comfortable, this room. Overall, it's the office of a highly successful person. *I* am a highly successful person. I am very good at my job.

Or at least I used to think I was.

I take in a slow, deep breath through my nose and let it out through my mouth.

"Rome, huh?" I say it out loud and the words seem to float around the room, hanging in the air like clouds.

I do actually think about it. For the entire day—the entire day of not writing, let me clarify. When I'm not writing—and when I'm supposed to be, but struggling, I do other stuff. Laundry, for example. I walk Reggie. I watch TV. I bake. I surf the internet under the guise of "research," but really, I just look for cool clothes and things for my house. I would leave and go do stuff, except I feel like if I stay in my house, I'm at least *trying* to work. This block is bad, though. Worst I've ever had. I'm trying my best not to drown in concern, so I decide to scrutinize my own face in the mirror while I ponder Rome. Why? Because I want to see what a procrastinating and completely creatively empty writer looks like? I don't know. Don't ask me stuff like that.

It's not a bad face, if I do say so, but it seems like there's a new line every time I look. My eyes are a pretty cool blue, and now they crinkle at the corners when I smile. They didn't used to do that. I've got decent teeth, an oval face, and a strong jawline, thanks to my dad. Because of my amazing hair stylist, my hair is a nice rich shade of light brown, and I don't have a single gray. Today. Ask me again in about three weeks. I always wanted to be taller, but I've had to settle for an average-to-shortish five foot five. I tuck some hair behind my ear and tip my head as I stare at my reflection and think about how there are still only two words on my computer screen.

"Well, Lily Chambers, what do you think? Maybe we should go to Rome, yeah?"

CHAPTER TWO

"How was the cruise?" I'm on the phone with my mom. I've been in Rome for a week, but she and my dad were off on a ship in the Caribbean when I left, so I haven't talked to her since I decided to hit up Europe in search of something—anything, at this point—to get me writing.

"No, no," she says, and I can picture her waving my question away like a pesky fly. "My cruises are always the same. But you are *in Italy*. I want to hear all about it. How is Rome? Is the pizza as good as they say? How 'bout the wine?" If her voice is any indication, my mom is practically bursting out of her skin to hear all about my self-imposed retreat.

"Rome is…" I don't want to tell her that I haven't really done much more than walk Reggie and eat at a little café around the corner from my hotel, because I'm trying so hard to work. She'd get worried, probably decide I'm sick and/or dying, and she'd be on the next plane to Rome. That's the last thing I need. "It's good!" I'm likely overdoing the cheerfulness, but I push on. "The pizza's amazing. The pasta is even better. And the wine? Incredible. And no headache!" None of those are lies, at least. "I'm gonna come home with several extra pounds, I think, and I'm not even mad about it."

"And have you made any new friends?"

"Ma. I'm here to work. I'm not in college." I try to keep my tone light because she's just asking a question, and my mother is the most salt-of-the-earth, kind person you'll ever meet. Even when she's mad at you, she's nice about it.

"I know. I just don't want you to be lonely while you're there."

"I'm not lonely. I have Reggie." At the mention of his name, Reggie lifts his head from the pillow on the couch that he's decided is his now. I hold up the phone like he's a toddler and tell him, "It's Grandma. Say hi." She baby-talks to him like she always does, and his ears prick up, and his head tilts, and I'm pretty sure he's really listening to her. They have a thing, my mom and my dog.

We talk about a few more mundane topics like we usually do. My mom and I have always been close, and we talk just about every day, if we can. That means there's rarely anything new for each conversation, so that's where the mundane stuff comes in. Recipes we've tried or want to, books we've read or want to, movies and TV shows we've seen or want to. It's mundane, and also wonderful. I do know how lucky I am to have such a great relationship with my mom. I promise.

After we've hung up, I glance over at Reggie. "What do you think? Walk?"

At the mention of the W-word, he uses the step I made him from the ottoman in the sitting area to get off the couch, then he spins in a fast circle at my feet, his way of saying yes, he would absolutely like to go please, Mom. Right now.

One thing I didn't expect in Italy—and don't ask me why, I have no idea, I checked WeatherBug and everything—is the heat. Yes, it's August. Yes, August is hot. But I didn't expect it to be surface-of-the-sun hot. Living-in-a-cast-iron-frying-pan hot. I have sweat more in the past five days than I have all summer back home, which says a lot because back home is *humid*. Here? It's just fucking hot. So, I snap my doggie kit bag around my waist and make sure Reggie's little water bottle is full, because the heat's kind of rough on him, too. Then I clip him into his harness and leash, swoop him up, and we head out to the elevator.

The name of my hotel is Hotel Cavatassi, which I love saying out loud. Such a cool word, Cavatassi. I've actually caught myself whispering it as I enter or leave. I like the way it feels, and since words are pretty much my life, it kinda makes sense that I do it. I wave to Marco, the concierge sitting behind the small front desk, and he waves and smiles back. He is a beautiful Italian gentleman with dark eyes and thick black hair, both on his head and on his face. His greetings always seem very genuine to me, but I realize I'm also staying in the penthouse, so maybe he feels obligated. Regardless, I appreciate his kindness, especially being so far from home.

It's late morning and the sun is high, and because it's closing in on lunchtime—and there are many restaurants close by the hotel— scents hang in the air. Basil. Tomatoes. Garlic. Fresh bread. Italy smells goddamn delicious, that's for sure.

My hotel opens onto what I would consider an alleyway back home but is actually a narrow street. I know this because yesterday, I saw a small delivery van maneuvering its way down it, his side mirrors *barely* clearing the buildings, and for a moment, I assumed the guy had made a wrong turn. Nope. He was delivering something to the shop with the gorgeous leather bags in the window. The cobblestones don't help the idea that this is a street and not an alley, but they look cool, and Reggie and I stroll lazily as he stops to sniff the corner of the next building.

It has a small, gated courtyard. The gate is open today, and as we walk past, I see a woman trying to navigate her door while her arms are full of bags. I give Reggie a tug in her direction.

"Here, let me help you," I say as I take two of the bags from her arms. She smiles at me in relief.

"Thank you so much," she says in an American accent. "I almost lost 'em." She goes inside, sets down the bag she has, then comes back out and takes one from my arms. "You're a lifesaver." She glances down at Reggie, and a flicker of recognition twinkles into her eyes. "Oh, you're staying next door, right? At the Cavatassi? I've seen you walking."

I nod and glance back at our building. "Yup. It's nice. I like it."

"Well, the least I can do is offer you something to drink, it's so damn hot." She holds out a hand to me. "I'm Serena. Come in for a bit?" I like her quirkiness. From her flowy yellow dress with the bright orange wrap to her cat's eye glasses and blond hair piled on top of her head, quirky is the perfect descriptor. Plus, it's nice to meet a fellow American.

"Lily," I say and shake her hand. Her nails are painted orange and turquoise, and they alternate colors. "Why not? Is it okay—?" I look down at Reggie.

"Oh, absolutely. Come, come." She opens her door, and we enter what is the most elegant entryway I've ever seen, all light marble and high ceilings. Not at all what I expected from the street. Reggie's nails click on the shiny floor and Serena squats down to give him some love. "And what's your name, kind sir?"

"This is Reggie," I say. Reggie is usually reserved with strangers—it takes him a while to warm up—but he seems to like Serena instantly, his tail swooping back and forth.

"I'm pleased to meet you, Mr. Reggie. You're very handsome."

"He knows it. Believe me." I feel like I'm in a movie because this is exactly what I would picture a wealthy Italian's house to look like, even though Serena is clearly not Italian. "Is this your place?" I ask. "It's beautiful."

"It is," Serena says, then indicates her grocery bags with her chin, silently asking me to follow her. I swoop them up and lead Reggie down the hall after her, trying not to gape at her stunning house.

The kitchen is massive, with a large island, shiny pots hanging from a rack above it. A Sub-Zero fridge and an oven with eight burners are appliance standouts, and the windows look out onto another courtyard, this one in the back. "Wow." I don't mean to gawk, but I can't help it.

"You like it?"

"It's gorgeous."

"Well, thank you, honey." She waves a hand at Reggie. "Unclip him. He's fine."

"You're sure?" Reggie's well-behaved, but I don't want him deciding to lift a leg on anything for no reason. I don't think he will, but he's a Chihuahua and they do whatever the hell they want.

"He's fine. Wine?"

I manage not to glance at my watch because I know it's not noon yet. But I'm also in Italy, where wine knows no time of day. "Sure."

Serena disappears through a door I didn't notice and returns with a bottle of white that's unfamiliar to me. "I don't know about you, but I prefer white when it's this hot. Must be the unrefined American in me." At that, she laughs, and it's high-pitched. Almost comically musical, and I kind of love it immediately. "And don't judge me, but I'm gonna put ice in mine."

"I wouldn't dream of it," I say with a chuckle. "In fact, I'll take some ice, too."

"Atta girl."

"Where are you from?"

She works the corkscrew. "Born in Michigan. Moved to New York City, where I was a dancer for many years."

"Wow, really?"

"I was a Rockette."

"No!" I gasp my surprise. "That's so cool!"

"Yup. Twelve years. Then Anthony and I moved to Nyack, and then we came here." She pours the wine, adds ice cubes to each one, then hands me a glass. She touches hers to mine. "*Cin cin.*"

We sip, and good Lord, it's delicious. Scott had not been kidding about the wine in Italy. "I've had a glass of something different every day I've been here, and I have yet to be disappointed."

"Oh, the wine here is next level. Truly. Nothing compares. Come." She heads out of the kitchen to back doors that lead into the courtyard visible from inside. While I'm not thrilled to be going out in the heat, Serena leads Reggie and me to a lovely, shaded patio with cushy looking furniture. We sit, and being out of the sun definitely helps us not overheat. "So. Lily. Where do you hail from, and what are you doing in Rome?"

I feel myself begin to relax with another sip. Something about Serena's presence is comforting, and I feel the tension in my shoulders ease up. Though she can't be more than a handful of years older than me, there's something almost motherlike about her aura. Reggie hops up on the little love seat next to me, turns in a circle, and makes himself a little napping spot, clearly feeling as comfortable as I am. "Reggie and I are from a small city in upstate New York called Northwood. We still live there. And I'm here for work." I don't like to dive right into what I do for a living. That'll come up sooner or later. I'd like to get to know Serena a little better first.

"And you're here on your own?"

I nod. "It's my first time here."

Serena sighs, tucks her feet up underneath her butt, and sits back. She takes a sip of her wine before speaking in a dreamy tone. "I remember my first time. Magical. Romantic. Just lovely."

"What about you? Are you here alone?" I've stopped assuming people have husbands or wives, preferring to let them tell me.

"Oh, yes. My Anthony died two years ago."

"I'm so sorry."

"He was a good man, if a tiny bit old-fashioned," she says, and the fondness in her voice matches the wistful expression in her eyes. "But he left me this house, and I can't bear to leave it. So here I am, a completely eligible bachelorette in the most romantic city in the world, all by myself." I can't tell if she's sad about that, but then she laughs heartily. "Who needs men?"

We cheers again.

I like Serena. A lot. We're talking about dogs when an older Italian woman appears out of nowhere, laden down with a tray of charcuterie, and I almost jump out of my skin. That sends Serena into a fit of laughter I am not sure she'll recover from.

"This is Ria, my Housewoman Extraordinaire," and the capital letters are implied by her tone. "She makes sure I eat and that my house is clean." Then Serena says something in Italian that I think referred to the groceries I helped her carry in, and Ria smiles, gives one nod, and is gone.

We've polished off a bottle and a half of the wine before I even start to feel it. We've decimated the charcuterie, only two green olives and one lone piece of bread left on the tray.

"Do you want to stay for dinner?" Serena asks, and I really, really do. But I also know I've used her as an excuse to avoid trying to work today, and that's not good.

I frown. "Rain check?"

"How about Friday? I have guests coming to visit from the States and I'm throwing a very small dinner party. I'd love you to come."

Dinner parties with strangers are certainly not this introvert's idea of a good time, but like I said, I like Serena, I feel exceedingly comfortable with her, and her blue-eyed gaze gives me a gentle nudge toward a yes. Apparently, that's all I need, and I hear the words come out of my mouth before I even realize I'm about to say them. "That sounds great."

❖

I'm nervous.

It's always like that when I'm about to spend time with a group of people I don't know. I'm not sure if it's the introvert thing or if

I've got some social anxiety or what, but the butterflies in my stomach have become drones, going from a weird flutter to an uncomfortable knocking around in my stomach, and I seriously consider texting Serena my regrets.

A glance at the desk with my closed laptop gives me the poke I need, because if I stay here, I have to try to work. I spent all day trying to force words—and I got some. Just not many. And I don't know that they're any good. The storyline is feeling very weak to me. Never a good thing. If I'm not excited about my characters, how can I expect my readers to be? And currently? I am *not* excited about my characters.

"All right. Fine," I say to my reflection. I'm wearing a cute ivory sundress with spaghetti straps and a yellow pattern that feels very summery. Serena's place is air conditioned, but I've noticed she also likes to open her windows and doors, so I'm not taking any chances. I don't want to be sweating like a farm animal in front of people I've just met. "What do you think, Reg?"

Reggie's on the bed watching me get ready. He tips his head to one side, then sighs and puts his head down on his paws.

"Great. Thanks a lot." I go to him and swoop him up, not caring that my dress will now be accented with tiny brown hairs. "It's a good thing you're so cute, you know that?" I can feel his tail whacking against my arm, and he licks my face with affection. I give him a squeeze. I love my dog more than most people. I'm not even kidding. We take care of each other. "Okay, you stay here and watch our place. Make sure nobody breaks in and steals anything." I glance at the desk again, at my laptop. "Except that. They can take that. I won't be late."

I give Reggie some treats, grab my jean jacket, just in case Serena changes her mind about the open-air atmosphere in her house, and the bottle of wine I purchased yesterday, and I head out.

The feeling outside is different on a Friday night than during a weekday. It's busier, yes, but there's also an element of celebration in the air. It's kind of hard to describe other than to say people seem more…festive? Which makes sense. It's the weekend. I merge into the throng of bodies moving down the street, catching snippets of different conversations as I make the short trek. Italian, of course, but I also recognize some English, also a little French. Lots of people here from lots of different places. Serena's gate is open. I approach her door and am just about to ring the bell when suddenly, I hear cheers. Like, from every direction. Joyous, ecstatic cheering fills the air, echoing all around me as Ria opens the door to greet me.

I must have a question in my eyes because she laughs and says simply in her glorious Italian accent, "Football game."

"Oh," I say, and draw the word out as I step inside, and Serena greets me. I forget how insanely popular soccer is in Europe.

"Lily!" Serena breezes in like she's on a hoverboard, and once again, she's wearing a flowy caftan or something. This time, she's all in royal blue with some lighter accenting shades. Her blond hair is down and slightly disheveled, though I think that's intentional. "I'm so glad you're here. Come, come." She thanks me for the wine, hands it to Ria, hooks her hand around my elbow, and leads me into the house, past the kitchen, and into a living room I haven't seen yet, and I start to realize Serena's place is way bigger than I thought, much bigger than it looks from the outside.

The living room is typical of the rest of the house: elegant, expensive, slightly ornate, but not unattractively so. There are two couches facing one another, a cool fireplace on the wall between them. The walls are a crisp white, the floors marble, the furniture a deep gray. It feels modern and classic at the same time, and before I can take in the art on the walls or the vase of flowers to my left, Serena is introducing me to the people sitting on the couches. "Lily, these are my dear, dear friends from back home in Nyack." She indicates the man and woman on one couch. "This is Margie and Robert." Across from them on the other couch are three more people. "Their daughter Bethany, her husband Chris, and their daughter Sophie."

I put Margie and Robert as slightly older than Serena. So, early sixties maybe? Bethany and Chris are younger—I guess mid-thirties. Sophie is clearly a teen. They're all smiling, and I step forward and shake everybody's hand.

The evening goes by quickly, and I'm surprised to realize it as we sit around the dining room table talking, plates empty, our bellies full of pasta and wine. I'm having a better time than I expected. Margie and Robert are super sweet, and they have lots of stories about Serena and her husband. While Bethany and Chris lived elsewhere during Serena's time in Nyack, they must've been around for many of the gatherings, as they also have stories.

"So, I have to ask," I say, gesturing with my wine glass. "Did any of you get a chance to see Serena as a Rockette?"

"Oh, I wish!" Margie says with a laugh, and the tender look on her face tells me she absolutely does.

"No, I was retired before Tony and I moved to Nyack," Serena says. "Met these guys after."

"Make sure she shows you her photo albums, though," Bethany says to me. "She's got some incredible shots. You'll be blown away."

Serena waves a hand, but her face has tinted pink.

"I will take you up on that," I say to her.

"So, what do you do, Lily?" Margie asks.

"Oh, I'm a writer." I sip my wine, trying to remember how many I've had. Ria is far too good at keeping glasses full, so I'm not sure how much I've actually consumed. But I feel warm, a little fuzzy, and very, very happy. So...three glasses, maybe?

"Really?" Bethany asks. "Sophie writes." She indicates her daughter sitting next to her, scrolling on her phone. When Sophie doesn't look up, Chris nudges her.

"Soph."

She glances up. She's cute, with blond hair and too much eyeliner. Her blue nail polish is chipped as she holds her phone and looks around. "What?"

Bethany swallows a sigh, and I figure she probably does that a hundred times a day. "Lily here is a writer."

"Really? That's cool," she says, and it seems like she might really think so. "What do you write?"

"I'm mostly a romance writer. I've done a few articles here and there." I sip my wine. "A couple screenplays. A series. A bunch of books." Sophie's eyes get a little bit bigger with each item in my list, which is fun to watch, but I steer the conversation back to her. "What about you? What do you write?"

She lifts a shoulder in that teenage shrug that seems to be more of a tic than anything. "Mostly fantasy."

"She writes about dragons and vampires and stuff," Chris says, but rather than sounding dismissive, his voice is tinted with pride.

"Well, romantasy is very big right now," I say.

Sophie sets her phone down and leans forward, and I can see in my peripheral vision how her mother and grandparents exchange a glance. "It *is*. I know! I'm working on one right now, and I'm trying to add some romantic stuff, but it's hard."

I wrinkle my nose as I nod. "It really can be, huh? But you, you have to build *worlds*. That's pretty impressive."

She nods and smiles. "Thanks."

"Maybe I could read some of your work sometime?" Then I wave my hand. "No pressure, though. Some writers don't like to share their work. I get that."

But Sophie's face has lit up, brighter than it's been since before dinner. "Yeah, that'd be awesome." And she looks like she really thinks so.

"Remind me to give you my email address when we go," I tell her. Then I look to her parents and their parents. "How long are you all staying?"

"A week," Bethany says, then looks to Serena. "Serena's got a few things set up for us, since she knows the city."

"We're doing a food tour tomorrow," Sophie says, and her eyes are bright, a sparkle I recognize. She's found somebody who gets her passion for words. I've felt the same way on occasion. "Hey! You should come, too!" She looks to Bethany. "Right, Mom?"

"Oh, I don't—" I start to protest, but I'm cut off by Serena.

"Absolutely," she says. "You should join us. I take every visitor who comes to see me on this tour. They're fantastic."

"We went last year," Sophie says. "I was *so full*." Her tongue lolls out and she slides down in her chair, making me laugh softly.

"But this is your visit with Serena," I say, my gaze on Margie and Robert. "I don't want to impose."

Margie makes a *pfft* sound and waves a dismissive hand, much like Serena does. I can see their friendship in their shared mannerisms. "You should definitely come. It's a blast. Good food"—she gestures around the table—"great company," and we all laugh.

I like these people. If I didn't, I'd have headed back to my hotel not long after dinner. But as it is, it's after nine and I'm still here, still enjoying the conversation, not at all in a hurry to get back. I'm sure Reggie is crashed out on my bed, and other than him, the only thing waiting for me back there is my barely begun manuscript. And pressure.

"You know what? I'd love to come. As long as I'm not stepping on any toes, I'd love to come."

Serena's smile is wide, and it occurs to me that she might be lonely in this foreign country alone. She has a house; I wonder if she has friends here. Or if they're all from other places. "Fabulous!" She reaches over and grasps my forearm, and I can tell from her expression—wide smile and blue eyes crinkled at the corners—that she's happy I'm joining them.

And in that moment, I'm happy, too.

CHAPTER THREE

R ome is reminding me a little bit of Manhattan.
       I think that as I lie in bed in my hotel suite the next morning.
I'm not sure if the sun is up yet. The street I'm on has some tall buildings
that block a lot of it until it gets high, but I can see the beginnings of
light through the sheers on the tall window across from my bed.

It's not quite as busy and not quite as loud as Manhattan, but it's
still both busy and loud. Not this early, of course, though I can still hear
muffled movement and hushed voices outside. A glance at my watch
tells me it's just before seven. That means the bakeries are opening.
It's been so hot that I've kept my windows tightly closed and the air
conditioning on, but I know if I were to open one, the scents of freshly
baked bread and pastries will already be wafting in the air.

Reggie is curled up next to my hip and snoring like a chain saw.
He was on his back not long ago, all four paws in the air, his body
vulnerable to any outside attack. I love that he's so comfortable with
me. I don't love that I'm going to be leaving him here again today, but
I can't exactly take him on a food tour with me. I decide I'll take him
for a lengthy walk this morning, in the hopes he naps while I'm gone.

In no hurry to get up, I reach for my phone and see that Scott
texted me while I was asleep. He and I both tend to forget the time
difference, so he was sending me messages at two in the morning. The
first one is very simple.

Update?

I sigh. I can't help it. He's doing his job. I am *not* doing mine.

His second message is easier to swallow.

Sorry about that. Got a call. Hit send before I meant to. Then a smiley emoji and a shrug. The next message reads, *Hey there. How's Rome? I am texting to see how the work is going and to ask if you have any updates. Also, I miss your face.*

I lay there and chuckle, wondering how many times he went over that text to make sure he got it just right, just business-y enough, but also friendly, while making sure to ask his question. I type.

Can't talk. Full of pasta and wine. And I find the emoji with the puffed out cheeks and send it. Then I send a second text. *I miss you, too. Let me get up and moving and I'll be back.*

I feel immediately guilty for putting him off, but I don't have much to report back, and I'm not sure I want him to know that just yet. Of course, there's also the fact that I can't keep it a secret forever.

I push my way out of bed and head out into the small kitchen in my suite. There's a coffeepot, and I set it to brewing before I hit the shower. When I come out of the bathroom, Reggie has moved to my side of the bed, his head on my pillow like he's a little furry human. It's freaking adorable, and I grab my phone and snap a couple shots. I also notice another text from Scott.

Stop stalling. I need an update.

I groan and let my head roll around on my shoulders. I can't be mad at Scott—again, he's doing his job—but I am mad at him. Because I'm mad at myself and I'm trying to point that anger elsewhere.

I toss the phone onto the bed and towel off my hair while I head out of the bedroom to grab my coffee. Without thinking, I open my laptop and have a seat at the desk to read what I've written so far.

It's fine.

It's not great. It doesn't suck. It's fine.

More groaning as I flop backward in my chair and blow out a long, slow breath. I'm not okay with "fine." I don't do "fine." I'm a perfectionist, and the fact that I can't seem to find my groove lately is seriously messing with my head.

I read it again, slam the laptop shut, and shake my head, then go back for my phone.

Doing some tweaking, but so far, so good. Not ready to show you yet, but soon. Promise. And then I overdo it on the emoji, sending a smiley, a wink, a typewriter, a pen, and a book.

I run my eyes over the message four, five, six times before I send it. Scott won't like it, but it should appease him.

"Jesus Christ," I whisper into my empty suite, feeling a roiling in my stomach that comes with stress.

I've never been in this position before, and I don't want to analyze why I'm there now. Instead, I turn on some music and, combined with the blow-dryer, drown out the thoughts in my head with noise. This is all stuff I will deal with later. Like tonight. Or tomorrow. Or next week.

Today, I have a food tour to go on.

❖

I am at Serena's place at 10:30 sharp, after having taken Reggie for a two-mile walk all around our neighborhood. We didn't go too far out of the way because many of Rome's streets look alike and I didn't want to get lost. So we went around blocks and backtracked and did laps of some blocks we'd already visited, but it's good. We also beat the heat, which was good for Reggie. Now, he's tucked up in the air-conditioned suite, probably curled up on the bed and snoozing, and I am ringing the bell outside Serena's gate.

Her front door opens just as a large, black van pulls up behind me. Serena and her houseguests all file from the house and out the gate. We exchange hellos and good mornings as we all pile into the van, which I realize is basically a cab that fits all of us. Serena sits in the passenger seat and the rest of us cram in. I'm in the back row, sandwiched between Bethany and Sophie.

"This is gonna be so much fun," Sophie informs me as we start driving to the place we're supposed to meet our guide. "We go every time we visit Serena."

"Yeah?" I ask. "How many times have you been here?"

Sophie looks across me to her mom, eyebrows raised in question. Bethany furrows her brow as she thinks. "Three? Four?"

"Serena," Sophie calls up to the front seat. "Are we gonna have Marina again?"

"I requested her," Serena says. "So I hope so."

"You're gonna love Marina," Sophie tells me. "She's so freakin' cool."

I love her enthusiasm, and her excitement is contagious, and pretty soon, I'm looking more forward to this than I was earlier. The drive doesn't take long, and in a blink, we're turning into a parking lot surrounded by what seems to be a bunch of little shops. The driver hops out and opens the door, and we all spill out like clowns from a mini car.

Serena spins in a slow circle as she looks around. "I don't see her yet." She points to a red awning. "We're meeting her there." And without waiting, she walks in that direction.

"This is Trastevere, right?" Sophie asks as we fall in line behind Serena, who nods in answer to the question. Sophie puts the accent on the "ver." One thing I've noticed in my slightly more than a week in Rome is that pretty much all Italian words are fun to say. They feel good in your mouth, I don't know how else to describe it. I don't speak one single word of Italian, but I could listen to it all day long. I find myself whispering *Trastevere* to myself.

Serena sidles up to me with a pamphlet in her hand. "I don't know why I have this," she says. "I know this tour by heart." She hands the pamphlet to me, then waves above us at the awning. "We start here, where we'll have an appetizer of some sort. Marina mixes it up for us, since we're regulars now. Then we'll go here," she points to the next name on the list, which says it's a wine bar, "and have wine and probably cheese." She continues down the list. "Then here for lunch and here for gelato."

"Oh, my God, this sounds amazing," I tell her. I try to offer her money for my ticket, and she makes a *pfft* sound and waves me away. Listen, I have plenty of money. Some would consider me wealthy. But I don't think my bank account would come close to Serena's. Still, I insist, and still, she waves me off.

"Absolutely not," she says firmly.

Bethany catches my eye. "Are you trying to pay for your ticket? Yeah, don't bother. She'll have none of it." And she smiles at me like knowingly. "Been there, done that, about a million times."

Serena smiles at me. She's got one front tooth that's slightly turned, giving her face a unique look. Today, her hair is piled on her head and she's wearing white wide-leg pants and a flowy turquoise tank top. Her earrings are also white and turquoise, and they dangle close to her neck. She has her own sense of fashion, and I love that about her.

"*Buongiorno!*" comes a cheerful voice from behind me, and when I see Serena's face light up, I turn to find the source.

"Marina!" Serena says and opens her arms to hug the woman.

They're like long lost friends, hugging and rocking back and forth as they do.

"How are you, my friend?" Marina asks, and her English is better than mine. Which is not surprising. One of my big concerns coming here was the language barrier since, as I said, I don't speak a word of Italian. But I had nothing to be worried about. So many young Italians also speak English, Marina being a clear example.

"Let me introduce you," Serena says. "Or reintroduce you." There's no need, as Marina remembers everybody's name and says them as she shakes hands with each person.

"And this," Serena says, "Is my new friend Lily."

Marina meets my gaze. Her hand in mine is warm and soft, and she's absolutely stunning, but in that unassuming way. Like she has no idea how fucking beautiful she is. Her eyes are dark, like the darkest roast of coffee imaginable. She's in her mid-thirties, I'd say, with gorgeous hair, thick and nearly black, cascading over her shoulders like dark waves. Her brows are wide and precise, and I get the impression that she doesn't miss much, that those eyes take everything in, like they are now. She's taking me in, all of me, I can feel it.

"Lily," she says. "So nice to meet you."

"You as well. I've heard a lot about you."

At that, her cheeks get a slight pink tint to them, and she glances at the others. "Don't listen to their lies. I'm a nice person."

The others laugh and I say, "Well, they've told me you're going to feed me better than any other woman in my life." I realize the double entendre too late, but she seems amused by it.

"Challenge accepted." She's still got my hand, and I'm not even mad about it. As if suddenly realizing it, she finally breaks eye contact and lets me go, and I feel every inch of her skin that touches mine as it slides away.

What the fuck?

She addresses the group, and I take a moment to clear my throat and try to reclaim my bearings, because this woman has thrown me completely off-balance mentally. My head feels a little fuzzy, and when I shake myself back to the present, Marina is telling us about the restaurant we're standing in front of, how it's been here for more than fifty years, and how its specialty is what's called a supplì.

I have no idea what that is, but if it tastes half as good as it smells just standing outside the door, I'm in.

Marina leads us inside, through the small main dining area, and down a narrow hall through the back, nodding and saying hello to everybody she passes. The air is heavy with the scents of garlic, basil, and cooking oil. My mouth waters.

The narrow hall spills us into a small room with a table set for seven with nice plates and shiny silver utensils, and we file around it and take seats. I'm at the end and Marina stands near me as she begins to tell us about the restaurant, the owners, and the food, and while she's doing that, she uses a wine key to open a bottle of wine. I barely hear what she's saying because I'm too busy watching her hands. Her fingers are long, her nails neatly manicured and polished black. I've never liked super-dark nail polish colors on myself—black, plum, burgundy—but against Marina's olive skin, it looks classy and perfect.

She goes around the table and fills each of our glasses, and when she gets to Sophie, she glances at Serena, who looks over at Bethany and Chris, eyebrows raised in question.

"Just a tiny bit," Bethany says, and Sophie fist pumps with a "Yesss."

Marina sees me watching and explains. "The drinking age in Italy is technically eighteen, but it's not super highly enforced, and teens are usually not hassled if their parents are present and say it's okay."

"When did you have your first glass of wine?" I ask her.

Marina's laugh is husky, surprisingly so, and her expression goes a little wistful. "I think I was nine or ten. My grandfather gave it to me. My mother was *not* happy about it."

"I bet," I say, as we all laugh.

Marina pours herself half a glass and holds it up. When we all join her, she says, "*Cin cin!*" We cheers and sip.

"What does that even mean?" Sophie asks. "*Cin cin?* Is it, like, put your glass to your chin and drink?" She juts out her chin to emphasize her point, and Marina laughs again.

"No, but I like your definition," she says. "You don't know the story? Okay, I'll tell you. Way, way back in Ancient Rome, people had enemies all over the place. Nobody trusted anyone because everyone was trying to get ahead in some way. But everybody drank wine, and they drank it often, so if you wanted to—how do you say?—*dispatch* your enemy, one of the best ways to do it was to poison their wine. Yeah?" She takes a sip of hers, and I watch her throat move as she swallows. "Now, they didn't have glasses like this back then. You couldn't see through them. They were—" She rolls her hand like she's looking for a word again, finally coming up with it. "Steins. Yes? With handles. So, when you'd cheer with another person, you'd say, '*cin cin*,' which was supposed to represent the sound of your steins hitting, and you'd do it hard. Like, crash them together. Because if we do that, then there's a good chance some of my wine will splash into yours and some of your wine will splash into mine. And if you *cin cin* with me and then don't drink, I will know you've poisoned my wine." She looks at Sophie. "And then we will have words, my friend."

Laughter rolls around the table, and Sophie looks thrilled by the story.

"That's so cool," she says.

"Not if you're getting poisoned," Marina says.

Sophie sips, and I think she's trying hard to appear as if she likes the wine, but I'm not sure that's the truth. It's cute, though.

Speaking of cute, Marina starts telling us about our first taste on this tour: the supplì. She starts off by telling us that it's a rice ball and we're going to think it's arancini, but it's not and here's why, but her words fade, I'm finding, because I'm too busy focused on everything about her. Her hair, her mouth, her hands, the way her ass looks in her jeans…

I clear my throat and try to focus on her voice as two waiters bring us plates of supplì. They're balls of rice and mozzarella, rolled together and fried, and when I push my fork through mine and the cheese oozes out, my entire mouth fills with saliva. I take a bite. "Oh, my God," I mutter without realizing it, and Marina's dark eyes are suddenly on me.

"Pretty wonderful, yes?"

"Beyond. Way beyond wonderful." I take a second bite. "Holy crap."

Marina's smile feels like it's made of light.

The table is now quiet, aside from all the humming and moaning as we eat, and as we each look around, I think we realize that and suddenly start laughing.

I like these people.

"So, Lily," Marina says as she refills all our glasses except

Sophie's. "I know Serena now, and I've met the others a couple times, but you're new. How do you know Serena?"

"Well, we just met this week. I'm staying at the hotel next door to her house."

Serena sends a smile down the table at me. "Lily was walking her adorable dog and saw me struggling with my groceries and stopped to help me. It was the start of a beautiful friendship."

I hold up my wine and Serena does the same.

"I didn't know your place was next to a hotel," Marina says.

"Mm-hmm. It's very unobtrusive, though," Serena tells her. "If you're not looking for it, you'll walk right by it. The Cavatassi."

"No," Marina says, and her eyes go wide for a split second. She turns to me. "My family owns that hotel."

"What?" I say, surprised.

"Yes." She's grinning. "You've met Marco?"

"At the front desk?" I think of the well-groomed gentleman who always says hello to me. "I see him every day."

Marina points a finger at her own chest. "My brother." And the second she says it, I can see the resemblance. It's all in the eyes, the shape and tilt and placement.

"I had no idea," Serena says, obviously just as surprised as I am.

Marina nods. "It's been in my family for four generations. My mother's grandfather opened it in..." She shakes her head. "I don't even remember what year. It's been passed down and the family always works it."

"Do you work there, too?" I ask, clearly unable to filter my questions before asking them.

She shakes her head. "Much to my parents' dismay, no. I do not."

Well, that's a bummer. I picture myself coming out of the elevator in the morning to see that face of hers smiling at me. What a way to start a day.

"But now," she says to Serena, "I know exactly where you live."

"Uh-oh," Robert says with a sly grin.

"And I know where you are, too," she says, turning to me. Her dark eyes capture mine, and I couldn't look away if I wanted to. Which I absolutely do not. "How long are you in Rome?"

"I don't know yet," I say truthfully.

"Huh." She nods and our gazes hold for what feels like a really long time. God, she's beautiful. Then she claps her hands once and says, "Okay. How was the supplì? Ready for our next stop?"

❖

The strangest thing starts to happen as the food tour goes on…
Creativity strikes.

It's happened to me like this before, but not for a long, long time. Back when I was very young and writing for the fun and pleasure of it, I'd write when an idea or a spark of creativity hit. Then it became my career, which meant I lost the luxury of waiting for an idea to pop up in my head. I had to start forcing them, coming up with them on my own, even if I wasn't "feeling it," as my friend Jessie would say. She's also a writer and one of the few people in my life I can talk to about such things because she gets it. While I write romance, Jessie writes horror, so it's not unlike her to text me in the wee hours and ask me if something scares me. It usually does.

I try not to focus on why creativity has chosen this moment to strike, but rather just roll with it. We're finishing up at the wine bar, having stuffed ourselves with the most amazing charcuterie I've ever had in my life, when I pull a small notebook out of my bag and begin jotting the things that have appeared in my mind. They are tweaks to the current plot I'm working on, and also some changes to my main characters, ways to enhance the chemistry, and I scribble down everything in my head so I don't forget it all.

"New story?" Sophie asks as her parents and grandparents chat with Serena and Marina is filling glasses.

"Current story," I tell her, finishing my notes. "That's why I'm here. In Italy. I'm trying to finish a book." I frown and correct myself. "Well, I'm trying to write a book. Can't really finish something I haven't quite written yet."

Sophie sighs like her fourteen years of life have given her endless experience, and she gets it. "Blocked, huh?" and she grimaces with sympathy. I really like this kid.

"Like I'm behind a brick wall," I say.

"Ugh. I hate when that happens." Sophie shakes her head with a sigh, and I catch myself before I say anything that makes her feel ridiculed. Because while part of me is thinking *How could she possibly understand*, I see by the expression on her face and the empathy in her eyes that, surprisingly, maybe she does. Maybe she understands completely, one writer to another.

Then I shoot a glance at Marina. "But…maybe not for long."

Marina catches my eye then and smiles at me, and I'm a little shocked at the quick zap of a thrill I feel low in my body. "Taking notes for the awesome Yelp review you're going to leave?" And when she winks at me, that zap becomes a pulse. A throbbing. Jesus Christ.

"Lily's a writer," Sophie supplies with a proud grin, and my fondness for her surges.

"Oh, wow," Marina says. "Really? What kind of a writer?"

"Novels, mostly," I say. As she looks at me, I feel like I'm bathing in the light her gaze seems to shed.

I've gotta write that down.

"Wow," she says again, and her smile grows as she hands me my refilled wine glass. "I've never met a writer before."

"No?" I take it and sip.

"Never. What a cool job."

"I mean, I don't get to eat amazing food and drink fantastic wine all day, but I guess it's okay."

She laughs that husky laugh again and nods. "That's a good point." How is it that something as simple as eye contact can affect a person's entire body? Because that happens. Marina's eyes meet mine and I feel it from the top of my head all the way down to my toes, across every millimeter of my skin. She holds it for only a couple seconds before breaking away and addressing the group. "So? What did you think?"

I don't even know what the others say. I barely hear their voices over the rushing of blood in my own ears. Thank God everybody starts to stand up, so I know we're ready to head to the next place. I jot down more notes, specifically about a character being shockingly affected simply by the mere presence of another person. Physically affected. Very physically affected. Then we file out of the wine bar and begin our leisurely stroll to the next restaurant on our tour.

"Are you enjoying yourself, Lily?" Marina is walking next to me. I like the way my name sounds in her accent.

"Very much," I say truthfully. "I didn't expect to be doing something like this when I came. Just thought I'd work."

"And then you met Serena," she says with a chuckle.

"And then I met Serena."

"I imagine she's hard to turn down."

"Impossible." I laugh softly. "How long have you known her?"

Marina wrinkles her nose, and her gaze shifts upward as she does the calculations. "Four years now?"

"Longer than I thought."

"I think she's been here for five. She and her husband used to come here for a month or two at a time, then they moved here permanently. Then he passed away a couple years ago, but she keeps bringing her friends and houseguests to the food tour."

"And I bet she always requests you." I say it with a knowing grin.

Marina blushes softly. "She does. Makes me feel good. She's a good person."

"I bet she'd say the same about you."

She lifts one shoulder and adds a smile to it. "I hope so."

"Well, you're certainly good at your job. I'm having a great time." It's the truth. Marina is fun and knowledgeable, and this tour is not at all what I was expecting. *She* is not at all what I was expecting.

"*Grazie,*" she says, her grin seeming almost mischievous. Then she touches my arm and scoots past me up ahead to direct the group into the next restaurant. That throbbing low in my body has picked up speed. And intensity.

"All right, Chambers, pull yourself together," I whisper, then follow the group into the next establishment.

This is our third stop, and every place has been warm and welcoming, the owners smiling, the staff friendly. They all know Marina, of course, and she chats with them in Italian before directing us to follow her. Again, we head to the back of the restaurant, but this time, we go down some stairs that lead us into a large room that seems to be a blend of a wine cellar and a basement but set up like a dining room. The walls are cement, and it's cool—a nice change from the heat outside—a long table set for us. Twinkle lights are strung all around, and they make it feel warm and festive.

"Okay," Marina says, and I've learned that's the word she uses when she wants our attention because she's about to explain. "Okay. This is where we will be having lunch." She goes on to explain the restaurant's background, but I don't really hear her words because I'm busy watching her mouth. I really want to pull out my phone and record her because everything she's doing, every move, every mannerism stokes my creativity, and I don't want to forget any of it.

I come back to myself when I realize she's finished talking and is opening another bottle of wine. Serena is at the opposite end of the table from me, and she calls my name to get my attention.

"Doing okay down there?" she asks. "Drunk yet?" She winks, and her laugh is almost a giggle, as is Margie's, and I think *they* are both feeling no pain, as my dad would say.

Marina hands me a glass of wine, and I hold it up. "Not yet, but it won't be long."

Serena and Margie dissolve into more giggles, and Marina shoots me a knowing grin. I'm not actually close to being drunk. I was kidding. I've been pacing myself. I don't generally cut loose with alcohol when I'm with new people, and I'm very aware of not getting drunk in front of Marina. Not that she'd care. But I do. It's not the impression I want to make, you know?

Marina begins her presentation on this restaurant, and before long, the waitress is bringing us salad, bread, and plates of pasta.

Can we just stop and talk about pasta in Italy for a second?

It is…life-changing.

It's dense and flavorful and not at all artificial. So far, on this trip, I've had carbonara, pesto, Bolognese, and lasagna. I plan to eat more. In fact, I may eat my weight in pasta on this trip. Today is gnocchi. It's to die for.

"When the room gets quiet," Marina says, "that's when I know everybody is happy with their food."

The sounds that go around the tables are mumbles and humming from people with full mouths. My gnocchi is heavy and cheesy and freaking delicious.

"How is it?" Marina asks me. The others are chatting amongst themselves now, and it feels like it's just me and her.

"There's no way I can finish this plate," I tell her. "But I will be taking all of what's left home with me. No way is this going to waste."

She grins, clearly satisfied with my answer.

"Want a bite?" I ask, and hold up my fork loaded with ovals of dense pasta.

She hesitates, and it occurs to me that maybe she's not allowed. This is her job, after all, she's not here to hang out. Just when I think maybe she's going to turn me down, she opens her mouth and slides the gnocchi off my fork.

Good God.

The move is sexy and sensual, and those two things combined make me swallow hard as I look into her dark eyes. My heart rate kicks up, and I wonder if she can hear it pounding against my rib cage.

"Mmm," she says. "So good."

I clear my throat and nod, apparently unable to form words at this point.

Again, when she grins at me, it's like she knows something.

Maybe she does.

After lunch, we're off to our last stop: gelato. Because of course, it's gelato. You can't end any meal in Italy without at least floating the idea of gelato. We're walking once more—which I have to say is nice, all this walking—but the heat is oppressive. Again, not as humid as home, but it's pushing a hundred degrees, and we're all feeling it. Even Serena looks a little bit wilted.

But the gelato place is air-conditioned, and we all sigh with relief as we enter. Orders are placed quickly, because we don't need any background from Marina on Italian ice cream, and soon, we're all sitting down, eating happily, and my pistachio is so good I feel like I might weep. Creamy and dense and delicious. It's when Marina points to a parking lot across the street and tells us that's where her scooter is parked that I realize this is where we say goodbye to her. Her work is done, and we will catch our own ride back from here, and all of a sudden, I feel a wave of sadness that I don't know how to combat.

And then I don't have to.

"Hey, I was wondering…" Marina pulls up a chair and sits next to me as Robert and Serena debate politics, which I am staying way far away from for the moment. I try not to focus on how good she smells, like sunshine and fresh rain rolled into one, a walking dichotomy of scent. Her hair is in large, spiral waves, and it takes a conscious effort on my part not to reach out to touch it. "Would you be at all—"

She interrupts herself to clear her throat, and I see light pink blossom on her cheeks, and I wonder absently if she's nervous about something.

Her voice is soft and low as she continues. "I mean, you probably already have this taken care of but, would you need or want somebody to show you around the city? 'Cause I could do that. If you wanted. No charge. I'd be happy to." And then she catches her bottom lip between her teeth like she's unsure, and she *is* nervous, and it's adorable.

I lean in close to her. "You know what? I would love that. Absolutely."

"Really?" And her face floods with something. Relief? Happiness? Anticipation? All of the above? I'm not sure, but as she hands me her business card, complete with her personal cell number scribbled on the back in her barely legible handwriting—which I make a note to tease her about later—her smile is wide and her eyes sparkle, and something within me shifts. I don't know how else to describe it. I can literally feel my world move in some weird way, like this is the beginning of some big change in my life. It's weird and comforting at the same time, which doesn't seem possible. I shake it off as best I can and meet those rich brown eyes.

Taking the card from her hand, I tuck it away someplace safe.

The ball is now in my court.

CHAPTER FOUR

I keep that ball in my court for a couple days. Longer than I should, really, but I think I've freaked myself out. It's annoying, because I am a grown-ass adult woman who should know what she's doing by now, but instead, I have the business card of a girl much, much younger than me propped up on my desk, apparently so I can stare at it in confusion every time I sit down to write. I am not prone to silly crushes or obsessions over women I barely know. I may write about those things, but they are not my reality.

That being said, Marina Troiani has been on my mind for days now, and that's new for me. And it's the reason I've been sitting on her number and not reaching out.

Because I'm not sure I should.

I don't know a thing about her, least of all whether she even plays on my team. I don't think my gaydar works in Italy. I haven't been able to pick out a single gay person since I've been here, which is slightly worrisome. They're going to take my lesbian card if I'm not careful.

As I sit at my desk with my laptop open, a very sparsely worded page on the screen, my phone buzzes. It's a text from Serena.

Lonely. Lunch?

It makes me grin what a woman of few words she is when it comes to texting, but she can talk your ear off in person. I also feel a little pang for her, because I know her company is gone. But I've already gotten a DM from Sophie. I think we're going to be fast friends, that kid and me.

As for going to Serena's, I'm torn. I really should work. But I also need to eat, or I'll collapse from hunger and won't be able to write anyway, so it only makes sense that I should have some lunch. Right? Okay. Fine. Not so torn. I text back.

Lunch sounds great.

I really want to buy her a meal, because the woman has fed me since I met her, but she won't hear of it and tells me to bring Reggie and come on over to her place.

Twenty minutes later, Reggie and I head out. Mother Nature has decided to give the Italian people a break for a day or two, and it's cooled off enough so that I don't feel like the soles of my shoes are melting into the cobblestones as I walk. Ria meets us at the door as if she's been waiting for us—which she probably has—and greets us with a smile and a cheerful *Ciao*. She gives Reggie some scratches on his head, and I appreciate that. It bothers me when people ignore my dog. Like, say hi to him. How hard is it?

Ria leads us straight through the house and into the back courtyard, where Serena sits under an umbrella that's opened over a round table laden with dishware, utensils, and a bowl of fruit. She's wearing bright yellow today, and her hair is up and wrapped with a yellow scarf. Her cat's eye sunglasses complete the look of wealthy eccentric, and it's a role she plays magnificently. I have grown very fond of her in a fairly short time.

"Lily, darling," she says, standing up and opening her arms. "So good to see you." She air-kisses both sides of my face, then sits back down and beckons for Reggie to hop into her lap. Which he does without hesitation, the traitor. "How goes the writing?" she asks after Ria pours us each a glass of sparkling water from the bottle in the center of the table.

I groan and pluck a green grape from the bowl.

Serena cocks her head and studies me.

"What?"

"Sweetheart, that's been your response every time I've asked you how the writing is going."

I nod. "Yup."

"Seems to me that somebody of your success and—well, dare I say it—fame in your industry wouldn't struggle so much."

I squint at her, noting the slightly smug, satisfied look on her face, and then I point at her. "Somebody's been googling me."

Serena grins and takes a sip of her water before responding with,

"Yes, but not me. I don't google my friends. If I were, however, fourteen and had just met a writer I connected with, I might."

"Sophie googled me," I say with realization.

"Of course she did. She's a teenager. They google everything." Serena waves a hand. "God forbid they have a conversation about something or ask a question. Nope. Google." She sounds a bit like my dad right then, and a small poke of homesickness hits. She sips again, then looks at me and asks, "How come you didn't tell me?"

"Tell you what?"

"That you're famous! That you wrote *Heartbreaker* and *Emily* and more. Do you know how many times I've seen *Heartbreaker*?" She's leaning over the table now, and I realize she's not being hurt or critical. She's *excited*. "Like, a thousand. Easily."

"I'm not famous," I say, and it's true. The writer of a movie rarely is. Directors, actors, even producers, sure. Writers? Not so much.

"You're famous to me. And to Sophie." She sits back in her chair and regards me with a grin.

"Now what?"

She shakes her head as Ria appears with salads for lunch. "Nothing at all. Just looking at my friend. My famous friend."

"Stop it."

She snorts a laugh and puts Reggie down so we can eat. "I'm just pokin' at you."

We dig in, and I wonder how it's possible that even something as basic as salad tastes better in Rome. It makes no sense. I munch happily.

"So, what are you working on?"

I sigh as I gaze off into the courtyard where birds flit around a couple of olive trees and I chew.

"Oh, well, that's ominous," Serena says.

"I'm blocked," I tell her, just blurt it out. "Like, not in the 'ha ha, every writer gets blocked now and then' way I told Sophie. I mean, seriously blocked. I haven't written anything worthwhile in weeks." I catch myself and close my eyes as I amend my words. "Months. I've been blocked for months. I owe my publisher a new novel by mid-fall, and I can barely write my own name." I blow out a forceful breath and take a slug of my water, feeling a surprising sense of relief at having told somebody. I don't think I understood just how much it's been eating me up inside.

"Is that why you're here?" Serena asks. Her voice is soft and her eyes are kind. I don't want her sympathy, I want her to take a whip and make me go back to my desk and write. But the sympathy also feels nice. I won't be getting it from Scott, that's for sure. Not that I blame him.

I nod. "Yeah. My agent is also a good friend, and he thought sending me to one of the most romantic cities in the world would…" I grimace. "Unstick me."

"It hasn't?"

"Not so far."

"Maybe you haven't seen enough," Serena says, leaning forward on the table again. "Rome is filled with inspiration. *Filled*. Overflowing. The architecture, the art, the history, the *food*. Maybe you need to explore more of it."

"I mean, you're not wrong. I haven't seen a ton." I think about the business card on my desk. "Marina did offer to give me a tour."

"She knows this city like the back of her hand. You should take her up on it. Speaking of inspiration…" She grins at me over the rim of her glass, then grabs a grape and pops it into her mouth, still grinning as she chews.

"What do you mean?"

"Nothing. Just that you two seemed to really…" Serena clears her throat. "Hit it off."

I narrow my eyes at her and search her face. "And what does *that* mean?"

A snort. "Honey, if you're not picking up what I'm laying down, I'm afraid I can't help you." She chuckles and adds, "Sophie taught me that."

"I mean, Marina's definitely cute and all, but she's super young and I'm not here to hook up and—" I'm interrupted by Serena opening and closing her hand like a mouth.

"Blah, blah, blah. You're here. She's here. You're obviously attracted to each other. Have her show you the sights. Why not? You already know she's fun. I've told you she's knowledgeable. And you might find some inspiration to…unstick you, as you said. You know? Where's the harm?" She sits back in her chair, clearly satisfied with her argument, and I have to admit, it's a good one.

"I mean, she did offer," I say softly to my plate.

"She did. I'd take her up on it if I were you." Serena is so matter-of-fact that I almost laugh. "She was flirting with you like crazy during the food tour."

I look up at her, surprised.

"Oh, honey." She smiles and reaches across the table to pat my hand as she shakes her head. "Please tell me you are not *that* blind."

I make a face because sometimes, yeah, I am that blind.

❖

Hi there! I think I'd like to take you up on that offer of a guided tour...

I sit up on the rooftop terrace of my hotel and stare at my phone. Then I set it down without sending the text and pick up my wine glass. And then I sigh like a woman with the weight of the whole goddamn world on her shoulders, which makes me roll my eyes at myself because what is my problem, anyway? Jesus.

And I pick up the phone again.

Reggie is lying next to me on the outdoor couch, and he lifts his head to give me a look that says, "Seriously? What are you doing?"

I set the phone down, text unsent.

Reggie groans and lowers his head, clearly disgusted with me.

I am officially ridiculous. Even my dog thinks so.

More sighing and more wine, and I gaze out at this incredible view that I'm shocked isn't taken advantage of more by the guests of this hotel. I guess maybe it's similar to living someplace like Denver, where the view of the mountains on the horizon is just normal, and you get so used to it after a while that you barely notice. This hotel isn't tall. I'm in their penthouse on the top floor, and that's only five stories up, but I can see the tops of so many buildings. Rooftop gardens and living spaces are prominent. There's a little party of some sort going on to my left about four buildings over. I can hear the music faintly, see the mingling bodies. And then church bells begin, and when I say they ring through the air like it's a Hallmark Christmas movie, I am not exaggerating. They're not obnoxiously loud, but they're clear. Melodic chimes that must echo through the city. And as I'm thinking that, another set of church bells begins to chime from behind me. Soon, there are at least four different sets of bells singing to Rome. A glance at my watch tells me it's six o'clock. I sit and sip and listen. Even Reggie is paying attention now.

It's beautiful. An almost religious experience, which I'm sure is the point.

When they finally end, I pick the phone back up. I don't know why I'm hesitant. Marina offered. It's not like I'm asking her a favor, right? She offered. And Serena's right: I clearly need something to help me with inspiration, or Scott's gonna have my head. The last thing I need is for my publisher to request I return their advance. It's hard to come back from *had to give back her advance 'cause she didn't deliver.* Finding another publisher after that—because I'd likely have to—would be a challenge, to say the least.

"That's how I'll look at this, right, Reg?" When my dog meets my gaze, I go on. "As research. Work." He stares at me for a good five seconds before putting his head down and snuffling out a breath that makes me think he's just done with my crap. "Fine," I say, then snatch up my phone and hit send on the text before I can think about it any more. I drop it face down on the couch and take a slug of my wine.

Okay. It's fine. It's done. She's probably having dinner or she's got—

Ping!

Holy shit. That can't be her already.

I pick up the phone and slowly turn it over.

It is. It's her.

Fantastic! her text reads. *How about we start with lunch or dinner so I can learn what you'd like to see?*

This seems reasonable. I mean, how will she know what to show me if she doesn't know what I'm interested in, right? I text back.

Sounds perfect. When?

The gray dots bounce and her text comes quickly. *Tomorrow? Lunch?*

It's not like I need to check my super busy schedule. I know what it'll say. Work. That's it. Or maybe some variation of it. Write, maybe. Or Try to Make a Living, that's a good one. Pretend You Know How to Write is a favorite, one that's being used more and more often lately.

Great, I type back.

How about I pick you up? Meet you in the lobby at half past eleven?

Gotta say, I like a woman who doesn't wait for me to make all the decisions. Been there, done that, it's fucking exhausting. I type back, *Looking forward to it*, send it, and set the phone down, feeling like I've just run a race.

I reach for the wine bottle and refill my glass. It's a lovely white with a name I can't pronounce that Marco left in my room when I arrived. I sit back on the couch cushions, sip my wine, and go back to admiring the view. Reggie is snoring now, so he's clearly *over* the view, but I'm not sure I ever will be. It's too magnificent.

Something many people don't understand about being a writer is that there is a large portion of the job that doesn't involve the physical act of writing at all. There's the thinking and the working out of plot lines and the development of characters and a lot of that stuff happens—at least for me—when I stare off into space. It also happens when I do other things. Tending to my houseplants is a good way for me to work out a kink in a storyline. Many of my ideas have come to me in the shower. Running the vacuum often helps me create just the right Dark Moment for whatever I'm working on. I can remember being accused more than once of being lazy, of lying around, and now I shut that memory down before it can surface all the way.

No, thank you. I'm going to sit here on this lovely rooftop, drink my fabulous Italian wine, and try hard not to look forward to the idea of seeing Marina again.

Two out of three ain't bad. Right?

CHAPTER FIVE

"M aybe this will get the juices flowing," Jessie says over the phone. She will text with me, but she prefers to "speak to a live person," as she always tells me, so I call her whenever I can.

I snort a laugh, and she playfully scolds me.

"Mind out of the gutter, Chambers. Jesus. The *creative juices* is what I meant. Though the other juices would be fine to flow as well..." She lets the thought trail off, but I put the kibosh on that instantly.

"No. Please. No way. I don't need that kind of complication. I'm not in a good place creatively, and you know how cloudy things get for me if I mix business and pleasure."

"Oh, I remember that crazy bitch. Let's not have that happen again." We both laugh, but there's a tinge of ick in both our tones because that was a nightmare that I don't want to relive. "You know," Jessie goes on, "it's too bad you write romance when you're feeling shitty like this. If you wrote horror like me, you could just create some horrific monster and have it mutilate all the problem people in your life."

I let go of a dreamy sigh. "That sounds lovely."

"It really is cathartic, not gonna lie. A few beheadings here and a few disembowelings there, and I feel better."

"I'm jealous. The worst I can do is kill off a character's nemesis. Or ex. Or mother-in-law."

"I mean, none of those things sound awful."

I take a deep breath and let it out slowly. "I'm worried, Jess." My voice is quiet, just above a whisper, because it's the first time I've actually said it out loud. Yes, I've admitted I'm behind. Yes, I've even admitted I'm blocked—something I don't let a lot of people in on. But putting voice to the concern? Yeah, that's a big deal for me. "I have this stress hanging out in my stomach. I don't like it."

Jessie's voice softens, the light playfulness gone. "What do you think it is?"

"I think it's passion. Or a lack thereof." To my horror, I feel my eyes well up. "I haven't enjoyed my job in a long time. I used to love it. It used to be something I lived for."

"And now?"

"It feels like a chore. An impossible, heavy chore. I've never felt like this. It scares me."

I hear Jessie let out a breath similar to mine, a thinking breath, like she's looking for a solution to offer me. "I'm sorry, hon. That really sucks. Maybe this guided tour will stir things up a bit." She has no suggestions, that's what that means, and I understand it. She can't fix this. Nobody can. I have to either ride it out, give up completely, or force myself to write something.

"Maybe," I say, with as much conviction as I can muster, because I don't want to give up. I love my job—loved my job—and I want to love it again. I want to get back there. I'm just not sure how. A glance at my watch tells me I need to get moving. "Listen, I gotta go. But thanks for letting me vent."

"Anytime. You know that. Let me know how it goes today, okay? I've never been to Rome. Send me pics. I wanna live vicariously."

"Will do," I say and hang up. Then I stand there in front of the mirror. "What do you think, Reg?"

He's been napping on my bed, and he opens his eyes to look at me. Apparently, lifting his head requires too much effort, so he just stares at me with his enormous brown marble eyes.

The heat is back, so I'm wearing a pair of navy blue shorts and a blue and white striped tank. I've slathered myself in sunscreen—I will tan just fine, but I don't want to burn. Or get skin cancer. My mother is all about sunscreen, barely leaves home without it, and she's rubbed off, no pun intended. I check my bag to make sure I've got sunglasses and lip balm with SPF. Then I step into my sandals, give Reggie a couple treats and a kiss on his furry head, and leave my room.

As I said, I'm on the top floor—the fifth—and while I tend to opt for the elevator up, I do like to take the stairs down. Makes me feel like I'm at least *attempting* to exercise. The stairwell spits me out into a hallway where I pass a janitor's closet and an office before I get to the lobby. There are heated voices coming from the office, a man and woman arguing in Italian, and I hurry past without looking in. I don't want it to seem like I'm eavesdropping, not that it would matter since I don't speak Italian.

In the lobby, there's a small table with a big jug of ice water, and I help myself to a cup, as Marina isn't here yet and I am never hydrated enough, according to my doctor. Why is it so hard to drink water? Now, if they told me I had to drink more wine to stay properly hydrated, I'd be all over that.

I'm just crumpling the paper cup in my hand, about to toss it into the small wastebasket, when Marina and Marco come around the corner from where the stairway is. Neither of them look happy, and I realize it was them arguing in Italian. They part without looking at each other, Marco to behind the front desk and Marina toward the small lobby area. The second she sees me, the stress on her face vanishes, replaced by a smile that seems genuine to me—though I have to admit I don't know her well at all and would have no idea if she was faking it.

"Lily," she says, running a hand down my arm, and I love the way my name sounds in her accent. "So good to see you." And then before I can comprehend it, she pulls me into a hug and air-kisses both sides of my face. It's a traditional greeting here between friends and a bit intimate for me...though not with Marina. She smells amazing again, like apples and comfort. When she pulls back and meets my gaze, she's still smiling, the perfection of her teeth telling me she likely wore braces as a kid. "I've got some great ideas for your tour, but first, I want to hear what you like. I have a great place for us to go to lunch. It's close. Okay with you?"

"You're the boss," I say. "Lead the way."

She chuckles and shakes her head. "Oh, no. You are the boss." But she turns for the door anyway, and I follow her, waving a goodbye to Marco as we pass. Marina doesn't wave.

"The restaurant is close," she says as we start walking along the cobblestones, falling into step alongside each other. "I know the owner. I've taken some of my food tours there. Excellent food, great wine, fun to—" She stops and looks up, and I remember from the tour that this is what she does when searching for the right words. "People watch. Good views."

"Sounds perfect. I do a lot of people watching for my job, so that sounds right up my alley." I wonder if she's familiar with that phrase, but she doesn't ask me to clarify. We walk in silence for only a few seconds before I can't help myself and ask, "Are things okay with you and Marco?" I wince internally because it really is none of my business, but they both looked so upset after their discussion. Plus, my curiosity has been known to drag me lots of places I probably shouldn't go.

Marina makes a *pfft* sound and waves a hand like it was just a normal disagreement. And maybe it was—I wouldn't know. "My brother," she says on a sigh. "Every time I come to the hotel, he tries to tell me why I need to be working there with him and the rest of my family." She looks at me and widens her dark eyes as she stresses, "Every. Time." Then she grins, and I feel a little better about the unsettled look she'd sported earlier.

I smile back at her, and it's clear to me she doesn't really want to delve into the subject, which I'm fine with. As I said, none of my business. Plus, we're at the restaurant now. Marina walks right up to the man standing at the small podium at the doorway and hugs him. He's clearly thrilled to see her and begins speaking in Italian, which she reciprocates. I don't mind; it gives me a chance to look at her.

Italians dress differently than Americans. It's one of the first things I noticed when I got here. A bit looser, both in clothing and in attitude, and very European, unsurprisingly. Marina's wearing a pair of wide-leg black pants and a tan tank that I don't think I'd call cropped, but it's short enough that if she reaches over her head, I'd see her stomach. I wouldn't mind that at all, I decide. Her sandals are black, her toenails are polished candy apple red, and her hair—God, her hair. I've never seen such a gorgeous head of hair on a person in my life. Dark and wavy, she has it partially pulled back and it all just falls in loose curls down her back to her shoulder blades.

"Lily?"

I blink myself back to the moment to find both Marina and the man at the podium looking expectantly at me. I shake my head. "Sorry. What?"

"I asked if you wanted to sit inside or out."

The sweat suddenly making itself know between my breasts answers for me. "Inside, if that's okay."

Marina nods and points inside, and the guy leads the way.

The restaurant is small and narrow, with tables on each side along the walls, and we walk between them to a table for two in the back. Marina looks at me with her eyebrows raised, and I nod my approval.

"Cute little table for two. It's good, yeah?" She pulls out my chair, and the chivalry isn't lost on me.

"It's perfect."

We sit, and the waiter asks us about wine. That's another thing I've learned about Italy—it's never too late or too early for wine. I nod at Marina.

"Red or white?" she asks me.

"Surprise me," I say, and it comes out a little flirty, and I sit there wondering if I meant it to.

She orders in Italian, then tells me, "I ordered us a red blend that I had last week. It's so good. Not too dry, but not sweet. A little fruity, but not too much." Her passion is clear, and I can't help but smile at it.

"I'm sure it'll be great," I said. "I trust you." A weird thing to realize is true, but it is, and I am somehow not surprised.

The waiter is back before we can even begin to have a conversation, and I think Marina has some pull here. The staff all seem to know her, and the waiter chats with her in Italian while he opens the wine. When we each have a glass and he's left to give us time to look at the menu, Marina holds up her wine.

"To a lovely day, a lovely wine, and a lovely lunch companion," she says, and the words are genuine and heartfelt, I can tell by her face.

I smile at her and touch my glass to hers, and we both sip.

"Oh my God," I say. "That's fantastic." The wine is exactly as she described, and I take a second sip.

We don't need much time with the menu, as we both choose the Caprese salad pretty quickly, then have a little laugh about it. Marina also orders us some bread with olive oil for dipping, and when the basket arrives, it's warm and carries that wonderfully yeasty scent that tells you it's fresh.

"So." Marina pulls a small, very battered notebook and pen out of her bag. "Let's talk about what you like." She clicks the pen with her thumb.

"Old-school notes, huh? I'm surprised."

"Yeah? Why?" She picks up her wine and looks me in the eye as she sips, and I feel it all the way down to my toes.

"I don't know. I guess I just assumed somebody your age would be all digital. Phones, tablets, things like that."

"Somebody my age, huh? How old do you think I am?" She seems more amused than affronted, and her eyes twinkle. "Or maybe I should ask how *young* do you think I am?"

"I would guess thirty-five," I say, and those dark eyes go wide.

"Yes. You are exactly right. Wow. Impressive."

"Did you think I'd guess too high or too low?"

"Too low." She laughs softly. "You talked like I'm still in high school."

"I apologize," I say, both of us grinning. "I just meant you're a lot younger than me."

"Am I?"

I snort another laugh. "Um, yes."

"How old are you?" she asks and leans closer, looking me in the eye.

"How old do you think I am?" I ask, and I lean toward her, and yeah, this is definitely starting to feel a lot like flirting.

"Oh, no, that question is a trap," she says with a laugh, wagging a finger at me.

"But you asked me the same question," I whine in protest.

"Yes, but that's because you very nearly insulted me." She's grinning, so I know she's just teasing me.

I laugh and say, "Fair enough. I'm forty-nine."

Marina waves a hand and makes a pfft sound. "You're young."

I make the same sound back. "On what planet?"

"This one. You are as young as you feel," she says.

"Then I must correct my earlier response. I'm about eighty."

She laughs outright, and I think it's the first time I've heard it. I've seen her grin, I've heard her chuckle, but this? No, this is new to me. She throws her head back and lets loose a husky, throaty laugh that's so beautifully contagious, I have to join her. Several customers at other tables clearly feel the same way.

She pulls herself together. "You are young and beautiful. Embrace it."

Okay, yeah, she just called me beautiful. I let that settle over me like a warm blanket as I hold her gaze and say quietly, "Thank you."

She holds up her wine in salute, then sips, and before I can say anything else, the waiter arrives with our lunch.

"It's crazy to me that tomatoes, mozzarella, and basil can look so gorgeous together on a plate. It's so simple, yet so perfect." I take a photo with my phone—yes, I can be that person at times—before I dig in.

"It's a classic," she says, and the next few moments consist of us chewing and humming our approval. "Okay," Marina says, picking up her pen. "What kinds of things do you like?"

I tip my head and think. "Hmm."

"Architecture? Art and sculpture? Religion? Sports? Philosophy? Food?"

"I mean, that's quite a list," I say with a grin. But her dark eyes hold mine, and while her expression is open and friendly, there's also an edge of seriousness to it. It makes me want to be completely honest with her. I set my fork down, dab at my mouth with my napkin, and set my elbows on the table. Wine in hand, I say to her quietly, "I need help with inspiration. Romantic inspiration. As you know, I write. Mostly books, all romance. And I've been struggling lately with…" I let my thought trail off as I inhale slowly, then let it out. "I've lost my passion for my work." I say it quietly, but in earnest, and I can tell by the shift in Marina's face that she understands exactly what I'm saying.

"Oh," she says, her pen stilling as she frowns. "I'm sorry. That's hard."

I nod. Something about the genuine sympathy in her voice has created a small lump in my throat, and I don't trust myself to talk in the moment.

"Okay." She gives one nod of her head. "Passion and inspiration. I have ideas." And then she's scribbling away in her little notebook.

"I can almost hear the wheels turning in your head," I say with a soft laugh.

"I have ideas," she says again, then sets her pen down, picks her wine back up, and looks at me. She holds her wine up and says, "To getting your passion back."

I touch my glass to hers, and we sip, watching each other over the rims. There's something then, something I can't explain. A feeling? A realization? A knowing? I can't put my finger on it, but it feels…

Hopeful.

❖

Meals tend to be leisurely in Rome, I've noticed. People here aren't in the same kind of hurry as Americans, New Yorkers in particular. While I do keep an apartment there, I don't live full-time in New York City—the place everybody's brain goes to when you mention New York—but people who simply live in the state of New York have similar attitudes. We're very nice folks. And we are in a hurry, so *please* get out of our way.

It's not like that here, and the first few times I walked down a street in Rome, I had to consciously slow my speed. I was zipping past people, getting annoyed when I got stuck behind friends walking three across and leaving no passing room. It didn't take long for me to understand that it wasn't them, it was me, and now I do my best to meander, wander, stroll, to take in my surroundings and breathe the air and fucking *relax already*.

It's not easy, but I'm working on it.

Marina and I take our time and finish our lunch leisurely. I hit the ladies' room, and when I return, find that Marina has paid the bill. I give her a look, and she just laughs that husky laugh that I have already decided I adore.

"I have a tour to give," she tells me as we step outside. "So, I must go." The air-conditioning in the back of the restaurant was lovely, and now I feel like I've walked into a wall of heat.

"But I just made you eat," I say, jerking a thumb over my shoulder.

Her smile is gorgeous, it's official. "It's okay. I don't eat as much with tour groups I don't know. Serena is an exception. I feel comfortable with her."

"Easy to do."

A nod. "Okay, can you find your way back?" She points to my left. "I have to go this way." She points right.

"I'm totally fine."

"Good. I'll text you tonight with some ideas and we'll get to work for you, yes?"

"Sounds perfect."

There's a slightly awkward moment where she seems like she's going to hug me, thinks better of it, then overrules herself and suddenly, I'm in her arms. Her scent almost distracts me from the feel of her body against mine. Almost. And then it's over.

"*Ciao*," she says softly, stepping backward.

I give her a little wave, and she turns away, and I indulge myself by watching her as she moves down the cobblestone street, the gentle sway of her hips, the way the heavy and hot breeze lifts her hair just enough to rearrange the ends. She's attractive even from the back.

I give myself a literal shake so I'll stop gawking. Jesus, what am I, a fifteen-year-old boy? I turn on my heel and head back toward my hotel.

I take my time, putting that strolling thing into practice. The street is lined with little shops, and I wander in and out of a couple. The third one I step into holds shelf after shelf of little notebooks and journals and diaries. Exactly the kind of shop I can lose hours in. I move slowly, pulling things off the shelves to open them, feel them, smell them. Many are leather-bound, and I inhale quietly. The blank paper also has a scent that I love, and I lift one of the journals to my nose and take a sniff. The reality is that I don't need another notebook or journal. I have dozens at home. They are my kryptonite when I shop, and especially when I shop away from home. I find one with a deep green cover that speaks to me, then move further into the shop where the next shelf features small, pocket-size notebooks. My brain flashes me an image of the battered notebook Marina used, spiral bound at the top like the kind a TV detective would use when interrogating a suspect. I find a beautiful one bound in black leather, and before I can second-guess myself, put it on top of the green journal in my hand.

Ten minutes later, I am on the street again, my bag filled with three journals and a small notebook. I have no idea when or if I'll actually give the notebook to Marina, but I don't regret buying it. I hit a couple more shops before heading back to my hotel.

Marco is at the front desk, as usual, and I wonder if he's ever not sitting there. His friendly smile is the complete opposite of the expression he wore this morning, and I remember the heated discussion he had with his sister.

"*Buongiorno*, Ms. Chambers," he says, and looking at him now, I'm shocked I didn't notice the physical similarities between him and his sister sooner. Same nearly black hair. Same cheekbone placement. Same slightly almond-shaped eyes. Where Marina's are dark like roast espresso, Marco's are lighter, more like cedar or mahogany.

"*Buongiorno*, Marco," I say back as I push the elevator button.

It's amusing to me how worried I can get about leaving Reggie on his own for too long versus how often I come home, shouldering that worry, only to find him dead asleep on the couch/bed/floor in a sunbeam, all my worrying for nothing. Today, he's curled up on the couch in the living room, a furry little ball up against one of the pillows. Sleeping hard, judging by the amount of blinking and yawning he does after I walk in.

"Dude, you could start pulling your weight around here, you know," I say affectionately as I sit next to him and scoop him up. "I mean, throw in some laundry once in a while. Get some groceries. Bake cookies. You know?"

He looks at me with those marble eyes, then swipes his tongue across my nose, which makes me laugh.

"I missed you, too, sweetie."

We spend the next few minutes snuggling. I know he needs a walk, so I leash him up and take him out in the heat, which hasn't gotten any less oppressive. Luckily, Reggie is a couch potato and outside is simply a necessity. Within fifteen minutes, we're back in the hotel suite and I'm staring at the laptop sitting closed on the desk.

I've never looked at it as a nemesis before. It's always been an extension of me, my partner in this very solo job I have. I've never looked at it as something ominous. It's hard to do that now, and I try my best to breathe, to think, to let the creativity in.

I owe Scott an update at some point today. It's still morning at home, so I've got some time. But instead of pulling out the chair and sitting, I move to the window, push the sheer curtains aside, and stare at the buildings beyond and the street below.

It really is gorgeous, even here in my own personal cobblestone alleyway-street-thing. I'm learning who everybody is: which man owns the coffee shop and what the woman looks like who always opens the bag store at eight o'clock sharp. I can see all the activity from my large windows, and I've learned that I find it relaxing to people watch from there. I make myself a cup of tea, pull a chair up to the windowsill, and just observe. I breathe in the scents of Rome—the basil and the bread and the tomato sauce—and wonder if I will ever find myself again.

I sigh, pull my dog into my lap, and sip my tea.

CHAPTER SIX

Two days later, I'm at my desk staring at my laptop. I've written about half a scene and can't decide if I like it. I've got two female characters that I do kinda like. The main characters are pastry chefs who have a negative history and haven't seen each other in a long time, and I need to get them to fall in love. Which should be easy, given how many times I've done this, but it's been a struggle.

My phone rings, and I glance down to see that it's Scott. I can't put him off any longer. I take a deep breath and answer.

"Hey, Scott." I inject my voice with some cheer.

"Hey, how's Rome?" He also seems to be adding an extra note of cheer, and I appreciate the effort.

"Hot," I say, then laugh softly. I stand up and start pacing. "It's ridiculously hot. But it's good. Things are moving in the right direction." It's not exactly a lie. I don't say *things are moving in the right direction super slowly, as I'm writing about seven words a day*, but that's still the right direction.

"Oh, that's great. That's good." He clears his throat, and it's perfectly clear to me that he's being pressured by those above him. Guilt settles in my stomach like a peach pit, sharp and ridged and unpleasant. "Will I be able to see something soon?"

Scott doesn't normally ask to see pages up front. He trusts me. Or he used to. Now he wants to cover his ass, and I can't blame the guy. I've become untrustworthy, and that realization sits on me like an elephant parking on my chest.

"Yeah," I say, trying hard to keep that cheer in my voice, but it's difficult. "Sure. Give me a few more days, okay?"

There's a beat of silence. It's awkward. It's uncomfortable. Scott and I have never had trouble communicating before. Not once. "Lily… are you okay?" His voice has gone soft now, laced with concern, and it puts a lump in my throat. He's a good guy who cares about me, and I'm putting him in a terrible position by not holding up my end of the business arrangement. "You don't seem like yourself recently, and if I'm being honest, it has me worried."

The lump has grown. I struggle to swallow it down in order to speak, but Scott goes on before I can.

"Do you need anything? Is there something I can do to help?" The care in his voice brings tears to my eyes, and I'm incredibly grateful he can't see me right now. "I'm worried," he says again.

I clear my throat, wandering through the suite to the bedroom where Reggie is curled up on the bed. "I'm okay. Really. Just—" I clear it again and finally feel like I have my voice back. "I'm just working through a few things is all. But I'm okay."

"You're sure?"

"I'm sure."

"Promise me there's nothing wrong." Oh, he's pulling out the big guns now.

I swallow and lie to him. "I promise. It's all good."

A beat goes by, and I can picture him at his desk, his handsome brow furrowed with concern, his bright blue eyes a bit clouded, which happens when he's worried. Finally, I hear him take a deep breath and let it out. "All right. As long as you tell me you're okay. You know you can talk to me, right? About anything."

That's the truth. Scott's a good man and a good friend, and I probably should tell him the truth: that I'm blocked, that my passion for writing is currently nowhere to be found, that for the first time in my career, writing a story about two people falling in love feels like a slog uphill along a muddy road in a blizzard instead of the joy it used to be, and I don't want to do it.

But I don't.

Instead, I force a smile onto my face so that it tints my voice because I want him to hear it. I want him to hear that I'm smiling and there's nothing for him to be concerned about. "I know," I say. "And I appreciate that so much. You have nothing to worry about. I'll have something for you soon. I promise."

God, Lily, so many false promises. Who the hell have you become?

I hang up with Scott—who seems pacified, at least for the moment—and fall onto my bed face first, apparently worn out from all the lying. Reggie lifts his head and gives me a look.

"*I know*," I stress to him as I roll onto my back. "I know. Ugh."

I have no idea how long I lie there staring at the ceiling. It must be a while, because when I tune back in to my surroundings, Reggie is snoring loudly. I absently wonder what it's like to have such an easy, peaceful life. If only.

My phone pings near my hand, and I groan softly, thinking Scott has more to say. But when I pick it up and look at the screen, my stomach does a pleasant little roll.

Marina.

You free this afternoon? Around 3?

"I don't know, let me check my very busy social calendar," I say out loud to my empty room, then smile at my own sarcasm. I type back. *I am.*

The gray dots bounce, showing me she's typing, then her text comes. *Great. I'll pick you up then.*

She gives no details, and I surprise myself by not asking for any. There's something about Marina, a comfort around her, and it doesn't occur to me for a single second to question where she might be taking me. While I'm sure she's not taking me to some remote location to murder me and leave my body splayed in one of the many fountains in Rome, the point is that *she could be*. I don't know her well at all. I barely know anything about her. And yet I've agreed to go wherever she's taking me, and I'm not even a little worried about it. That's very unlike me, and I am kind of enjoying the mystery element of it. The excitement feels almost new to me.

Of course, instead of making me sit down and get some work done, having a plan in a couple hours makes me focus on my wardrobe instead. Anything to not write.

"Man, this is getting old, Reg. Very, very old." I sigh as I stand in the spacious closet where I've hung the majority of the clothes I brought with me on the trip, not knowing exactly how long I might stay. There aren't a ton of options, but I brought a lot of mix-and-match kind of stuff. Tops and jackets and tanks and short-sleeve button-downs. Since I have no idea where we're going, I opt to stay fairly casual.

I shower and dress in white linen pants and a royal blue and white patterned sleeveless top. A quick check of the weather app on my phone tells me it's in the low nineties, so I decide no jacket is necessary. I style my hair, glad that Rome has slightly less humidity than the northeast part of the States. Adding a bit of jewelry always makes me feel like I'm dressing something up a bit, so I add gold hoop earrings, a couple bangle bracelets, and a necklace with a teeny-tiny replica of Reggie's paw print that my niece had made for me for Christmas. Once my makeup is done, I stand in front of the full-length mirror and check myself out, looking with a critical eye before I give my head a shake.

It's not like this is a date, Lil.

No. It's not. At all. In fact, if anything, this is a business meeting. Marina and I never touched on payment, but my intention is to—obviously—pay her for her time. So, yeah, this is a business transaction.

"Nothing wrong with looking nice for business, though, right?" I glance over at Reggie, who looks like he wants to shake his head and roll his eyes at me. I sigh. "Shut up."

I head down to the lobby around two forty-five, after loading Reggie up with some treats to tide him over, and I'm surprised to find Marina already here. She's chatting with a woman maybe ten years older than me that I've seen helping set out the continental breakfast the hotel offers each morning. She has dark hair shot through with sporadic strands of gray, pulled back into a neat bun. Her brown eyes are kind and crinkle slightly at the corners when Marina makes her smile.

Marina sees me across the room, and—does her face light up? Maybe. She waves me to her with a rolling gesture of her hand, and just as she's about to introduce me to the woman, it clicks in my head because their smiles are exactly alike. I mean, exactly. Like a painter painted one, then made a perfect duplicate on the other face. This is Marina's mother I'm sure of it.

"Lily, I'd like you to meet Roseanna Troiani, *mia madre*. Mamma, this is Lily Chambers, the woman I told you about."

Roseanna turns to me and holds out a hand. When I clasp it with mine, she closes her other one over them, holding my hand in both of hers. Her English isn't as good as Marina's, but it's better than some Americans I've met. "So nice to meet you," she says, her accent much thicker than Marina's. "I hope you are enjoying your stay."

I nod, my hand still sandwiched in hers. "I love it here. Truly. The rooftop terrace is my favorite."

She looks to Marina, who translates what I said into Italian, I assume. Roseanna looks back at me with a big smile. "My idea."

"A good one," I commend her.

She and Marina have another back and forth in Italian before Roseanna lets me go and Marina takes my elbow and leads me to the door.

"Gotta get you out of here, or she'll talk to you for hours," Marina says quietly as we exit. "Americans fascinate her."

"Really? How come?"

"Lots of people feel that way. America is a fascinating country."

It's not really an explanation, but she's also not wrong.

We get out onto the street and she says, "Okay. Today, we walk. Yeah?"

I nod and she heads to our left. Most of the shops and restaurants I've experienced so far here have been to the right, so already, I feel like I'm heading into new territory.

"It's not far," she promises, and I fall into step next to her.

"What are we doing today?"

"Well…" She stops at a corner, and we wait for traffic.

Have I mentioned the traffic in Rome? Drivers here are nuts. Like, certifiable. Too fast, careless, reckless. Worse than drivers in Massachusetts, and that's saying something.

"You said you needed romantic inspiration, and one of the things I find couples enjoy greatly is taking a cooking class together."

"Okay, you've piqued my interest," I admit.

"Good." We don't have to go far. In about fifteen minutes, we reach our destination—a small restaurant that I probably wouldn't have even noticed if I was hurrying down the street. Marina holds the door open for me. "Let's cook."

❖

It's a pasta-making class. I can see that as soon as we walk in and are led to the back of the tiny restaurant, then down a very narrow flight of stairs. There are a few other people there, and the space is surprisingly large, given the small area we just went through upstairs. There are six tables set up, three on each side, and one in the front where a woman stands. She's wearing a white chef's coat and a smile, which gets even bigger when she sees Marina, and she squeals like a teenager at a boy band concert.

Marina goes to her and they hug, clearly happy to see each other, babbling in Italian and laughing. After a moment, Marina holds out an arm to me and says, "Anna, this is my friend, Lily Chambers."

I hold out a hand to shake Anna's but she waves it away and hauls me into a tight hug. "Any friend of Marina is a friend of mine," she says in perfect, accented English. "Welcome."

I thank her and she indicates one of the three empty tables for us. The other three are occupied by what I observe to be a married couple (they're wearing matching wedding bands), a family of three (the young daughter looks just like the father), and another couple, marital status unavailable to me.

Two burgundy aprons are folded neatly on the table, along with utensils and bowls. Marina hands me one, then puts the other on herself. It looks great on her, of course. She pulls her hair back into something messy and cute as what looks to be a family of four filters in from the staircase: a mother, father, and two twin boys of maybe eight or nine. They take the table behind us.

"I think we're all here," Anna says. "We've got quite a mix today, and everybody speaks English, so that's what I'll teach the lesson in, okay? Let's go around the room and say where we're from, shall we?"

"Introvert's nightmare," I whisper to Marina, who grins at me. The first couple is from Australia, the family of three is from Germany, the couple behind them is Canadian, and the family of four is also from Australia. "I'm from the United States," I say. "Specifically New York."

Anna gives a nod. "We usually have more Americans, so you'll have to represent your country on your own." She smiles at me, then looks at the class and holds out her arms as she says, "Today? We make pasta."

From a doorway to her right, which I hadn't noticed before, three more people in chef's coats enter the room carrying trays. They supply each table with ingredients. Eggs and water and semolina, to name a few.

"Have you done this before?" I ask Marina.

Her smile is instant. "I've taken Anna's class dozens of times, and I've made pasta with my mother about a million."

I frown. "I hope it won't be too boring for you."

"No way. I'm going to enjoy watching *you* make pasta." She bumps me with a shoulder, and for reasons I can't explain, I like her answer. Then she lowers her voice and leans close. "I think you should pay attention to that couple." She indicates the married pair from Australia. He's tall and a little gangly, and she's cutely plump. They haven't stopped smiling since we got here. "Anna says they're on their honeymoon."

"Well, that explains the canoodling," I say in a whisper.

Marina's dark brow furrows. "Can—what?"

I laugh quietly. "Canoodling. Like, being touchy-feely, heads close together, that kind of thing."

"Oh. Being in love, you mean."

I blink at her once before nodding. "Yeah. That."

She holds my gaze for a beat before Anna interrupts us with her first instructions, and soon, I am knuckle-deep in flour and eggs.

"You can mix this with a fork if you like," Anna tells us. "Some people find that easier. But my mother and my grandmother used their fingers and hands."

"Mine, too," Marina chimes in.

"I think it's better. Gives the dough a bit more love. And who can't use a bit more love, eh?" Murmurs of agreement and soft chuckles go around the room. I do a scan to find the twins behind me both with their hands in dough. The young girl across the aisle is concentrating hard, her tongue poked out at the corner of her mouth, and I'm impressed with the effort they're putting in. Both sets of parents are helping, and it's sweet to watch.

Also, Marina's not wrong about the newlyweds. They're also supplying me with an example of how this can be a romantic thing. Their heads are close together, their voices soft, both mixing the dough. I can't make out specifics of what they're saying, but I know they're talking. Every so often, the woman giggles, and the man looks very satisfied at having cracked her up.

"Good research, yes?" Marina says quietly.

"I forgot how wonderful it can be to have somebody make you laugh," I say kind of absently as I watch the couple.

"It's the best." There's a beat of silence before she adds, "This pasta isn't going to make itself, you know. Get mixing, woman."

I laugh and turn to look at her. She's smiling at me and gives me a wink and points at my unfinished pile of flour and eggs. "Yes, ma'am."

We each have a pile that we're mixing, and it's surprising how quickly it becomes a dough. Marina is much faster and better at it than I am, of course, but she's also patient. When I get frustrated, she moves to my dough and demonstrates how to knead.

She has great hands.

It's a fleeting thought that zips through my mind and then is gone. But I noticed it.

"Like this," she says as she rolls the dough back, then pushes it forward with the heel of her hand. "You try."

I do my best to imitate her movements. Anna strolls down the aisle. "Nice, Lily. Perfect."

I glance at Marina and smile like a kid who just got the math lesson correct.

"If your dough is too dry, you can add a teaspoon of olive oil to soften it up," Anna says loudly to the class. "If it seems too wet, add more flour."

Marina is standing close to me, and a glance across the aisle shows me that the newlyweds are nearly touching. Okay, yeah, I can see how this class could be kinda romantic.

"What are you smiling at?" Marina asks.

I shrug and shake my head. "Nothing. Just happy." It's true, I realize. I haven't enjoyed myself this much in quite a while.

"Good. Me too."

And then Anna is telling us we need to let our dough rest for an hour, and if we follow her through the mysterious door I didn't see, she has a light snack of charcuterie and wine for us.

"I love charcuterie and wine," I whisper to Marina.

She smiles that smile at me, and I can't help the thought that runs through my head: oh, yeah, this is definitely romantic. I picture my pastry chefs and wonder if putting them in some kind of class together would start some sparks flying.

"Ready?" Marina's voice pulls me back to the present. The rest of the room has filed through the doorway behind Anna's station, and Marina has her arm out, waiting for me to go first.

With a nod, I follow the others through the door.

❖

The charcuterie and wine was nice, but nothing rivals the actual dinner we have. While we were rolling and cutting our pasta dough, preparing it for cooking, the assistants were setting the table in the other room for the eleven of us, and it's gorgeous. Formal place settings, candles, a huge bowl of salad and a pile of fresh bread, complete with olive oil for dipping.

The assistants take our fresh pasta away while we all grab seats. It's snug, and Marina and I sit quite close, our knees bumping here and there. The room buzzes with conversation, everybody talking and laughing. The atmosphere is happy, excited.

"I'm having such a good time," I say quietly to Marina, and it's true. "This is the best time I've had so far on my trip."

"Really?" Marina smiles, and her cheeks tint just the slightest pink. "I'm so glad to hear that. Are you getting what you need?"

I hold her gaze for an extra beat. I know what she's asking. Am I getting inspiration for my writing? And I am. But I'm getting something more as well, something I'm not ready to examine quite yet. I nod. "I am. Thank you. *Grazie*." I try my hand at what tiny bit of Italian I've picked up.

"*Prego*," she says quietly. And then the assistants arrive with our dishes and the room is filled with gasps of delight and scents of tomato sauce and basil and I am honestly so happy to be here that I feel my eyes well up a bit. I feel Marina's hand on my thigh and then she's leaning in close. "Hey. Are you okay?"

I turn to meet her gaze, and the concern in her eyes is so real, so genuine, and that doesn't help the wetness in my eyes. I do my best to smile and reassure her. "I'm actually great. Just…enjoying the moment."

Her response is to smile and pat my thigh, and I can admit that I'm a little bummed when her hand leaves.

Dinner is fun, with lots of cross-table conversations, all in English with various accents attached. It really is a study in international friendship, and I can't remember the last time I enjoyed myself so much. We finish up, and when I try to pay, I'm told it's not necessary. I can't tell if Marina already paid or if they let us participate for free, but either way, they won't take my money. I finally talk them into letting me leave some extra to tip the employees.

"I think they only let me leave money to get me to go," I say to Marina as we exit out onto the street.

She laughs. "Probably." She doesn't tell me how we didn't have to pay. I don't push. For now. "So?" she asks as we stroll leisurely down the street, in no hurry to get where we're going. "Did you find some inspiration?"

"I think I might've felt a bit, yeah." The street is bustling, dusk beginning to settle over the city.

"Well, I have some other ideas as well. But I will leave—" She makes a face like she's thinking, then looks at me, her brow adorably furrowed. "The phrase has to do with a ball?"

"You're leaving the ball in my court."

"Yes!" She points at me. "That's it. I am leaving the ball in your court."

"Got it."

"So, you text me if you'd like to be inspired more. Okay?"

I realize as we walk that I have mixed emotions about that. Ultimately, though, it's probably a good thing that it will be up to me to reach out. I'm not okay verbalizing that. At all. Even in my head. But I know it's true. Another thing I know is true? I'm probably going to text her again. Yeah.

"Gelato?" Marina asks, pulling me out of my spinning thoughts. She's stopped at a little gelato shop and indicates it with her thumb.

"Absolutely," I say, even though I am stuffed beyond belief. "I'm so full, but I am never going to pass up gelato in Rome. Never."

"This is a decision I approve," Marina says and holds the door open for me.

The shop isn't terribly busy, but the wonderful smell hits me the second I enter. Why does Rome smell so good all the time? This place smells like chocolate and coconut and almonds, and I inhale deeply as the door closes behind me.

"Nice, eh?" Marina says, noticing my sniffing.

"Amazing." There are easily fifteen flavors under the glass display, and they don't look like ice cream at home at all. The tops are wavy, like the gelato has just been poured into the bins recently. It probably was. "Okay, what flavor do Romans choose most often?"

Marina lifts a shoulder. "I don't know about all Romans, but I can tell you my choice."

"Which is?"

"Pistachio." She says it differently, though. She doesn't say it with an SH sound, like Americans do. She says it with a CK sound. Like, pi-STAHCK-io.

"It's not pistachio?" I ask, saying it the way I always have.

She shakes her head and says it again.

"I say it wrong."

"Yes."

I correct myself and say it like she does.

"*Bene.*"

I'm pretty sure that means "good," and I feel like I just got a gold star from my favorite teacher.

Most places I've been to so far have employees who speak at least some English, but this doesn't seem to be one of them. Marina speaks in Italian, then looks over her shoulder at me. "Pistachio?"

"Yes, please."

A few minutes later, Marina and I both have pistachio, mine in a cone and hers in a dish. The heat is still a thing, despite the sun having set, and I have to work fast to keep my gelato from melting down my cone and all over my hand. I do the lick-and-spin move my mom taught me when I was a kid, and when I glance back at Marina, she's watching me. Just…watching. And the look on her face is something I'm not sure I have right. Wishful thinking, maybe?

"How's yours?" I ask, indicating her bowl with my eyes.

"*Perfetto.* Yours?"

"The best I've ever had. Hands down. So good. Thank you for suggesting we stop."

She seems to study me for a moment, like she's not sure she should say what she wants to say but then decides to. "I wasn't ready for the night to end," she says simply, and does that half shrug thing again.

"Same," I say, and when she gives me a puzzled look, I add, "It means me too. My niece says it all the time."

"Ah." She nods, and I'm pretty sure her smile grows.

My cone is now manageable, so I can pay attention as we stroll toward my hotel. When we get to the front door, I stop and look at Marina. I clear my throat. "I also wasn't ready for the night to end," I admit, my voice quiet. "But I have Reggie. He's gonna need to go out and eat and all that good stuff, so…"

"He needs his mamma, as all good dogs do."

"Exactly."

"Well, I will leave you to him. Please give him a pet for me." She eats the last bite of her gelato, then says, "And remember, text me if you need to."

What if I want *to?* I almost ask but catch myself. "I will. Thank you, Marina."

With a nod and a last glimpse of the sultry smile, she turns to go.

I watch. I admit it. Just like last time, the sway of her hips holds my attention. Damn, she is incredibly sexy. I can admit that to myself now that she's not standing next to me. Something about thinking that while she's right there in my space feels weird to me, but now that she's gone, the thoughts come rushing in like a dam just broke.

"All right, Chambers," I mutter to myself as I pop the last of my waffle cone into my mouth, and Marina disappears around a corner. "Get your mind out of the gutter."

I haven't been interested in another woman in quite some time, and I'm not about to start with somebody who's more than a decade younger than I am. No. She's fun to look at, but that's all. Well, she's fun to look at, and she's great company. But *that's* all.

CHAPTER SEVEN

A day and a half has gone by since my cooking class with Marina, and guess what I'm doing.

That's right.

I'm working.

Well. I'm trying to. And I've done a bit.

Not a lot. Not nearly what I need to. But I'm writing and it's the teeniest, tiniest of starts. I'm sending my pastry chefs to a retreat. A very sought-after, exclusive, invitation only retreat, taught by a renowned pastry chef mentor. They don't know the other will be there. A little forced proximity—especially for two people who already have a history—ratchets up the sexual tension, I have discovered, so that'll help. Another day or two and I should have enough to send to Scott, to tide him over for a while. My relief is so solid, it feels like I could hold it in my hands.

Marina definitely helped with inspiration, that's true. One of my chefs has to make some dough, and her kneading of it becomes a very sensuous thing for the other character to watch. I remember Marina's hands as she taught me how to knead the pasta dough, pulling it in with my palm, pushing it out with the heel of my hand. Honestly, how can something as simple and basic as kneading dough become sexy? How does it stir up desire? I have no idea, but as I was writing the scene, it absolutely did.

And now I sit back in my chair in front of the window of the living room and blow out a breath of relief. It's a scene. Not an entire screenplay, but a scene. A start. I still don't feel quite right, not super creative, the words aren't flowing out of my fingers like they so often have, but it's a start. I'll take it. At this point, I'll take just about anything.

Serena invited Reggie and me to join her for dinner tonight, so I take a quick shower and dress in a lightweight sundress. It's still stupid hot out, and I know Serena will likely have us sitting out back with that light, warm breeze.

When we arrive at Serena's, Ria leads us out back, as I predicted, where Serena is already sitting on a cushioned lounge with her feet tucked under her. She gets up to hug me and waves a finger up and down in front of me. "Love that dress."

I give a soft laugh. "I was wondering if you'd seen it already. My supply of clean clothes is running low. Do you know if there's a laundromat or something around here?" Ria hands me a glass of wine as I sit.

Serena makes a *pfft* sound and waves a hand. "Bring your laundry here. Ria will do it for you."

I scoff. "I'm not going to make Ria do my laundry. Absolutely not. I can do it myself." I see Ria hiding a grin as she heads back inside.

"That's fine, too. I even have a dryer." She reclaims her place on the lounge, and Reggie jumps up to curl up next to her, the traitor.

I frown. "Is that unusual?"

"Italians generally hang their clothes outside to dry." She pushes herself up a bit in her chair. Her hair is piled high on her head, a bright blond messy bun wrapped in a sheer red scarf. "But over the past few years, the humidity has gotten so bad, the clothes don't dry, they just hang there. So, they've started selling way more dryers than they used to."

"And you have one."

"Listen, I can't be hanging my fine washables outside for everybody to see. Gotta leave some things to the imagination." Then she laughs, and it's very nearly a cackle, which makes *me* laugh. "So? How did things go with your tour guide?"

I narrow my eyes at her, because how did she know I took Marina up on her offer? Then it occurs to me that I need to stop questioning what seem to be the magic powers of Serena DuBois and just answer her questions. "It was fantastic. She took me to a cooking class where we made pasta. I had a blast."

"And?" Serena says before sipping her wine. "Did it help?"

"A little bit. Yeah." It feels weird to get into the whole idea of my passion for my work and how much it's been ebbing and flowing lately. But I nod. "A little bit." I don't mention that after I wrote the dough kneading scene today, the creativity was done. I'm trying not to dwell on that, because one scene does not a screenplay make. I decide a subject change is in order. Well, a partial subject change. I don't want to talk about my work anymore. I do want to talk about Marina. "So, what's the deal with Marina and her family?" I relay what I saw between her and Marco.

"Oh, that." Serena sighs, and then Ria arrives with some charcuterie and tells us dinner will be ready in about half an hour. "Marina comes from a somewhat traditional family, and the hotel has been part of it for four generations now. Simply put, her father expects her to work there for the rest of her life."

"I see." I sip my wine, which is rich and peppery.

"And Marina, bless her, wants something different for herself. Something more." She sips and watches me over the rim of her glass, as if she's contemplating her next words. "She must really be fond of you if she picked you up at the hotel. She avoids that place like the plague for exactly the reason you described: Her brother is always giving her hell about not helping out with the family business."

"It was pretty heated," I agree.

"Marco's a nice boy," Serena says. "But a bit of a chauvinist. Thinks because he's the male in the family, he gets to boss his sisters around."

I grin. "I don't get the impression Marina takes kindly to being bossed around."

Serena laughs. "Oh, no. She does not. She is her own woman, that's for sure."

"I did meet her mom, though. She seemed nice."

"Oh, Roseanna? She's lovely. I've had her over for drinks once or twice with Marina, but she's quiet. Kind of shy." Serena smiles off into the distance, like she's remembering. "She did exactly what her husband and son expect Marina to do now: played her role. Helped her parents run the hotel." She sits up and holds out a hand, palm facing me. "And don't get me wrong. It's a gorgeous hotel. Very successful. Elegant. It does *very* well. But I think Roseanna would have liked something different for herself, so she doesn't push Marina the way the rest of the family does. She's…" She taps a finger against her lips as she searches for the right words. "Quietly defiant. I think that's a good way to describe her."

I think about the woman I met the other day, how she was cleaning and quiet and how much she looked like Marina. And also how happy she seemed simply to be in Marina's presence. "So…the hotel is hers? Her side of the family?" At Serena's nod, I say, "I've seen her cleaning, and I know she helps set up breakfast. I'm surprised she wasn't behind the desk."

"Oh, she hates the front desk," Serena says with a chuckle. "Plus, the kids speak better English. And Marco can be a bit of an egomaniac, so he likes to be the point person for guests. Makes him feel important, I guess."

Ria appears to let us know dinner is ready, and we trek inside to sit. Reggie trots in behind us and hops up on Serena's couch in the living room where he can see us but also be comfortable. He must realize he doesn't need to beg, as both Ria and Serena make sure he gets scraps. My dog is no dummy.

"I think I'm going to text Marina again," I say once we start eating, unaware that I'm going to say it until the words are actually out and floating in the air over the table.

"Oh, yeah?" Serena asks, her brows raising up to the edge of the scarf.

"She knows so much, about the city, the people, the buildings…" I look up and meet Serena's knowing gaze, and I shrug one shoulder. "And I like spending time with her."

Serena's smile isn't exactly smug, but it seems to say that she knows something.

"What?" I ask.

She shakes her head and tears a piece of bread to dip in the small saucer of olive oil between us. "Nothing. Nothing at all. I'm just happy to hear you've hit it off."

Hit it off.

Okay, I suppose that's accurate. Right? We enjoy each other's company, or so it seems. "Yeah, we have," I say. "I mean, I'm kind of a client to her, though, so…" I don't mention that she wouldn't take my money for the cooking class.

Serena lifts a shoulder. "Maybe. Maybe not." She pops a cherry tomato from the salad into her mouth and gives me that knowing smile again.

"Why do you always look like you know something the rest of us don't?" I ask her. I laugh, but it's also a serious question.

"Maybe I do," she says cryptically, then laughs softly and sips her wine.

❖

"Clearly, she's trying to set you guys up." Jessie's talking with her mouth full, and I can hear her fork against her plate. Or more likely when it comes to Jessie, her spoon against her cereal bowl.

"Are you having Fruity Pebbles for dinner again?" I ask with a chuckle.

"Nope." I can hear the crunching. "Cocoa Pebbles tonight."

"Oh, well, that's better."

"Stop changing the subject."

I sigh. I'm lying on my bed, watching the fan spin slowly on the high ceiling. It's still hot, but I have the window open so I can hear the sounds of the city—which has quieted, as it's nearing midnight. "I mean, it's not like I announced my sexual orientation," I say, to which Jessie snorts.

"Please. All you have to do is google, and it sounds like your neighbor lady did, so…next argument?"

"I have no idea of Marina's…preferences."

"I bet the neighbor lady does. Next?"

"She's a child, Jess. A zygote."

"You said she's thirty-five."

"Yes. Exactly."

"That's hardly a child. Age gaps are super hot, Lil. For fuck's sake, you write romance, how do you not know this?"

I drape my arm over my eyes and groan. "Well, my life is not a romance novel."

"Maybe it's time it was." She sounds so nonchalant, so matter of fact, that it takes me a minute to absorb her words.

Huh.

One of the biggest complaints from readers who are not diehard romance fans is that romance is "unrealistic." And while I can see why they might think that, I disagree. There's no reason your life can't be a romance novel—within reason, of course, as Jessie goes on to explain.

"I mean, you're probably not gonna marry a rich duke—or in your case, a rich duchess—but that doesn't mean you can't have a good time with a hot, young Italian girl you met while traveling, does it?"

"I guess not?" I form it as a question because that's how I'm thinking.

"You don't have to propose, Lil. But aren't you in one of the most romantic cities in the world? And isn't the reason you're there to gain some inspiration for your story? Seems to me the universe just handed that inspiration right to you on a silver platter, as my grandma would say. Maybe, say thank you and take it."

I manage to change the subject, but her words stay with me long after we hang up. My life has never been a romance novel. I've never been with anybody for longer than a couple years, and my last relationship was nearly ten years ago. I am woefully out of practice when it comes to love or even just dating. At this point? It terrifies me.

And yet...

Marina's face seems to float in the air above me. That smile. All that gorgeous hair. Those dark eyes that seem to know much more than they should. Without stopping to think about it, I snatch my phone back up and type out a text.

I'm ready for my next dose of inspiration.

It's not until after I hit send that I realize how late it is. "Oh my God, Reggie, why didn't you remind me what time it is?" My dog is sleeping hard and can barely be bothered to open his eyes and give me a look.

And then my phone pings. I freeze, afraid to look, but then I do.

Are you free tomorrow?

"Okay, so I will eventually take you someplace farther away, where we can't walk to it." Marina grins as she leads me down the street, then off in a direction I have yet to travel.

"Everything is so close here," I say. "I feel like I can walk to just about anything. Kind of like New York."

"True, but there's also so much more of the city, also like New York. You just happen to be staying in a very populated section."

She's wearing a pair of black shorts today, giving me the gift of her bare legs, which I have trouble not ogling, because *damn*. And I don't mean "damn." I mean "*day-um*." Because wow, her legs are beautiful. Muscular but shapely, deeply tanned. My mouth goes suddenly dry, and I clear my throat before I speak. "I don't mind the walk," I say, and it's true. The heat has eased up for us a bit. Instead of the high nineties, it's in the high eighties, and it's amusing how the high eighties can seem almost cool when you're so used to temps close to a hundred degrees.

"I will also, one day, take you someplace that doesn't involve eating or drinking," she says as she stops and turns to face me with a big grin. "That day, however, is not today." She reaches for the door to her right and pulls it open, then waves me in. "After you."

This isn't a restaurant, I don't think, and it almost seems closed. But then a woman greets us with a cheerful *buonasera* and gives Marina air-kisses on both cheeks and a big hug. They speak in Italian for a moment and then Marina turns to me, her arm out. "This is the woman I told you about. Lily Chambers, this is my dear friend from childhood, Angela Petrillo."

I expect to shake her hand, but Angela Petrillo pulls me into a warm hug, and I get the same two-cheek air-kisses Marina got. Angela is plump and soft, and her hug feels like comfort and home. I like her instantly.

"Welcome," she says. "Welcome. Marina has told me so much about you. Come." She waves us into the empty room where there is a long table, chairs, and wine. So much wine. Wow.

We sit in the closest two seats, and Marina leans close to my ear. "When you ask for inspiration, my mind goes to wine. I can't help it. The depth and flavors and stories behind wine…" She lifts a shoulder and whispers. "Inspiring."

It's easily the most fun I've had in longer than I can remember, and by the time we leave Angela's place—with longer hugs this time and promises to keep in touch—I'm more than a little bit tipsy. I don't know Marina well enough to know if she is as well, but she looks happy, her grin near constant.

"That was amazing," I say as we stroll down the street, which has come alive since a couple hours ago. Lights and music and people. The scents of food. The sounds of a soccer game emanating from every bar and restaurant we pass, including the collective, seemingly city-wide cheer whenever there's a play in Italy's favor.

"I'm glad you enjoyed it," she says, and I find myself leaning into her a bit, holding her arm for steadiness.

A couple passes us, a man and a woman, and the woman is beautiful, elegant in very fitted black pants and heels, and both Marina and I turn to look, follow her with our eyes as she passes. Turning back, our gazes meet. She grins and her eyes sparkle and I roll my lips in and bite down on them.

"She had a very nice…behind," Marina says diplomatically.

"She did," I agree.

"So, is that your, um, preference?" She doesn't look at me as she asks the question.

"What, behinds?"

That yanks a laugh out of her. "No. Women." She clears her throat, and it occurs to me that she's nervous asking this question.

"Ooohhh," I say, drawing the word out. "Women." I lean into her a little more, the wine making me braver than usual. "Yeah. It is. Though I'm more of a leg girl than an ass girl."

"Ah, I see."

We walk for another moment before I say, "Yeah, you don't get away with not sharing, too. So, is that your preference as well?" I hold my breath as I wait for her answer because I don't know what I'll do with the information, no matter which way it goes.

"Yes. I have always been gay."

"Always?" I ask, teasing her.

Her cheeks pinken, I can see it even in the low light. "Well, since I knew what it was to like somebody."

"I see," I said.

"You?"

"Oh, I was later than you. Not exactly a late bloomer, but later than you. High school. Fell in love with my best friend. That old song and dance."

"She was straight." It's not a question. Marina knows, as do most of us.

"Are they ever gay?" I say it with a chuckle. We can laugh about it now, but when you're sixteen, it's not even a little bit funny.

"Nope."

We walk along, enjoying the night, the atmosphere, the softness of slight inebriation, and it feels a little bit different between us now. I can't really put a finger on exactly how, but we've shared something personal, and the air between us has shifted because of it. I still hold her arm, and she doesn't seem bothered by that at all. In fact, she closes her hand over mine, and we walk along that way, and it doesn't feel weird at all. Quite the opposite, which would probably be more confusing for me if I had less wine in my system. But we continue to meander, and I think I sigh, because I'm so incredibly content right now. Marina tightens her arm, which kind of squeezes my hand against her body, and everything in this moment could not be any more perfect if I wrote it myself.

"Oh!" I say, remembering something. "I have something for you." I reach into my purse and pull out the little notebook I bought. Handing it to her, I say, "I noticed you could use a new one."

Her face is hard to describe in that moment. She's surprised, yes, but I think she's also really touched. I don't know her that well, yet, but I'm pretty sure she likes it, which thrills me.

"This…" She swallows and runs her fingertips across the cover, then looks up at me, her eyes soft. "Thank you, Lily. This is very kind."

"You're welcome," I say, and a warmth runs through me as we continue to walk.

We reach the hotel too soon. "We're here already? Well, that's a bummer." I say the words before I can think about them—stupid wine—and Marina's grin widens.

"We can always do it again," she says. "We're searching for inspiration, no?" She catches my eye. "Have we found any yet?"

I practically swallow my tongue trying to keep the words inside and not let them fly out into the Roman evening. "I think we're doing pretty well," I settle on, and it's not a lie. "But I'd like to do more." That's not a lie either.

Marina reaches past me and punches the code into the keypad on the door. The hotel's front entrance is locked after hours. She holds the door, then says softly, "You know how to find me." She gives me a kiss on the cheek—this isn't an air-kiss; I feel her lips against my skin—

smiles at me, then holds up the notebook. "And thank you again for this." She holds my gaze for a beat and then turns to go.

I watch her walk away, and maybe I *am* an ass woman, because that's where my eyes are glued. Again. She turns the corner out of sight, and I practically collapse against the doorjamb as I blow out a breath.

Good God, the woman knows how to make an exit.

CHAPTER EIGHT

My pastry chefs have chemistry!

Well, at least they do for this scene, and it's a relief. I've been writing all morning, and I don't hate what I've written. That alone is an accomplishment I haven't achieved in a while, and I want to keep going, but I've got a written interview I need to complete before the end of the day, I owe Scott a phone call, and I've got a Zoom meeting with an executive producer about one of my series she has questions about.

None of these people know how I've been struggling lately, and it's kind of a relief to bang out nearly an entire scene this morning and not freak out about it.

Of course, the source of this inspiration wasn't Italian food or even Italian wine. It was one Italian woman, and I'm not so naive that I don't get that. What to do with it is another story entirely.

Because I want to text her.

I want her to inspire me some more.

Is that a bad thing? "I don't think so," I whisper aloud, and Reggie lifts his head from his place on the couch and looks at me with what I'm certain is suspicion. Or possibly judgment.

"What?" I ask. He stares for a moment longer, then sighs the most put-upon sigh I've ever heard and rests his head again.

"Nice," I say. "Nice."

I decide to put the pastry chefs to bed—not literally; they're not ready for that yet—and take Reggie for a walk before I start in on my afternoon work. It's hot again, no surprise there, but September is closing in and the weather forecast promises slightly cooler temperatures in the next couple of weeks.

Will I still be here then?

It's a good question, one I contemplate as Reggie and I stroll down the block, but before I can dwell too much on it, my phone buzzes in my pocket. When I look at my watch, I see it's Chloe, my sixteen-year-old niece, a kid I have adored with all my heart since the second she was born.

"Hey, Thumper," I say in greeting, using the nickname I gave her when she was six months old and used to lift her legs in her crib and drop them back down, thumping loudly and shaking the whole house.

"Hey, Aunt Lil. How's Italy?"

"Hot," I say with a chuckle as I stop so Reggie can sniff the corner of a building where I'm sure dozens of dogs have already peed. "But good. How are you? Getting ready to head back to school?"

"I got a couple more weeks. Hey, how much do you love me?"

I grin. This is the question she uses just before she's about to ask me for a big favor.

"More than the whole universe," I say, my standard reply. "What do you need? New shoes? Taylor Swift tickets?"

"I need a week in Italy." She laughs, but there's an edge to it.

"Are you serious? What do your parents say?"

"They said okay, as long as it's okay with you and I wouldn't be in your way." I can picture her, slight grimace on her face, nibbling on her thumbnail while she waits for my response.

"Sweetie, you're never in my way."

"That's what I told them."

We both laugh, and just like that, we start setting it up. By the time Reggie and I get back to the hotel and I reserve a room for Chloe—listen, I love my niece, but I still need to work, and her teenage lifestyle of late nights and sleeping until noon doesn't jibe with mine—I'm super excited for her arrival.

"She's a great kid," I say to Serena later that evening as we sit in her courtyard sipping a crisp Pinot Grigio. "I really want her to meet you."

"I look forward to it," Serena says, stroking my dog's back as he sits draped over her thigh on her glider. "When does she get here?"

"Next week," I say. "My brother is notorious for waiting until the last minute. I'm guessing Chloe's been asking him about it since I got here. So, I used my points and got her booked."

"And she's okay flying alone?"

"Her parents are big travelers, so she's flown several times already. She's an old pro." It's one thing I don't worry about when it comes to Chloe. She's smart and savvy and takes no shit. She's got tons more confidence than I had at her age.

"Well, I'm thrilled you're going to have a visitor from home."

"Me too." We sip our wine, and it's still surprising to me how comfortable I feel hanging with Serena, despite only knowing her for a very short time. "Do you think some people are just meant to meet? Meant to be friends?" It's a sappy question, and I give her a look that I hope tells her I'm aware of that fact.

She grins, though, taking away any of my worry. "You mean like me and you?" At my nod, she says, "Absolutely. I think people come into our lives for a reason. We don't always know what that reason is, but we learn something from everybody that crosses our path."

"Yeah? What are you learning from me?" My tone is slightly teasing.

Hers is not, and her voice goes soft. "I'm being reminded what it feels like to have a good friend."

I don't know where the lump in my throat came from, but it's suddenly there. "That's really sweet. I'm very glad we met." I hold up my wine glass in salute and she does the same, and we sip. "So, what am I learning from you, then?"

"You're learning how to lighten the hell up and see things that are right in front of your eyes."

"Interesting. Like?"

"Like joy. Like contentment. Like opportunity."

I tip my head slightly as her words land. "Interesting," I say again. "Are you therapizing me?"

"Is that even a word?" She scoffs, but she's teasing me. "I thought you were a writer."

"That's what they tell me."

We laugh softly and then she says, "How's Marina? Seen her lately?"

And then we're off, and I'm telling her all about the wine tasting from the other day and how much fun we had. "I think she shook something loose because I'm writing. Not a ton. And maybe not that great, but it doesn't suck. I wrote this morning and was actually happy with it."

"It sounds like she's been helpful."

"She really has. In fact, I want to text her again. She said she had a list of other places to show me."

"She's a fabulous guide," Serena says. "I'm so glad you two are enjoying each other's company."

I give a little snort-laugh. "I mean, I'm enjoying hers, but I'm sure it's work for her, so…" I shrug and reach for my glass, but Ria is suddenly there and tops it off for me. Seriously, the woman moves like a ninja.

"Oh, I don't think it's work for her." Serena sips her wine and gazes over the rim at me like she knows something.

Hmm. Cryptic. Well, kinda.

"Regardless, she's been amazing. And I really want her to meet Chloe. I think they'd hit it off." I had a vision earlier, after I booked Chloe's flight, of her and Marina. They were laughing and joking, and I don't know where it came from, but it filled me with such joy.

"I'm sure they would." Reggie shifts his position against Serena and sighs happily. I just shake my head as Serena laughs and continues to stroke him.

"He's so uncomfortable here," I say with a roll of my eyes.

"I see that." There's a beat as we both gaze at my adorable dog, and then Serena says, "Hey, circling back to the subject of wine tasting, I'm having a wine tasting here next week. A few friends, a bunch of different wines, Ria's going to whip up some munchies. Do you and Chloe want to come?"

"That sounds fun. Let me see how she feels about it."

"She's welcome to come and bring Reggie, and if she gets bored, she can hang in my guest room where there's a big TV and all the streaming services."

"Perfect."

❖

I thought I could at least wait until the next day before I caved and texted Marina, but I was wrong. It seems that wine lowers not only my inhibitions but also my resolve.

Hi.

A super creative text, it's true, especially for somebody who writes for a living, though I do follow it up with a smiley emoji. So, there's that.

It doesn't take long for Marina to respond. The dots start bouncing right away. *Ciao, bella. Can't sleep either?*

I frown, then notice the time. Nearly one in the morning. Apparently, wine also renders me unable to tell time.

OMG, I type, *I'm so sorry. I didn't realize it was so late. Ignore me. Go back to sleep.*

The dots bounce again, then, *I wasn't sleeping, and I have no desire to ignore you.*

A pleasant little flutter shows up in my stomach, and I try to pretend I'm not smiling, but I am. Of course I am. I type, *Why aren't you sleeping? It's late.*

The dots bounce, then stop for a moment, then bounce some more, then stop again, as if Marina's having trouble finding the right words. *Too many thoughts.* It's a simple, vague explanation that I admire. It's exactly something I'd send, too.

I can relate to that. I nod as I hit send. *My brain never stops.*

A beat goes by. Then, *How's the writing?*

That perks me up. *Much better than last week.*

Fantastica! I'm so glad to hear that.

I can't remember the last time somebody played cheerleader for me. It's nice. *Yeah. Feels a little better. Still a long way to go, but...* I let it hang and send it.

Well, I have another idea, if you need more inspiration. She follows that up with a Cupid's arrow emoji, a heart emoji, and a devil, which is an interesting combination, to say the least.

Oh, really? I type back.

Yes. But we don't walk. It's a bit farther, though not far.

I grin as my fingers fly over the keys. *Mysterious! I'm in. When?*

Her response is immediate, as if she'd already typed it and was just waiting to hit send. *Tomorrow?*

I literally feel it as my grin blossoms into a wide smile. I admit it.

I even laugh softly and try not to overanalyze how much I actually *want* to spend time with this woman. *That sounds perfect. I need to work in the morning, but pick me up in the afternoon?*

The dots bounce and her words pop up. *I'll be there by 3.* She follows that up with a heart eyes emoji.

Can't wait, I send.

Sleep well, bella.

I pretend that I don't notice it's the second time in this conversation she's called me beautiful. Lots of pretending tonight. Lots of ignoring what's actually happening in my head, in my heart. I'm very good at it, really, feigning obliviousness, and I continue to do so as I brush my teeth and wash my face and slip between the sheets and snuggle with my dog.

Nope. Nothing to see here.

But I'm still grinning.

❖

"I'm sorry, what is this?" I ask, looking at Marina in surprise, then to my hand, then back to her.

"It's a helmet," she says, the *duh* silent but totally implied. She taps my skull. "Goes on your head."

"I kind of thought we'd take an Uber or something," I say, looking uncertainly at the powder blue moped in front of me. They call them scooters here. Or Vespas. But to me, it's a moped, and I've seen how Italians drive them. Crazily. Weaving in and out of traffic. Completely disregarding any kind of lane markings. Or traffic laws, it seems. It's shocking to me that I've been here for a couple weeks now and haven't seen a traffic accident involving a scooter. Yet Marina wants me to straddle one.

She's fastening her chin strap and glances at me as I continue to stand there, probably looking terrified. Because I kinda am.

"Oh, *bella*, don't worry." She laughs softly and wraps her hand around my forearm. Her grip is warm, firm. "I know how it looks, the way we are on our scooters. I hear it all the time from my clients who come to visit. But I promise you"—she squeezes tighter until I meet her eyes—"I *promise* you, I will drive carefully, and I won't let anything happen to you."

Her words are so soft and feel so genuine to me, and the fact that I weirdly trust this woman I barely know is confusing as hell. But I give her one nod, pull the helmet on, and fasten the strap.

The seat has a tiny back to it, which helps me feel a little less worried—a little. When I was a kid, I was riding a dirt bike with my brother. He was driving, I was behind him, no back on the seat. He hit a rut, and I went flying off because there was nothing to keep me from doing so. I wasn't terribly hurt, but it instilled a fear in me. I never rode with him again, and this situation now is giving me flashbacks. Marina gets on and flips up the kickstand, then makes room for me. She pats the seat, and I throw my leg over, and I was so busy worrying about dying in a horrific traffic accident that it never crossed my mind how close I'd be to Marina, how I'd have to wrap my arms around her, hold her tight, feel her body, smell her hair. Jesus Christ. I am feeling completely overwhelmed by, well, feelings. Fear, concern, arousal, excitement.

What the hell am I doing?

"Ready?" Marina asks, interrupting my internal meltdown. When I nod, she grins. "You're gonna have to hold on, you know."

"Right. Right." I slide my arms around her torso and clasp one forearm with the other hand.

"Don't worry," she says as she starts the engine. "I've got you."

It's very possible I'm squeezing the life out of her as we merge into traffic and head off to wherever she's taking me. I left Reggie with Serena, who was only too happy to take on dog-sitting duties so I could spend time with Marina, so she could be taking me for miles and miles. It's not like I can stop her; I'm kind of a prisoner at the moment.

But…it's not so bad, I must admit. We're going at a reasonable speed, she's not weaving in and out of cars like I've seen others do. At one point, though, it seems like she almost does, and I realize she is making a conscious effort to be extra careful with me on her scooter. I smile as I move my head to the left so I can see over her shoulder.

"Doing okay back there?" she asks as we sit at a red light.

"I'm good," I say. And I am. I tighten my grip on her, and she puts her hand on mine for a moment before the light changes and we're off again.

It's not a long ride. Maybe fifteen or twenty minutes, and after we cross the Tiber river, we're parking in a public lot. It surprises me that I'm sad to let go of her. We take off our helmets, and I gaze around.

"Welcome to Trastevere," she says.

"Trastevere," I repeat. "I've been saying it wrong. I've been saying tras-ta-VAR-ay." Her pronunciation is tra-STEV-array.

"I forgive you," she says, and takes my helmet so she can lock the two of them together on the scooter. "Okay, so, I wanted to bring you to Trastevere because it's—how do you say?" And she squints into the middle distance, something I have begun to find very charming. "Off the path?" The crinkling of her nose says she's unsure, but I'm not.

"Off the beaten path."

"Yes. That. Off the beaten path." We start to stroll as she waves an arm out like she's Vanna White presenting a prize. "This is a much more authentic Rome."

And I get it instantly. I do. It's still clearly Rome, from the cobblestone streets to the rows of cafés and shops, but there's something about the atmosphere. "The vibe is different," I say, a bit to myself and a bit to her. "It's, like…" My turn to search for the right word as we wander, and I take in the people as well as the businesses. "Bohemian, maybe?" That feels right. Trastevere seems more laid back, more relaxed, like there's a bit less hustle and bustle than where my hotel is. "I like it."

"Yeah? Me too. I live in this area."

"You do?" I don't know why I'm surprised to get this piece of information, but I am.

She nods. "I have had my flat for about three years now."

"And you live alone?"

"Just me and my plants."

"No pets?"

At that, she sighs. "I had a dog for a long time. Enzo. I got him when I first moved out of my parents' house. I was twenty-two, and I adopted Enzo from the shelter, so I wasn't really sure how old he was. They told me he could be anywhere from two to five. I had him for eleven years before he passed. He was the love of my life." She rolls her eyes with a chuckle at that, as if she thinks she's being silly. But I don't think that at all.

"I'm so sorry," I say quietly. "Losing a pet is so hard."

"I was a mess. Couldn't eat. Cried all the time. I'd love to get another dog, but I also can't imagine getting another dog. You know?"

She looks at me, and her expression says she's longing for somebody to understand. I wonder if her family didn't.

"I do. I don't know what I'll do when Reggie goes." My eyes tear up, and I indicate them with a flapping hand, as I laugh softly at myself. "Look at me, it's something that hasn't even happened, and I can't so much as talk about it."

Marina grabs my hand as she joins my laughter. She brings it to her lips and kisses my knuckles. "We are a pair," she says with a sniffle as she drops my hand, and I realize she was choking up, too.

"We sure are."

"Okay. Topic change." We're still strolling—it's more of a stroll than a walk—and I love the feeling here. I revert back to "vibe" because it's the perfect word. The vibe is just ideal, and I can see why Marina lives here. "I thought we could go to this little café that overlooks the river, have some tea or espresso, maybe a pastry, and we can wander after that, do a little shopping if you want, hit an art gallery or two. Then"—she checks her watch—"then at six, there's live music at this bar I know. The band's really good. We can have dinner there, listen for a while, watch people…"

"People watch," I correct her with a grin.

"Damn it. People watch. I will get that." She stops walking and turns to face me, and she's fucking breathtaking. I'm not kidding, the air literally stops in my lungs. I'm paralyzed by how gorgeous she is, and for a split second, I wonder what it must have been like for God or the gods or the Universe or whoever or whatever created her to gaze upon their finished product. How proud they must've been to have made something so movingly beautiful. "How does that sound to you?"

I'm caught up in my swirling thoughts and don't answer right away, and a look of concern parks itself on her face.

"Or we can do anything else you want. You're the boss."

It's my turn to grab her hand, and I don't hesitate. "That sounds like the most perfect date ever." I don't realize I've used that particular word until it's out of my mouth and hovering in the air between us, but Marina doesn't seem to be fazed even a little bit.

"I think so, too." She still has my hand. Or I still have hers. Or… our hands are still linked when she tugs me. "Come on."

❖

Fifteen minutes later, we're sitting at a round little table for two on the second-floor outdoor balcony of a little café with a name I don't even remember. We've ordered espressos and a plate of almond cookies. Our table has an umbrella open over it, which cuts the heat considerably without disrupting the gorgeous view we have of the River Tiber.

I sit back in my chair with a contented sigh. "This is perfect. Absolutely perfect."

"Yeah?" Marina looks pleased when I turn to her.

"Yeah. Thank you for bringing me here. For bringing me everywhere. You've been amazing." She still won't let me pay her, although I was able to bully her out of the way so I could buy our coffee and cookies. Small victories.

Speaking of—the waiter arrives with a tray and our order. The espresso cups are small and adorable, the opposite of the enormous plate of cookies that have my mouth watering instantly. The waiter leaves and Marina reaches for a cookie.

"They make these right here every day. They're better than my grandmother's." She takes a bite and gazes off over the river. "If you repeat that, I'll deny it."

I laugh and pick up my cup. The espresso is creamy and strong and nutty and just incredible. I must make a sound I don't realize because Marina is smiling at me.

"Good?"

"Delicious. Wow. You Italians sure know how to make coffee. Even the worst cup I've had here is better than any I've had at home. I'll be so disappointed when I go back."

Marina smiles and sips her own espresso, but doesn't say anything, and I think I see a cloud cross over her face, but I'm not sure. I don't know her well enough yet to get all her expressions.

I grab a cookie and bite into it, and the noises I make come all on their own. The cookie is crispy on the outside, but wonderfully chewy inside, and the blast of almond flavor wakes up my palate. "Holy shit," I say, chewing and looking at Marina in amazement.

She laughs. "Your eyes are so wide right now."

"This is the best damn cookie I've ever had. In my life. Ever. Holy shit."

She's still laughing, shaking her head. She picks up her cup again and looks out over the river. "I have such fun with you." She says it quietly, and I'm not even sure if I'm meant to hear it. But then she turns and meets my gaze and shrugs as if saying, *What can you do?*

"I have fun with you, too." And I mean it.

We're quiet for a bit, both of us clearly lost in our own thoughts. Then Marina turns to me. "Tell me about your family."

Okay. Slight topic shift, but I'm good with it. "My family. Let's see. There's my mom and dad. I have one brother, AJ, who is four years younger than I am. He has one daughter, my niece Chloe, who I love more than life. In fact, she's coming to stay here with me this weekend. And she would *love* you. Do you have time to meet her?"

"I'd love to meet her," Marina says without hesitation, and I realize I'm thrilled to have another reason to see her.

"Great. She should be here Friday morning. She's only staying a few days because she's got to get ready for school, but it'll be fun. She's sixteen. She's great. Funny. Smart."

"You light up when you talk about her."

I nod and grab another cookie. "She's my favorite person on the planet."

"You close with your brother?"

I chew and think about it. "I don't know that I'd call us close. I mean, he's my brother. I love him. But we're very different people. If there wasn't Chloe, I don't know how often I'd see him or talk to him."

She nods thoughtfully, like she gets it.

"What about you? Are you and Marco close?" I frown and wrinkle my nose. "I passed the office the other day when you were arguing."

She smiles what looks to be a sad one. "Marco and I were very close growing up. Probably because I wanted to be a boy back then." We both laugh softly, understanding how that happens to lots of us lesbians when we're young. "He's a little older and I followed him around like a puppy. He was my hero."

"I sense a 'but' coming."

She takes another bite of her cookie and chews for a moment before continuing. "But he can be kind of sexist, to be honest. It's not a quality I love about him. Our father is very traditional, and instead of helping to educate him and bring him into a more modern way of thinking, Marco tends to…" She squints and does that searching-for-a-word thing. "Emalate?"

"Emulate."

"Yes." She snaps her fingers and points at me. "He emulates my dad. Which means he thinks I should follow in my mother's footsteps and do the cooking and cleaning in the hotel. Women's work." She scoffs, pairs it with an eye roll, and grabs another cookie.

"Oh, that's frustrating."

"It is. And my little sister Valentina doesn't help. She's sweet but doesn't have much ambition, so she's perfectly happy to work in the hotel. It's easy and convenient for her." She turns to me. "Don't get me wrong, I love my sister. She's sweet and kind. But she has no drive. The hotel will be all she knows. It makes me sad."

"It's her choice, though, right?" I don't like the worry I see in her eyes. I want to make it better.

"It is." She lets out a soft sigh. "I know. Still."

"You want more for her."

"Exactly."

"Well, that just makes you a good big sister." I drink the last of my espresso. "What about your parents?"

"I love them. Wonderful people. My dad can be hard. And as I've said, he's not exactly a modern guy. But he's a good man. And my mother? She is the kindest person I've ever known." When she talks about her parents, her expression goes soft, and there's a tender smile that I wonder if she's even aware of.

"I feel that way about my parents, too, though my dad is pretty modern."

"When did you come out?"

"I was a freshman in college. I fell in love with my roommate. My very straight roommate. Such a cliché, just like my high school best friend." I snort a laugh and shake my head. "She started dating a frat guy, and I was shattered. Which was…" I sigh. "Just so stupid of me. But I was eighteen and it was such a deeper love than before, at least to me, and so spent the second semester of my freshman year just crying and being heartbroken. I was a walking young adult novel. My poor mother had to put me back together. That's when I came out to her. She said she'd pretty much always known, which kind of took the drama away."

Marina's grin is both amused and sympathetic. "We all have those kinds of stories, don't we? I'm glad your mom knew. And your college roommate has no idea what she missed out on."

I feel my cheeks warm, and it has nothing to do with the heat of the day. "I don't know. We're still in touch and she's married to the frat guy now. They have three kids."

"Ah, so, not meant to be, then."

"Nope." A beat goes by and I say, "What about you? When did you come out?"

"A bit earlier than you. I was still in high school. Played on the football team, er, soccer to you. Had a major crush on my coach."

"Talk about cliché." I laugh and reach over the small table to give her a playful shove in the arm. "Your coach? Seriously? So unoriginal."

"Says the girl who fell in love with her straight roommate." We spend a moment of amusement before she goes on. "It became kind of clear that I was different—even though I'd always suspected. So, one day, I sat in a café not far from school and I watched every person who walked in. And I told myself not to think about it, to answer instantly if I found that person attractive or not. I was there for almost three hours."

"And?"

"Every person I found attractive was female except one." She bites a cookie and says with a grin, "And that one guy was kind of girly."

"And it was decided."

She nods. "It was. Just like that."

"Okay. First girlfriend. Go." This is fun, getting to know her.

"Angelina Martini." She says the name so fast, I wonder if she somehow knew I was gonna ask. "She was beautiful and funny and athletic, and she broke my very young heart."

"Oh, ouch. That first one is the worst, isn't it?"

"The *worst*. How about you?"

"Michele Burton." I let go of a wistful sigh. "She was older, more experienced, and I was head over heels. We lasted a whole ten months before she decided I was boring and started seeing a mutual friend of ours. She actually called me a marshmallow."

Marina grimaces. "Ouch."

"Yeah. Took me a long time to recover from her." I finish my espresso. "Like I said, the first is the worst."

"Okay, how about last girlfriend?" And I swear to God, her dark eyes twinkle with mischief, which makes me laugh.

"Funny how neither of us is asking about current girlfriends,"

I say out loud before I realize it. Marina just continues to grin and finishes her espresso.

"I made an assumption," she says, setting her tiny cup down on its tiny saucer.

"Same."

Our gazes hold and there's an electric current of arousal that runs between us. It's almost visible, I swear, like I could reach out and grab it, feel how taut it is, pluck it like a guitar string.

"How about we compare worst dates instead?" I ask, hoping she doesn't notice that I don't really want to discuss my last relationship. She does, though, I can tell by the way she looks at me, and how weird is that? That I can read what she's thinking already?

"Okay," she finally says. "You first."

I nod and clear my throat. "This was about two years ago. I'd been single for a short time and was trying to get back out there. I swiped right on this woman on a dating app and we set up dinner."

"Ah, there's your first mistake," Marina says, finger up. "You start with coffee. Something short you can escape from if you need to. Something with a time limit."

"Now you tell me," I joke. "But you're absolutely right. My friend Jessie told me the same thing—*after* the fact. Anyway, I meet this woman at the restaurant. Shockingly, she's more attractive in person than in her photo."

"Ah, it's usually the other way around."

"Exactly. So, I'm pleasantly surprised already. We shake hands, sit down and…" I turn to Marina. "She never. Stops. Talking." Marina barks out a laugh and I go on to say, "I'm not kidding. Not once. She started talking and that was it. She never asked me a single question but went from the subject of her job to her family to her education to her cats to the menu to her favorite foods." Marina is cracking up at this point. "I think I said a total of about seven words the entire night. And they were to the waiter."

"You needed to be rescued!" Marina is still laughing, and I decide right here that, just like her accent, her laugh is a sound I love and want to hear more of.

"I know! And I never thought to set that up with somebody ahead of time. I was so out of practice dating." I shake my head with an embarrassed chuckle. "That was nuts." I grab a cookie. "Your turn."

Marina looks out over the river. "All right, so I was doing a favor for a friend."

"Uh-oh," I say, and she laughs.

"Exactly. A good friend of mine had a good friend who had gone through a divorce. They'd been together for many years, she didn't see the split coming, and she was devastated by it."

"She sounds like *lots* of fun," I say with a grin.

"The divorce was over a year before this date, and my friend was trying to convince her friend to get out there, to try dating, to stop staying in her house like an old woman."

"Good advice."

"Against my better judgment, I agree to take this woman out for coffee." She points at me. "See? I've already beaten you."

"Points for you."

"You say your date started talking and never stopped? Mine started *crying* and never stopped."

"Oh, no."

"Oh, yes. And I don't mean little sniffles and tears running quietly down her cheeks. I mean big, loud sobs. Blowing her nose. Streaking her mascara." Marina's eyes are wide as she tells the story, and it's my turn to crack up.

"Oh my God."

"That's right. Oh my God is right because how was I to get away? The woman is clearly heartbroken. Going through something. And the people in the coffee shop thought it was me! That *I* was breaking her heart. Oh, the looks they gave me. You should have seen. So, I couldn't just get up and leave, I had to hold her while she cried."

"No!" I say, drawing it out as I continue to laugh, and then we're both cracking up so hard, we're doubled over. She can't catch her breath, and my eyes are leaking tears. It takes a few moments for us to collect ourselves, but we're both still grinning. "I don't know which of us wins worst date," I say. "I thought mine was pretty clearly the winner, but yours might take it."

"We can call it a draw," she says, her expression warm. She glances at her watch. "Ready for our next stop?"

I am and I'm not, I realize. I'm learning that just about anything new with Marina is either fun or exciting or breathtaking or all three. But also? I could sit here with her, sipping espresso, gazing out over the

River Tiber, and telling each other stories from our lives for the rest of time, and I'd be perfectly content.

I push away from the table and stand. "Ready. Lead the way."

Marina holds out her hand, and I don't think twice before grasping it. Even as warning bells are chiming in my head, I know I'll go wherever she leads me.

CHAPTER NINE

The band is called Amore e Vino. Love and Wine. I have no idea why, but I kind of like it. The music is mellow but modern, sort of an amalgamation of jazz and new age. The lead singer sounds like a little bit of Diana Krall mixed with a little bit of Amy Winehouse. Sultry, deep, and soulful.

Marina somehow got us a seat up front, so our table for two had a fabulous view as we ate our dinners and sipped the most delicious Sangiovese I've ever tasted. Now our plates are gone, and we're both thinking about dessert but haven't decided yet. Our wine glasses are refilled by the super stealthy waitress who I swear keeps materializing out of thin air, and I sip as the band does an impressive cover of Adele's "Easy on Me." Again, the main word I think of to describe the lead singer's voice is soulful. There is such depth of emotion in her notes, she moves me to almost-tears, leaving a lump of emotion sitting in my throat.

They finish the set with that song, and the lead singer announces they'll take a break and be back. I look at Marina with my eyes still wet. "Wow."

"Pretty amazing, huh?" She says it with a proud smile, and just as I'm wondering about that, she stands up and the lead singer approaches our table to wrap Marina in a clearly ecstatic hug.

The woman squeals something in Italian, then pulls back to hold Marina at arm's length. She's slightly older than Marina, but not much, and she's dressed in all black—wide-leg pants, loose-fitting tank, a drapey scarf or sweater or shawl thing that I can't really discern—and her ash blond hair is piled on her head. Her eye makeup is dark and heavy, but somehow, looks just right on her.

Marina holds her arm out in my direction, and I stand. "Gina DiGiuseppe, meet my friend, Lily Chambers. Lily, this is my dear, dear friend, Gina."

We shake hands over the table, and Gina sizes me up in a way that isn't even a little bit subtle. "It's nice to meet you," she says, her English perfect but her accent much heavier than Marina's.

"Likewise," I say, then gesture to the corner where the rest of the band is standing and chatting. "You guys are terrific. Seriously. Wow. Wonderful."

Gina looks like she's not sure if I'm being sincere or blowing smoke up her ass, as my dad would say, so I stop talking and glance at Marina, who I'm pretty sure levels a look at Gina. It's like they're having a conversation without any words.

Gina speaks in Italian, and Marina answers her in English. This happens twice before Gina sighs loudly and switches to English, and I realize Marina is doing it for my benefit. I add another tick in her Win column in my head. They chat a few minutes longer, then Gina excuses herself to the ladies' room, and Marina and I sit back down.

"I appreciate what you did just then," I say.

Marina takes a sip of her wine. "What did I do?"

"I have a cousin who married a guy that's French Canadian. He speaks fluent French, but my cousin doesn't. Whenever his family comes to visit, they all speak French and he speaks it back to them while my cousin sits there with no idea what's being said. I witnessed it once and found it so incredibly rude. So, thank you for not doing that."

"It's one hundred percent rude," Marina says. "And Gina"— she hesitates for a moment before continuing with—"doesn't love Americans."

"No? How come?"

Marina wrinkles her nose and her voice has a sheepish tone to it. "She thinks you're all dumb and spoiled."

I bark a laugh before tipping my head from side to side. "I mean, she's not far off."

Marina laughs at that and looks relieved.

"So, how do you know her?"

"Oh, we dated." Marina says it so nonchalantly, then picks up her wine and sips again, that it makes me reach across the table and poke her.

"Well, no wonder she doesn't like me."

"Trust me, that's strictly about your homeland." But there's a soft twinkle in her eye.

"Why didn't it work out?" My question is genuine, not teasing, and I hope she sees that.

"Well…" Marina wets her lips as she gathers her thoughts, and I try not to audibly clear my throat at the sight. She waves a hand toward the band. "First of all, the hours are terrible. She sleeps all day and is up all night. I don't work that way. I'm more of a morning person, and I need my sleep. Second, we are just very different people with different goals in life." She shrugs to punctuate the simplicity of it.

"And you stayed friends. That's awesome."

"We did. I like her a lot. We just made very bad partners."

"I get that."

The restaurant has really filled up since we got here, and as the band returns, the vibe is even more palpable. Applause breaks out as Gina returns to her mic and smiles.

Marina and I have slid our chairs around toward the back of our small table so we're sitting next to each other. I reach over and grab her hand, and when she looks, I lean close and say in her ear, "I'm having a really good time."

Her smile is bright and warm, and she squeezes my hand in return. She doesn't let go of it.

❖

We leave the restaurant before the band is finished. It's my suggestion, and I'm okay with that. I'm ready to have quiet, and also to have Marina to myself again. Plus, I don't want to take too much advantage of Serena, who has Reggie.

"Are you kidding?" Marina asks as we step out of the restaurant and onto the cobblestone street. "Serena loves that dog. She'd keep him forever if you asked her to."

I'm not sure if she's trying to make me feel better or if she's angling for more time, and I'm not sure I want to know which it is. Because I'm not sure which I want it to be.

We stroll casually, hand in hand, back toward where we left Marina's scooter. Her hand is warm, soft, and strong. I like the way it feels in mine.

"I can't remember the last time I walked holding hands with somebody." It's a thought in my head, and I'm a little surprised when it comes out of my mouth.

"No?"

I shake my head.

"I think holding hands is underrated," she says, and that somehow seems odd to me coming from somebody under forty.

"You do? How come?"

"Because it carries so much weight." Her voice gets softer. "You just said, you can't remember the last time you held hands with somebody. Which means you don't do it often at all. It's not a regular, everyday thing. But when you do hold somebody's hand, it's likely somebody you trust. Somebody you care about. Somebody you want to keep safe or that wants to keep you safe. Somebody who cares enough to lead you or be led by you." Her thought seems to trail off and she shrugs in kind of an offhand way, like she's worried I might think her reasoning is silly.

I don't think that at all.

"That's beautiful," I say, and I mean it. "I've never really given it that much thought, but I agree with everything you said." I give her hand a squeeze to punctuate my words.

We walk quietly for a bit, and I just take in my surroundings. It's fucking gorgeous here, there's no way around it. The heat has eased enough where I'm not actively sweating the way I have been pretty much since my arrival. There's even a bit of a breeze coming in from the direction of the river. Now that it's dark and all the shops and restaurants are lit up, now that there are lights all along the river, now that people are strolling, just like us, I feel like I'm walking in a painting. One titled *Evening Stroll Through Trastevere* or something factual like that, featuring cafés and bistro tables with wine glasses on them, maybe a faceless couple kissing in the shadows, the whole thing with a tint of moonlight blue. It's dreamy and romantic.

For a moment or two, I start to think about my pastry chefs—my fictional characters who've been ever so stingy with the chemistry—and I wonder about putting them in a similar situation. Someplace where they're together, physically close to each other in the evening light. Surrounded by other people, but feeling like it's just the two of them. There's nothing more romantic than that feeling of the rest of the world just melting away...

"You still with me?" Marina asks softly, giving my hand a gentle tug.

"I am. Just thinking about my current work in progress and the characters."

"Ah. So, would you say this evening was *inspiring*?" There's a teasing lilt to her voice, and it makes me laugh.

"I would definitely say that, yes. You've done well."

We reach her scooter and she drops my hand, sadly, to unlock the helmets. "Well, just so you know, I have more inspirational ideas. Other places to take you. I mean, if you need more."

Do I need more? What a stupid question. Of course I need more. I don't even take a moment to think about it. "I'm in."

She glances up at me quickly.

"What, are you surprised?"

Her grin is sheepish. Maybe. The light is low and it's hard to see, but I think I've made her happy. Which makes me happy. Ridiculously so. She hands me a helmet, then holds her thumb and forefinger scant millimeters apart. "Maybe a tiny bit."

"Well," I say, pulling the helmet on, "you shouldn't be. You're a wonderful date." *Hostess! Hostess! I meant to say hostess! Damn it.* I clamp my mouth shut and concentrate on the chin strap, and I can feel my cheeks heat up. I'm glad for the dark. When I do finally glance up at her, she's grinning like she just won the lottery.

"You're a terrific date as well." She says it softly and holds my gaze for a beat before getting on the scooter and making room for me. And this ride?

Oh, this ride.

She goes slower, I'm pretty certain. I wonder if it's because it's dark, but I suspect it's to make the ride last longer. I'm holding on to her, wrapped around her just like last time, but I'm closer. I wasn't sure I could be, but I've pulled myself up against her until every possible part of us that could be touching right now is. And it's glorious. *Can we just ride like this forever? Please?*

She takes her time getting us home. I actually think she takes a different route. It's hard to tell in the dark, but we pass a few things I don't remember passing on the way there. We stop at a light, and she puts her feet down, then lays a hand over mine on her stomach, and it feels like the most natural thing in the world. We don't say anything. My chin is on her left shoulder and we're both looking off slightly to the left where there's a café and a man with a guitar crooning a love song I vaguely recognize. We watch in silence until the light changes, and we're off again.

Even though she takes a longer route and drives a bit more slowly, we still arrive back at my street eventually. It's dark, and while there is less activity on the street, it's by no means not busy. People milling up and down, a few shops still open, bars still have tables outside and we can hear muffled music coming from a few places. We park the scooter, lock up our helmets, and even after my protests—feeble as they are— Marina insists on walking me the short distance to the hotel.

Again, we walk hand in hand. Again, it feels like an old, comfortable habit.

We don't say much, we just stroll. When we reach the corner of the building where the door of the hotel is, we stop, and Marina looks down the street. "You need to go get Reggie?"

"Yeah, Serena is up late, so I'm not worried about waking her."

She nods, still gazing down the street. A beat goes by, like she's thinking about something, and then she turns her head and her eyes catch mine, and she takes one step toward me, which makes me take a small step back, and then I'm leaning against the warm solidness of the building behind me. Her hand slides along the side of my neck and into my hair, and I'm not surprised or taken off guard at all when she kisses me. I think I've known all evening it was coming, and I welcome it now. In fact, I'm relieved.

Holy crap, she's a good kisser.

I mean, it's been a pretty long time since I've been kissed—and it's been an extraordinarily long time since I've been kissed this well— so maybe I just don't remember what a good kiss feels like, but this? This is beyond good. Way beyond. This is, like, damn near fireworks territory. Marina's mouth is warm and soft and just the tiniest bit demanding. Not overwhelming. Not control freakish. Just in charge enough to give me a little taste of what could be if we ever went farther.

The world seems to fade away. Yes, I know how clichéd that phrase is, especially as a writer, but there's no better way to describe it. The street sounds muffle. The other people who I know are wandering up and down the street mere feet from us no longer exist; they just disappear from my awareness. There's nothing and there's nobody except Marina Troiani and her mouth on mine.

Neither of us push. We just kiss. I can't speak for her, but for me, I know if I nudge anything along, if hands get involved and start to wander, I'll be dragging her up to my room, and I don't want to do that. Not yet. Not now. That's not me. I don't fall into bed with people, no matter how attracted I may be. I'm not wired that way. But Marina could be an exception, and that realization has me slowly and gently ending our kiss. For both our sakes.

We stand there in the shadows with our foreheads pressed together, as if we need a few seconds to recover, catch our breath. I do.

"Wow." She speaks first, and it makes me grin as I open my eyes and tip my head back a bit so I can look at her.

"Agreed," I say, and Jesus, she looks so freaking sexy right now. Her face is flushed. Her lips are plump and still wet and she's smiling. Her eyes are sparkling, and I'm not sure I've ever seen a more beautiful woman in my entire life. And I've met several celebrities. I take a moment to gather myself, because this woman has completely discombobulated me. My hands are on her waist, and I use them to find my balance so I don't simply melt into the cobblestones like I'm made of chocolate and was left in the sun. "Well," I finally say, and gesture with my hand in the vague direction of Serena's place, "I should go get my dog."

She nods. "Yeah. Yeah, you should do that." She clears her throat and looks around. For what, I'm not sure. Then she takes a step back, and my entire body feels her absence.

I grab her arm to stop her from going too far. "Listen, I had a great time with you tonight."

"You did?"

"I did. Best time I've had in a long time. Thank you. *Grazie*."

"*Prego*," she says softly. "Text me?" She asks it as she's slowly walking backward away from me, and her voice is steady, but her face has the most hopeful expression on it.

"I will."

Her smile bursts into light, the white of her teeth visible in the streetlight, then she turns away from me and heads back to her scooter.

Again, I watch until she's out of sight, then fall back against the building again as if all energy has completely dissipated from my muscles. "Jesus Christ," I whisper into the night. I take a moment to replay our kiss. How it felt, the taste of wine still on her tongue, the warmth of her hand on my neck. "Jesus Christ." Because it bears repeating.

CHAPTER TEN

Chloe's squeal is high-pitched and loud enough to snag the attention of at least half the people walking down the street as she exits her cab at the corner and sees me walking toward her.

While I don't squeal, I'm just as excited to see her. It's been too long. I spent much of early summer in my apartment in New York City, and Chloe was a counselor at a summer camp, so our schedules didn't mesh. I haven't seen her in nearly two months, which is unusual for us.

I only get close to her cab before she runs and jumps into my arms, wrapping her legs around me like a chimpanzee.

"Aunt Lily!"

"Hey, Thumper." I hug her to me. She's always hugged me like this: a full body hug. And she's tiny—barely five foot one—so it's not hard for me to hold her this way. I spin her in a full circle before setting her back down so she can help the cab driver who is unloading her stuff.

"How was the flight?" I ask as we walk toward the hotel. She's got a large backpack slung over her shoulder, and I'm pulling her wheelie suitcase.

"Are you kidding me? It was incredible. I stretched out and slept for a few hours. And the food was really good."

I treated her to a first class ticket, which made me happy. "I'm glad you enjoyed it."

"It slapped. Seriously. Thanks, Aunt Lil."

Chloe and I have always been close. I knew by the time I was forty that having kids was probably not happening for me, and I was okay with that. I wasn't somebody who never wanted kids, but I also wasn't somebody who had to have them, like some of my friends are. I figured if I ended up with a partner who really, really wanted them, I'd be happy to coparent. But that didn't end up being the case, so Chloe is about the closest thing I'll ever have to my own kid.

In the Cavatassi, I introduce her to Marco, who she whispers to me is "hella hot," and he takes us upstairs. While my suite is considered the penthouse, there are still three other rooms on the floor, and Marco puts Chloe in the room right next to mine. There's no adjoining door, but I don't worry about her. She's a responsible kid, and I don't expect for a second that she'll sneak out when I'm sleeping. In addition to being responsible, she knows I'd kill her. And then I'd send her home so her father could kill her again.

Serena is having that wine-tasting thing tomorrow night, and she's invited both me and Chloe. I have no idea who else will be there, but Serena has yet to introduce me to somebody I don't like, and when I tell Chloe about it—and that she can bring Reggie—she's thrilled.

Tonight, though, since Chloe's flight didn't arrive until midafternoon and she's tired from traveling, we're going to have a leisurely dinner nearby, just the two of us. It's been far too long since I've had my niece all to myself.

I take her to a little café that I've been to a couple times, so I know that the hostess speaks impeccable English, and if we sit outside, again we can bring Reggie. Chloe is pretty much in love with my dog, so bringing him along becomes her thing, and she holds his leash. When we're seated, he sits at her feet, not mine, which makes me feign hurt, when inside, I'm actually grinning. I love that he loves her.

We order; Caprese salad for me and gnocchi for Chloe, who doesn't understand why I'm in Rome and not having pasta, and I'm forever grateful she doesn't have body image issues. I hope she never gets them. I almost tell her to ask me that question when she's over forty but decide I shouldn't put that on her. "Because the fresh mozzarella here is to die for," I say. I order a glass of Pinot Grigio, and the waitress turns to Chloe, whose eyes go wide.

"Can I get wine?" she asks in a whisper, like the waitress wouldn't hear her.

"If you tell your father, I'll kill you," I say.

She gives a tiny giggle and asks me what kind she should have.

"Can you bring mine and I'll let her taste it?" I ask the waitress, who smiles with a nod and is off.

"So?" I say. "What's new at home? Ready for school?"

She lifts one shoulder. "Yeah. I think so. Mom got me some clothes. I have almost all my supplies."

"What's gonna be the hardest?" The waitress brings us warm bread and a saucer of olive oil for dipping.

"Ugh. Calculus, I think." Chloe is not great at math. Like her aunt, she struggles with numbers. But unlike her aunt, she keeps trying until she gets it.

"Your dad any help there? He's good with numbers."

"He tries, and yeah, sometimes he does help." She takes a bite of her bread and makes a humming sound of approval.

"Right?"

"So good."

My wine arrives, I let Chloe sip, and she nods with enthusiasm, so we order her a glass. My brother would have my head. But Chloe is so happy, and I swear she sits up taller, like she's acting older. It's adorable.

Our dinners come and again, Chloe's eyes go wide at her plate of gnocchi. That lasts for an entire five seconds before she's digging in. We chat about regular life stuff—how her summer went, her parents, my parents, my work—before she gets what I call her "serious face." Her eyebrows furrow just slightly. She rolls her lips in a lot, as if she's thinking about the best time to bring up whatever she's about to bring up, and she avoids eye contact.

All those things start to happen as I order a second glass of wine, but I know from experience to wait her out. If I push her to talk before she's ready, she'll clam up and say nothing. So I sip my wine and watch the pedestrians that stroll along past us as the night begins to fall. Reggie is watching, too, and not for the first time, I'm so glad he's not a typical yippy Chihuahua mix. He's happy to people watch, just like his mommy.

"So, can I ask your advice on something?" Chloe finally says.

Here we go.

"Always. What's up?"

"Well," she says, then looks off into the distance and sighs. "There's this guy…"

I manage to keep from saying "Excellent!" and instead shift in my seat so my elbows are on the table and I'm leaning toward her. "Mm-hmm." I sip and watch her.

"Oh, stop it," she says with a wave of her hand. "I know you're thrilled. You don't have to hide it."

I laugh. I can't help it. She knows me as well as I know her, clearly. "Sweetie, I have been waiting for the *there's this guy* line for a good three years now. I can't help if I'm elated."

"What if I'd said *there's this girl*?"

"Just as elated. Duh."

"Maybe more so?" Her eyes twinkle with mischief.

"Maybe," I tease back. "But tell me about this guy."

Listen, I know my niece well. Sometimes, I think I know her better than my brother does because I have a bit of distance in that I don't live with her or see her every day. This means I can see changes in her expression or her body language more clearly than if I saw her every day and she was trying to hide something. So now, sitting across from her at a small, round table outside a little café in Rome, I can tell immediately that this is serious. That she's seriously into *this guy*. I am simultaneously thrilled and terrified. Thrilled that she's experiencing such exciting feelings. Terrified *this guy* will break her heart.

"His name is Jordan and he's just so cool."

"Okay."

"He plays football, and the team has been practicing the past few weeks at the same time we've had tennis practice and, well, we've been talking."

I instantly don't love that Jordan is a football player, but I catch myself for generalizing before I say it out loud. "Talking is good."

"We have so much in common." When she says this, her entire face lights up, and it warms my heart. "He loves video games. We both love *Animal Crossing*—which some guys won't admit. We play *Fortnite* together. We both love scary movies. He wants to go to law school." She sighs the kind of sigh that can only come from a teenage girl with a crush. "And he's not just a snack, he's the whole meal." She picks up her phone and scrolls for a few seconds before handing it over.

It's a selfie of Chloe and *this guy*, and she's not kidding. He's super cute. Tall, sandy blond hair, smiling blue eyes. He's got his arm around

Chloe, who looks absolutely infatuated with him. I have to admit, though, they're adorable together. Chloe is the all-American girl with honey blond hair, her eyes a stunning green. The two of them together look like models in a professional photo shoot for tooth whitener or sunscreen. Or condoms.

"Wow," I say. "He's cute."

"Right?" She does that sigh again, and I smile at her.

"What do you need advice about?" In my head, I'm shouting *Don't say sex, don't say sex, don't say sex*...though if she did, I'd help her in any way I could. I would just cry afterward.

"How do I ask him out?" She frowns and wrinkles her nose at me.

I blink at her several times, then indicate the phone with my eyes. "You mean, you're not already?" Those selfies sure make them look like they are.

"No. We're just good friends right now, and I've kinda been waiting for him to ask me, but then I started thinking, hey, it's 2025 and I'm a modern woman. Who says *I* can't ask *him* out?"

"Nobody," I say. "Nobody says that."

"Good. The homecoming dance is at the end of September. I want to ask him to go with me."

"Great. You should."

"Great. How do I do that?"

I stare at her. She stares back. Minutes tick by until we both burst out laughing. I sip my wine and ask, "What part of my life makes you think I'm the person to ask?" I'm joking a little. And I'm not joking a little.

She groans like she's annoyed at having to explain herself. "Aunt Lil. Please. You're practically famous!"

"Practically being the operative word."

"You hang out with celebrities."

"I've *met* celebrities. Big difference."

"You're worldly."

"I don't even know what that means."

"Aunt Lil." This time, she says my name through clenched teeth. "Help me. Please." She glances down at her hands and adds softly, "I really like him."

My heart squeezes in my chest, and I shift my attitude. My favorite person on the planet is asking for my help. "Okay, first things first: Do you think he feels the same way as you? Meaning, does he want to be more than friends?"

Chloe looks relieved at my questions, like this is what she's here for. "I think so? I mean, I haven't asked." She looks like the thought of asking makes her ill.

I take a deep breath. "Well. Okay. Here's the thing: I think you're gonna have to risk it. You know? You're gonna have to just ask him to the dance."

She grimaces and I hear her swallow. "Yeah."

"If you wanted to ask him to go just as friends, you could do that, too."

Her face flinches. "I think he'll get asked by one of the cheerleaders if I don't make a move that's more than friends. You know what I mean?"

I want to say *damn cheerleaders*, but I was one, so I nod instead.

"Can you help me word how to ask? I mean, you're a writer and you write romance. Can you help me write up a script to ask him out?"

"Now, *that* I can do."

❖

"Do I look okay?" Chloe makes a face just this side of a grimace, as if my gorgeous niece is ever anything other than gorgeous in my eyes. But I do my duty and scrutinize her—or pretend to—carefully. Her blond hair is in a messy bun, and I can just see the faded blue streak in it that she got on the last day of school in June. She's not really somebody who enjoys dressing up as much as her friends do—she'd rather be in comfy things like joggers or shorts and flip-flops. But she's making an effort today, with no prodding at all from me. I think she wants to make a good impression on Serena. She's wearing a cute sundress that has a subtle paisley print on it in light greens and golds. Her sandals are brown. "I should've done my toes," she says, gazing down at the chipped black polish.

"Sweetie, you look great." And she does. I think it's so cute that she's nervous because normally, *I'd* be asking *her* for advice on my outfit.

"I don't want your friends to think I'm a loser."

"Listen, I don't even know who else will be there. It's possible Serena is the only person I'll know besides you."

"And Reggie," she reminds me, reaching toward the couch to give my dog some love.

"And Reggie. We can all be losers together."

"Well," she says, nuzzling Reggie with her face, "you and me can be losers. Not Reggie. He's the king." Reggie looks at me over her head like he knows exactly what she just said and is very satisfied by it.

With a roll of my eyes, I go back into my bedroom to check out my own outfit. I wasn't kidding about not knowing who will be there. Serena's cache of friends is nothing if not eclectic, so I've kept it simple. Some lightweight, wide-leg pants in a pale yellow and an ivory sleeveless button-down shirt. Seeing Chloe's cute messy bun makes me consider growing my hair back out, but for now, I tuck it behind my ears, put on some simple gold hoops, and I'm ready to go.

"Shall we?" I ask her, my standard question whenever we're off somewhere together.

"We shall," she says, her standard response. She clips Reggie's leash on, and we head downstairs, where we wave to Marco before heading outside. "God, he's so hot," she mutters, and I wonder if I was even meant to hear it. Then she and Reggie are off to sniff stuff on the other side of the street.

I laugh when we get to Serena's gate and I say, "We're here," because Chloe's eyes widen in clear surprise.

"Already?"

"I told you it was close." I hit the intercom and the gate buzzes open.

"Close? That was, like, next door." She doesn't even need to redirect Reggie—when he sees where I am, he pulls her my way and runs through the gate with her laughing behind him.

"Told you he loves Serena."

Ria meets us at the door, and I introduce Chloe, who sticks her hand out to shake. Ria looks surprised but takes it with a soft smile, then leads us into the living room where Serena is chatting with a couple of women I've never met before. She stops mid-sentence when she sees us, gets to her feet, and comes across the room to embrace me.

"So good to see you, my friend." She bends to scoop Reggie up and lavish him with kisses—which he absorbs happily, his tail wagging furiously—then turns her attention to Chloe. "And you must be the niece your aunt can't stop talking about."

Again, Chloe sticks out her hand, and my pride swells. I taught her how to shake hands when meeting somebody new. I explained to grip firmly and look the person in the eye. I can still hear her giggling laughter when I demonstrated a "wet fish" shake. She was twelve.

"I'm Chloe," she says, looking Serena in the eye. "It's a pleasure to meet you."

More pride swelling on my part.

"Well, you look just like your aunt," Serena says.

Both Chloe and I say simultaneously, "But in miniature." We've heard many times that we look similar, and I'm not tall, but Chloe is super petite.

"Come in, come in." Serena unclips Reggie's leash and continues to carry him with her as she leads us into the living room, where the other two people sit.

Chloe leans close to me and whispers, "Um, she just took my dog."

I do a quiet snort. "Yeah, you've got some competition for Reggie's affections, I'm afraid."

"So not cool."

Serena sits on the sofa and indicates the couple sitting opposite her. "Kayla Tennyson, London Granger, this is my friend Lily Chambers and her niece, Chloe." She drops a kiss on Reggie's head and adds, "And this is my boyfriend, Reggie." I swear to God, my dog straightens up in her arms like he's trying to make a good impression on the newcomers.

Kayla and London both stand as I cross and shake their hands, then feel another surge of pride as Chloe does the same. Both women are stunning, especially London. She's tall, blond, thin. Her big eyes are a gorgeously deep blue, and I get the impression she doesn't miss a thing. Kayla is equally observant, but she seems less interested in the people in the room and more interested in our surroundings.

"How do you know Serena?" I ask as Chloe and I take seats.

"Oh, Kayla did work for my husband," Serena says. "She's in security."

Aha. That explains her attention.

"She and London are on their honeymoon."

I don't know why I'm surprised there are another couple of queer women in Serena's life, but I am. Pleasantly so. As if she'd been lurking around the corner waiting for Serena's words, Ria appears carrying a tray of glasses filled with what looks to be Champagne.

"A toast to the newlyweds," Serena says, holding up her glass.

Chloe looks at me, and I nod for her to go ahead and take a glass.

Once all our glasses are raised, Serena goes on. "May you never wonder if you're loved. May the sun always be on your faces. May you walk side by side for your entire life together, and if you can't, may one of you have the strength to carry the other. *Cin cin!*" We touch glasses and sip.

"That was lovely, Serena," London says. "Thank you." She turns to me as I tuck away that she's American, judging by her accent. "And what brings you to Rome?"

"Oh, I'm here to work," I say, not lying but not telling the whole truth. "And Chloe starts school next week, so she wanted a quick visit." I lean into her. "Cuz she missed her old aunt."

Chloe gives the teenage girl eye roll, but grins to take out any sting. "And to see my boy, Reggie." She sends a mock glare his way. "Not cool to abandon me after one day, my dude. Not cool at all." In response, he seems to shift closer to Serena, which makes us all laugh.

"So," Serena says, addressing me. "I know last week I told you this was going to be a tasting, but I've changed it to a game night instead. I hope that's okay. We just have such a fun, laid-back group tonight, I thought it would be perfect. Plus, we can get to know each other a bit. And there will still be plenty of wine, don't worry."

"I'm always up for game night," I say, not at all disappointed by the change. "Sounds fun." I turn to Chloe to see if she'd rather not stay, and she's grinning like a fool, so I know she's in.

The doorbell rings, causing Reggie to yip twice in Serena's lap, and a moment later, two men are led into the room by Ria.

"Everyone, this is James and Brandon," Serena says, standing and waving her arm toward the two in a flourish. "They own a wine bar near my old home in Nyack. And the way I love wine? Trust me, these boys got to know me all too well." She laughs and they laugh and then hug and kiss her, and their affection for her is clear. As she goes around the room and introduces us all, I notice James and Brandon have matching wedding bands.

Chloe leans close as the guys shake hands with Kayla and London and whispers, "Is this a queer party? Should I go?"

I bump against her playfully with my shoulder just as the doorbell rings again and Reggie repeats his two-yip notification.

"Thanks, Reg," Chloe says, and then Serena gives him a kiss on his head and hands him over to her.

"Your turn." Serena gives my niece a wink.

Chloe snuggles my dog happily—something that's always warmed my heart, their mutual affection—and settles back against the sofa just as the next guest is led in by Ria.

My heart rate kicks up several notches, and I can feel my face get warm because Marina has just walked into the room. Serena hugs her tightly, and Marina meets my eyes over her shoulder. Her smile grows.

"I'm late," she says to Serena. "My apologies."

Serena waves a hand and makes a *pfft* sound, then leads her into the room by the hand and goes around the room making introductions. When she gets to me, she says, "And you know Lily. And Reggie. Have you met Chloe?"

"I have not." Marina reaches a hand out and shakes Chloe's, and before I can brace for it, she bends and hugs me. In my ear, she whispers, "You look beautiful."

I almost laugh at her words, because *I* look beautiful? Has she looked in a mirror lately? She's wearing jeans today, and it occurs to me that I haven't seen her in jeans. It's been too hot. And it's also very sad I haven't seen her in jeans because two words: her ass. Holy shit. Her ass is the most perfect specimen of a person's behind I've ever seen in my life. Like, ever. She bends to shake hands with London, and I can't pull my eyes away. On top, she's wearing a black sleeveless top, and her arms are lean and muscular and deeply tanned. Her dark, dark waves of hair have been pulled back into a ponytail which, instead of making her look even younger, just makes her look casual and fun. I clear my throat and manage to wrench my gaze away. Finally.

"Okay, we're all here," Serena says with a clap of clear delight. "Who needs wine?"

We're all here and we're all queer echoes through my brain. Well, besides Chloe, but I now realize there are two queer couples, plus me and Marina, and is this a setup? Marina catches my eye and very subtly lifts one shoulder, as if she's wondering the same thing. Did Serena invite us both to hang with other gay couples because she's trying to tell us something? I mean, I wouldn't put it past her.

Ria has collected the empty Champagne glasses and returns with several kinds of snacks. Charcuterie galore, grapes, olives, bread—we will not go hungry while we play, that's for sure. She then takes everybody's wine order, because Serena has just about every kind of wine you can think of, and I absently wonder if this gorgeous house of hers has a wine cellar. I wouldn't be at all surprised.

Marina sits next to me so it's her, me, and Chloe in a row. "How are you enjoying Rome, Chloe?" she asks across me.

Chloe leans forward to see her. "I've only been here since yesterday, but so far, it's pretty dope. Right, Reg?" My dog licks her face in response.

"Trying to think of some cool places to take her while she's here," I say to my lap. Part of me is afraid to look at Marina while she's so close. I'm not sure I could control myself. "She flies home on Monday."

"We should take her to the Spanish Steps," Marina says. "At night, though. Super cool there."

"I read about those," Chloe says, and I can tell the way her voice has kicked up a bit in pitch that she's excited by this suggestion. "And Trevi Fountain isn't that far from them, right?"

Marina shakes her head. "Easy walk."

"Can we do that, Aunt Lil? Maybe tomorrow?"

"I'm sure we could," I say, because who needs to work? Then I chastise myself internally. I haven't seen Chloe in weeks, she's only here for a couple days, and it's not like I've been a writing fiend anyway, right? I pretend spending the day with Marina isn't something I'd absolutely love to do. Nope. Not thinking about that at all.

Ria returns with a tray of wine glasses and hands them out. Some white, some red, one rosé for James. I notice Serena is missing, but she returns in a few seconds with a stack of game boxes.

"Okay, who wants to play what?" she asks, and our night really begins.

"Wait," London says as Serena is opening the box with the game Taboo in it. "Lily Chambers?"

I nod. "Mm-hmm."

London slaps her own thigh. "I know you. Oh my God." She gives Kayla a playful shove. "She's a writer." Back to me. "You're a writer, aren't you?"

"I am," I say, holding a glass of wine.

"What do you write?" James asks.

"Novels and screenplays," London answers for me, then immediately apologizes. "Sorry about that. I'm just so excited to meet you. I can't believe it took me so long to put it together." Kayla still looks a little lost, so London clarifies, "She wrote the movie *Heartbreaker*." Kayla's expression shows surprised recognition as London turns back to me. "Right?"

"I did, yes."

"God, I love that movie. I loved the book more," she says, lowering her voice.

"She also had a book series turned into a TV series on Hulu," Chloe says, and I smile and shake my head slightly. Chloe is always tooting my horn for me.

"Wow," Brandon says. "So you're, like, famous."

"I wouldn't go that far," I say with a smile. I always falter a bit in these situations. It's lovely to be recognized, to have my work praised. But it's also always just the tiniest bit uncomfortable. Chloe used to tell everybody we met who I was, and it drove me nuts until I realized she was just a kid and she was simply proud of me, and she wasn't sure where the boundaries of oversharing were. I finally had to have a conversation with her about how it was okay for her to talk about my work, but only if it was brought up by somebody else.

"I mean, she's kinda famous," Chloe says, her grin painted with pride.

"Well, *Heartbreaker* is in my top five all-time favorite movies." London solidifies that with a determined nod. "Definitely."

I start to thank her, but Kayla is squinting at me like she's trying to look into my brain. "Was Aria Keller in that movie?"

"She was. She played the teenage daughter."

Kayla points at me. "She's a big client of mine."

"Really?" Marina asks, jumping into the conversation. "What do you do?"

"I'm in security. I have several celebrities as clients, and Aria is a regular."

London runs a hand down Kayla's arm, clearly proud of her wife.

"What a small world," Serena says. "Right? What are the chances you'd have some kind of *Six Degrees of Separation* connection?"

"I guess it just means we were all meant to meet," Marina says simply, and murmurs of agreement zip around the room.

"So," Serena says then and holds up the box top from the game. "What do you say? Are we ready?"

Let me state here that I had no idea my niece was so good at Taboo. Like, how have I known her for her entire life and never realized this? She's a ringer.

So, the game Taboo has teams. We start out broken into four of them, but after over an hour, both Brandon and I decide we need a break. So now the teams are Kayla and James, London and Serena, and Marina and Chloe. The idea is you get a card with a word on it, say *book*, for example. And then there's a list of words that are taboo— meaning words you cannot use as clues. You need to get your teammate to guess the word *book* without using words like *read, pages, cover, story, New York Times bestseller*, things like that. Kayla and James are comically bad. London and Serena are quite good—though not nearly as good as London and Kayla when they were on the same team. We had to break that up pretty damn quick. Marina and Chloe, however, are absolutely kicking ass.

Everybody is doubled over with laughter at the moment, me included.

"The fact that you got *eggplant* with only *phone* and *penis* as your clues is alarming to me," I say to my niece through my laughter. "What would your father say?"

"If you tell him," Chloe warns me, also through laughter as she points a finger at me, "I will never speak to you again." She's sitting on one of the sofas next to Serena, and Reggie is curled up between the two of them, fast asleep. Not for the first time, I marvel at his ability to tune out a very boisterous room in order to nap. Chloe sees me looking his way and puts a hand on his furry head. "He's good," she mouths, as if understanding that I was checking on him. She's such a sweet kid, full of empathy. That's something I find seems to be lacking in a lot of youth these days, and it thrills me that my niece cares about others in her world.

I shift my gaze and catch Marina looking at me. She grins, and with her flushed cheeks and bright eyes, it's clear she's having a blast. Much wine has been consumed, lots of good nibbles have been had, and the night is winding down, I think, which James and Brandon confirm when they stand and one of them gives the usual "Welp" signal that's pretty universal for "Time to go." It's funny how it only takes one person to start the flow of everybody leaving.

A glance at my watch tells me it's going on ten. I could stay longer—I'm surprisingly not tired—but I know Chloe must be. Her body clock isn't as regulated as mine. I give her the raised eyebrow look of *Ready?* She gives me a half shrug, like she's not sure, and pushes to her feet. Reggie is not happy about it, and he makes a grumbling sound that makes both Chloe and Serena laugh.

"We've disturbed the little prince," Serena says, giving Reggie a pet and a kiss on his head.

One by one, we hug Serena and thank her for a lovely evening. When it's Chloe's turn, Serena keeps an arm around her as she looks at me and says, "I like this girl. You can bring her around any time." Chloe blushes adorably.

The handshakes the evening started with have turned into goodbye hugs, all of us feeling like old friends now. Kayla sidles up to me and asks, "Where's your phone?"

I pull it out, and she and I exchange numbers.

"Next time you're in New York," London says, "give me a shout. We'll do dinner or have you over or something." She glances toward Kayla, who nods with enthusiasm.

"Definitely. It was great to meet you."

More hugs and then everybody is on their way, waving over our shoulders to Serena.

Chloe has Reggie on his leash, and Marina is still with us, even as the others head down the street toward where they'll meet their Ubers. We wave some more until they turn the corner and are out of sight. The same corner I've watched Marina turn so many times.

"Well," Marina says, looking down the street that's still bustling, "you headed back to the hotel?"

"Oh, I don't know," I say, hedging a bit.

"I'm not tired," Chloe chimes in, bless her. And then, as if to punctuate her words, Reggie gives one yip from the end of his leash and starts to walk away from the hotel.

"Clearly, neither is Reggie," I say with a laugh. I meet Marina's gaze. "I could wander a bit."

And just like that, the three of us and my dog begin to stroll the busy streets of Rome at night. Shops are still open, much to my surprise. It's not just bars and restaurants. We pass a leather shop, the stationery shop I've been to, and a little handmade soap boutique, all lit up and open for business.

Chloe and Reggie walk slightly ahead of us, which is amusing because she has no idea where she's going. I walk next to Marina. Close. Close enough to feel the heat coming off her body. Close enough to smell that scent I've come to know simply as Marina: cloves, nutmeg, cinnamon. She smells warm and inviting and tempting, like apple pie on a windowsill.

"Take a left up ahead," she instructs Chloe, who holds up her thumb in response.

"Got it."

Marina and I look at each other and grin. "She's awesome," Marina says quietly.

"I'm glad you think so," I say. "I'm pretty in love with her myself. Have been since the day she was born."

"I understand why."

We amble for a bit and pass a pizza shop. The scents of tomatoes and basil practically slap me in the face, in the best of ways. Before I can mention it, Chloe turns back to us. "Man, the smells in Rome? Fire. Absolute fire."

As time passes and I'm just about to suggest we turn back, Marina points straight ahead of us. Before she can say anything, I hear Chloe gasp.

"Are those the Spanish Steps?" she asks. "I read about them!" The excitement in her voice is obvious as she swoops up Reggie and picks up her pace. "Meet you there!" she calls over her shoulder, and zips toward the attraction.

Marina puts a hand on my arm before I can call any warnings to Chloe. "She'll be fine. She can't really get lost there. It's just a big square. We'll catch up." Her hand slides down my arm and her fingers brush mine, but don't grasp on. "I want to hold your hand again, but I don't want to cause any questions while Chloe is here."

I turn my eyes to hers, and I hope she can see my gratitude in them. "She leaves in two days," I tell her.

Marina nods, and we keep walking.

❖

The Spanish Steps are something to behold, which is strange to say, because they're basically a big flight of stone steps in front of a fountain. But they're also pretty much completely covered by people. Sitting, standing, climbing.

"Well, these are some busy steps," I say, mostly to myself, but Marina hears me and laughs softly.

"It's a huge attraction. Thousands of people a day pass through here."

I turn to her. "How do you know so much about everything?" I say it with a bit of a chuckle. "Like, you're a walking travel guide."

Marina points to me. "Exactly."

I squint at her.

"That has always been my goal." Her expression grows serious as she looks off in the direction of the fountain, which is lit up and spewing water from stone sculptures I can't make out. She glances down at her shoes as she says, "I am always fascinated by the history of a place. I do research to find out everything I can. Sharing what I learn with others is something that brings me such joy." She shakes her head as she gazes off into the middle distance, as if there aren't hundreds of people milling about. "My family doesn't seem to understand that." Her eyes focus on me again, and I can see her face start to light up as she speaks. "Whenever I go to a new place, I spend hours on the internet, learning everything I possibly can about the history of the city, the buildings, the people. I find the best attractions, both well-known and hidden. And I'm good at it."

She's speaking with such passion, I can almost feel it coming off her in waves. This is something she truly cares about, it's so obvious to me, and I suddenly understand the strife with her family. "And being stuck in the hotel would keep you from pursuing this passion of yours."

She nods, and the shadow of sadness that passes across her face squeezes my heart. "It's why I love the food tour so much. Because my boss lets me work out the route myself. I get to find little out-of-the-way places and introduce people to them and watch as they have the best day or trip or meal *of their lives*. It...I can't describe it. It's such an honor to witness."

It's official. I've never met anybody like Marina before. Ever. I'm about to tell her so when I catch, out of the corner of my eye, frantic waving coming from the top of the Spanish Steps. When I turn, I see Chloe, standing at the top, Reggie in one arm, and waving like a fiend with the other. I start laughing and point her out to Marina, who joins me.

"Take a photo," she instructs, and I pull out my phone and take several. "She'll be glad to have those."

"How many steps is that?" I ask absently, wondering if she's exhausted and if she carried Reggie up.

"One hundred thirty-five," Marina says without missing a beat. I turn to stare at her, and a beat goes by. Two. Then we both burst out laughing.

"I can't believe you just...knew that off the top of your head."

"I told you. It's what I do."

I shake my head with affection, then lean into her. I don't mean to. It's not intentional. My body just kind of...tips that way, and I feel Marina's arm go around me, tightening, holding me close to her for a moment before she lets go. I swear to God, if Chloe wasn't here, it's very possible I'd drag Marina back to my hotel room and have my way with her. Part of me is bummed. Another part is relieved, thankful for the situation and for keeping me from doing something too spontaneous.

But damn.

We stand there for a long time—or at least what feels like a long time. Just stand there, leaning into each other. Anybody looking at us might not notice because we're not holding hands. We're not kissing. We're not even looking at each other. But our bodies are touching. From our thighs up to our hips, our sides, my shoulder is pressed against her arm, and I would stay like this forever if I could.

I watch Chloe descend the steps carefully with Reggie in her arms—which I'm glad about, because there are so many people here. She glances up every so often until she sees us, then returns her focus to her feet until she reaches the bottom. Then she sidles through the crowds and finally reaches us. Her eyes are bright and sparkling, and her smile is radiant.

"This place is amazing," she says, and drops a kiss on Reggie's head. I expect her to hand him off to me, but she keeps possession. "There's too many people here to put him down," she informs me. "He could get stepped on. Plus, I think all the legs make him nervous. Can you imagine? You're walking along, and suddenly all you see are long, tall legs? Nothing else. How creepy and scary." She kisses Reggie again, and my dog looks completely content to be carried like the prince he is. We're quiet for a moment before Chloe addresses Marina. "Why are they called the Spanish Steps when they're in Rome? Did Spain build them?"

Marina shakes her head. "No, they were built by Italians. They're just named for the area." She spins her finger in a circle. "This is the Piazza di Spagna—the Spanish Plaza. So…the Spanish Steps."

"Well, that's boring," Chloe says, clearly hoping for something more action-packed.

"It really is," Marina agrees with a sigh, and the two of them stand there, looking at the gorgeous Spanish Steps of Rome with twin looks of disappointment on their faces. I manage not to bark out the laugh that wants to shoot from my mouth, because oh my God, they're so much alike right now, it's a little bit unnerving.

We spend a little bit more time just wandering. Chloe hands Reggie over to me so she can get some photos with her phone, and then she's sending texts and smiling at the screen. When she finally slides it into her bag and looks at me with a big smile, I ask her if she's ready to call it a night.

"Not really," she says, then proceeds to yawn, which makes us all laugh.

"But clearly yes," I say, and we head back the way we came, taking our time, in no hurry to leave one another's company. The trip back to the hotel seems to take much less time than the walk to the Spanish Steps, and it's my turn to be disappointed.

At the door of the Cavatassi, Marina turns to us. "I had so much fun tonight."

"Me too," Chloe says.

"Me three," I add.

"Chloe, I don't know that I'll see you before you leave, but if I don't, it was an honor and a privilege to meet you." Before she can say anything more, Chloe wraps her in a hug, and because she's so small, Marina has to bend. She stands, lifting Chloe off her feet and making her laugh.

"You're super cool, Marina," Chloe says. "I hope we meet again."

Marina doesn't say anything to me as she steps forward and wraps me in a hug as well. But in my ear, she whispers, "Text me."

I nod and she lets go. "Be careful getting home, okay?" I say.

"Always." She takes a couple of steps backward before she finally gives us a wave and turns to go. As is my normal behavior, I stand there and watch her go until she turns the corner and is out of my sight. A sigh escapes me before I can catch it.

"Wow," Chloe says as she turns to the front door of the hotel and punches in the after-hours code to open it. "You've got it bad."

"What?" My voice is about six octaves too high on that word, which kind of defeats my whole pretense of being insulted.

Chloe laughs. "Okay, Squeaky McSqueakerson. Deny it all you want. But I have *eyes*." She waves a hand over and around her eyes to showcase them. "And they have seen things." Then she laughs and laughs as we head for the elevator.

I shake my head and follow her, trying to deny the soft smile playing on my lips and the subtle heat in my cheeks, but I stay quiet, and I don't deny anything.

Mostly because I can't.

CHAPTER ELEVEN

I can't believe it's time for Chloe to go already.

One thing about my success that brings me pride is that I can do things like spring for my niece to come join me in Italy for a long weekend. I'm very aware that most people don't have that luxury or privilege, and I'm so incredibly grateful.

That being said, I'm sad to send her home.

We're tucked into the back of a cab—I didn't want to waste the time she'll spend driving to the airport, so I decided to go with her—and our cab driver is singing to his radio. It's not a song either Chloe or I recognize, and he's not exactly pitch perfect, but he's making us grin.

I pat Chloe on the knee. "I'm so glad you came to spend some time with me."

"Me too," she says, looking me in the eye. A shadow crosses her face, and she glances away as she says, "I wanted to talk to you about something."

"And you wait until the car ride to the airport to do that?" I say, trying to inject a little levity, because her expression has grown very serious. When her smile only lifts one corner of her mouth, concern floods me. "Are you okay? What is it?"

She clearly senses my panic because she rolls her eyes in that way that only teenage girls can do—that way that makes you feel like you're a totally ridiculous human. "Aunt Lil. I'm fine. I want to talk about *you*."

"Me?" Well. That's unexpected. "What about me?"

"We're...a little worried about you." She grimaces as if that wasn't exactly how she wanted to say it, like she's concerned about how I'll receive her words.

"We? Who's we?" I ask.

She looks slightly guilty as she says, "Me and Grandma."

My mother. It figures. Leave it to her to drag her granddaughter into her Lair of Unnecessary Concerns for Others. Don't get me wrong, I love my mother. But she needs to get a hobby that doesn't include other people's business.

"Don't be mad," Chloe says in a rush, and it makes me fix my face.

"Look," I say, choosing my words carefully. The last thing in the world I want to do is hurt my niece's feelings. "I know Grandma's concerned, but she shouldn't be talking to people about my work. I mean, sure, I'm a little behind, but—"

"Work?" Chloe looks confused. "I wasn't talking about work."

My turn to look confused. "I'm lost."

Chloe sighs, and again, she seems to look for the right words, this time outside the car window. A scooter whips by way too fast, and I have a fleeting visual of Marina. "We're worried about you being alone." When Chloe finally says it, her voice is quiet. Soft. She frowns and meets my eyes.

"Oh," I say, just as quietly. "I was not expecting that."

"It's just…it's been a long time, and Grandma says you're not dating and…" She lets her voice trail off for a beat as I silently seethe over my mother discussing my love life with my teenage niece. "Don't be mad," she says again, and I see the clear concern on her face. "You've just been alone for so long and then…" Her smile comes back and lights her up. "And then I see you with Marina, and you're so happy."

"Whoa, whoa, whoa," I say, traffic-copping her with a hand. "Marina and I are just friends."

Chloe snorts like that's the most ridiculous thing she's ever heard. "Yeah, okay. You look at all your friends like that? Do you lean against all your friends that way? I was there, remember?"

I blink at her and let a moment of silence pass before I speak. "Well, damn, girl."

That makes her laugh. "Yeah. Clearly, you think people are blind. Mainly me."

"I don't," I say and glance down at my lap. "I guess…" I shrug, not really knowing what to say. My feelings around Marina are so blurry and convoluted and I'm not ready to give them voice yet.

"She's super into you. Just so you know."

I roll my lips in and bite down on them, trying to hide the grin, but I can't, and Chloe sees it. She leans into me with a shoulder.

"Aunt Lil, seriously. She's so cool."

"Sweetie, she's way younger than me."

"And?" When I don't answer, she asks, "Why is that a thing?"

"I don't know. It just is." I'm trying not to sound anything close to irritated or annoyed or oversensitive, but I think I'm failing.

"Well, she didn't seem to think so." Chloe isn't pouting, but she's close. We're silent for a few moments. Then she seems to gather herself and turns to face me.

"Okay. Remember how you told me if I wanted to ask Jordan to the dance just as friends, I could do that? And I told you if I do, somebody else will ask him to go as *more* than friends?" I nod. "Well, that's what will happen here."

I squint. "I don't follow."

She tips her head to the side. "How long do you think Marina will last out there before somebody snaps her up?"

I blink at her. That's a question I have avoided asking myself. I saw how the lead singer of that band looked at her, how strangers in shops and restaurants and on the street look at her. With curiosity. Interest. Desire.

I don't like it.

Still. "Chloe. She lives in Italy. I live in the US."

Chloe looks at me expectantly. "And? What's your point?"

"Honey." I don't want to make her feel bad, but she's a kid. She has no idea how—

"You think people don't do LDRs all the time?"

I shake my head. "What's an LDR?"

She groans, and it's brutal. Can't remember a time when I've felt quite this uncool. "Long distance relationship, Aunt Lil."

"Oh," I say, drawing the word out.

"People are in 'em all the time. And they make 'em work."

"Well. Good for 'people.'" I make the air quotes, really wanting this conversation to be over. I'm not proud of the relief that floods me when we pass under the sign reading *Fiumicino Leonardo Da Vinci International Airport.*

Chloe sighs, and I hope it's the sigh of somebody who has given up trying to make their point. And that seems to be the case until we get her bags out of the trunk, and I ask the cabbie to wait for me while I get teary and hug my niece so tightly, she starts to wiggle in protest. Then I hold her face in both my hands, like I've done since she was a toddler, and I kiss her forehead, then both cheeks.

"I love you," I say.

"I love you, too," she says, grabbing my forearms. "And you're awesome and gorgeous and somebody like you should be worshipped, not all alone. That's all I'm saying." She smiles at me as I let her face go. She shoulders her backpack, telescopes the handle on her pullman, and hugs me one more time. "You're worth loving, Aunt Lil. Remember that."

She turns and heads into the airport. Over her shoulder, she calls, "And come home soon!"

I stand there, misty-eyed, and watch her disappear into the crowd, wondering if she's actually sixteen or a wise fifty-year-old disguised as one. Shaking my head, I climb back into the cab.

Her words echo through my head for the entire drive back.

You should be worshipped, not all alone.

Worshipped, huh? I can't say I hate the sound of that. I wonder what it's like to be worshipped. Not that I need that level of devotion, but you catch my drift.

You're worth loving, Aunt Lil.

Yeah. That one. That one worms its way in and settles around my heart like the gentlest of hugs.

I stare out the window as we drive, my eyes wet.

It's quiet for several miles—well, quiet except for the cabbie, who is now singing to Lady Gaga—and then my phone buzzes. Two texts.

One is from Chloe, telling me she cleared security, and also apologizing for getting "hella serious" on our last day. I, of course, tell her it's fine. Because it is. She texts back, *I just love you and want you to be happy.* Ladies and gentlemen, my teenage niece, sounding like somebody's grandmother.

The second text is from Marina, and all it says is *Thinking of you...* There's one red heart, and what the hell? Three simple words and a red heart have me all gooey inside? Just like that, I'm a mushball? Have I always been this easy?

Okay, so maybe Chloe was right after all.

Maybe I *do* have it bad.

❖

The words are flowing today.

Like, flowing.

This hasn't happened in months. Months and months and months and I am not going to look a gift horse in the mouth over it. (What the hell does that even mean, anyway? I make a note to google later...) I keep typing, and the sexual tension between my pastry chefs is so thick, they could cut it with one of their pastry rollers.

My fingers fly over the keyboard.

This. This is what every writer lives for. Well, I can only speak for myself, but I'm pretty sure this kind of forward motion on a project is what we all strive for. This pace. This steadiness. This confidence.

I don't normally stop at the end of a scene—I like to stop mid-scene so I can hit the ground running when I sit down next time—but I write the perfect hook to keep readers wanting to turn the page to the next scene, and then I realize how stiff my body is. When I glance at my phone, it tells me I've been working for four solid hours.

I can't remember the last time that happened.

I take a quick look at my word count and am shocked. It's been so long since I wrote that much in one sitting. I can feel these characters. I can *feel* them. It's exactly what I need to write a believable story, and it's only right now, in this moment, that I realize how very nervous I've been that I wasn't ever going to feel a character that way again. My eyes well up, and the deep breath I take is audibly shaky.

I push myself to my feet. I need to stretch, to move, my muscles are stiff, and there's a throbbing ache in my back. Reggie is on the sofa, but his head is up and he's watching me.

"How do you feel about a walk, buddy?"

It takes him about 2.5 seconds to be at my feet staring up at me in expectation.

"I'll take that as a *let's go, Mom.*" I clip his leash on him, scoop him up, and we head out to the elevator.

I'm not even sure what day it is. Chloe left yesterday, so that would make it…Tuesday? I think. Yeah. That's right. It's Tuesday. The front desk is empty, Marco must be off taking care of some hotel chore, and Reggie and I head outside.

The heat is very slowly starting to break, which is such a relief. It's warm, but bearably so, and we merge into the bustling foot traffic on our street. The sky is cloudy and gray and I wonder if we might finally get some rain.

Reggie and I take our time strolling. It feels good just to be moving. The chair in my suite isn't the most comfortable, and after so long in the same position, my back is screaming. But the walking is good, the feel of solid ground under my feet, the fresh air in my lungs, the bustle of others in this world with me, my adorable dog's butt as he trots along in front of me—all these things are highly noticeable right now. It's what happens when I'm in the perfect creative frame of mind. I see and feel everything around me as if it's magnified. Again, it occurs to me just how long it's been since I felt this way, this kind of observance and creativity.

My phone buzzes in my pocket. I look at the screen and have zero control over the grin that busts out across my face.

Ciao, bella. How are your words today?

I've gotten to the point where I can hear Marina's voice when I read her texts. And the crazy part is that her accent does things to me now, right here in the street, with her nowhere near me, when I'm reading her words, and the sound is just in my head. I get a little flutter low in my body, and a quick throb between my legs reminds me that I'm alive. My brain immediately tosses me an image of the two of us kissing.

I inhale deeply and let it out slowly.

Yeah. This woman.

I type back.

Hi! Been writing like crazy but needed a break. Walking Reggie right now.

The dots bounce for a bit before her words appear. *I'm nearby. Need a break from the crazy writing? A glass of wine?*

And now my grin turns into a chuckle. *I'm in Italy…does anybody ever say no to a glass of wine?*

Never, she replies, then gives me the name of a café that I recognize, having walked past it many times in my strolls.

It's not far from where Reggie and I are, and when I reach it, Marina is already seated at an outdoor table for two, with a glass of wine in front of her and another waiting for me at my seat.

The throb hits me again, a little harder this time.

"I could get used to this," I say as I absently bend and kiss her cheek. I don't even think about it, like it's just the most natural thing to do. And it is. Something zips across her face, but it's gone before I can get a solid read on it. I sit and make sure Reggie's leash is secure, but there's really no need. I've learned in Italy that he seems to enjoy people watching as much as I do. He plops himself down near my feet, tongue lolling from that walk and the heat, and settles in as I pull his small collapsible bowl from my bag and pour some water from my own bottle into it. Satisfied my dog is good, I focus on my date as I lift my glass, the crimson wine absolutely gorgeous to look at. "Here's to having somebody who gets your wine for you ahead of time."

Marina smiles that sexy smile at me, and we touch glasses and sip.

"Oh, good God," I say. "That's delicious."

Her smile is satisfied. "Thought you'd like it."

Talking with Marina has become so incredibly easy. I don't know when that happened. It's like I've known her for years and know she gets me, and when she asks about my writing, I just open up like a faucet.

"I may have finally found my groove with this book," I say, and I can feel my own excitement rolling through me, the way I always get when the story is flowing along smoothly. "I can't remember the last time it came this easily."

"You were struggling earlier, no?" Marina puts her forearms on the table and leans toward me, clearly interested in what I'm saying. I can't remember the last time *that* happened either.

"I was, yes." I take a sip before I continue. "Honestly, it's been a long time. I've struggled for…quite a while now."

"I remember. What do you think has changed?"

Her question is so innocent and genuine, and I almost laugh. And then I toy with honesty. Do I tell her the truth? Do I make something up? Do I dodge the question altogether? When I look at her, when I fall into those dark eyes, when I'm caressed by that gentle smile, there's no option other than honesty.

"You. That's the change." I say it softly. Not quite a whisper, but close. "You've inspired me. And I'm not easily inspired, believe me."

Marina's cheeks blossom a pretty pink, but her expression is one of clear satisfaction. "Me, huh?"

"You."

"Well." And here, she gets what's just this side of a goofy grin on her face.

Yeah, she's definitely satisfied with my answer, and she's so fucking cute and sexy right now, I start entertaining fantasies about the two of us. Naked. Oh my.

"I did offer to help with inspiration, and you did accept that offer, so I guess we both win."

"I guess we do."

And then there's a lot of staring. Eye contact. Knowing half-grins. The throbbing between my legs is tapping away, making sure there's no way I can ignore it. My underwear is suddenly damp.

"So, I was thinking," she says.

"Uh-oh."

"Funny." That smile again. I'm focused on her mouth, and my brain sends me an image of kissing her. Then I lose myself and when I come back to the present, I realize she's waiting for me to answer the question she just asked.

"Sorry. What?"

Her grin is knowing—how is it that I feel like this woman I've barely known for a few weeks can see right into my soul?—and she repeats her question. "I asked if you're busy for dinner."

"Tonight?"

"Yes. It's actually why I texted in the first place. I wanted to invite you to my place for dinner."

The idea of getting to see where Marina lives, to be in her space and surrounded by her things is much more appealing than I even want to admit to myself, and I don't hesitate. "I would love that."

Her face lights up so brightly, I wonder if she thought I'd say no. "Yes? *Eccellente*."

"What can I bring?" I ask.

"Nothing. Your beautiful face. And Reggie." We both look down at my dog, who is happily watching the world walk by. When I glance back up, Marina is studying me. Her eyes on me feel like her hands on me, and I like it. We stay like that for a delicious moment before she breaks our gaze. "I will text you the address. You can take a cab or an Uber."

I nod. "And are you cooking?"

"Oh, yes. Is there anything you don't eat?"

I ponder for a moment before shaking my head. "If it's food, I tend to eat it."

"*Eccellente*," she says again, and there's that flutter again that her accent causes in me. She finishes her wine, and I follow suit.

"I should probably get back to work," I say. "You know, I'm usually sad when our time together is over, but now I know I'll see you later, so it's not that bad." I swallow, surprised that I let myself say those words out loud, but there they are, floating in the air between us. I brace, but Marina's smile just gets bigger.

"Me too," is all she says, and we stand, Reggie included.

"Thank you for the wine. That was a much-needed respite." She squints at me, and I smile as I edit, "Break. A much-needed break."

"I'm glad I could help." With a jerk of her thumb over her shoulder, she adds, "I am this way." It's the opposite of the direction Reggie and I are headed, so I nod.

"See you tonight," I say, and I really, really like the sound of that. So does Marina, given how her expression softens. This time, she bends to kiss my cheek, then strokes it with her thumb.

"Bye."

And yes, I watch her walk away. I am no dummy.

❖

This is a date.

I have to actually talk myself into accepting that as fact. Marina and I have been doing this dance long enough to understand that this is a date.

And therefore, I must dress accordingly.

That also means I must obsess and second-guess and try on everything I brought with me in order to find the best outfit. Because of course I do.

"I should've taken the time to go buy something new," I mutter as I whip off the top I'm wearing, utterly unimpressed with it. Reggie is on the bed watching me. He didn't look terribly impressed with that shirt either.

Here's the problem: I don't want to overdo it. I also don't want to underdo it. On top of that, I only have limited options because I didn't bring my entire wardrobe to Italy with me, obviously. I also didn't expect to be going on an actual date while in Italy. I'm supposed to be here to work. But after much obsessing and stressing and throwing items on the floor, I finally decide to walk the line between super casual and dressed up. I go with a simple pair of white capris and a light blue top with capped sleeves and an open-notch neckline that dips enticingly. I top the clothing off with wedge sandals that give me a tiny bit of extra height, some small gold hoop earrings, and a spritz of my favorite subtle perfume—a scent I found in Paris that's surprisingly soft and inviting.

I scrutinize myself.

I'm not tall. I'm not well-endowed. I have nice eyes, I guess. The blue of them is pretty unique, like my mom's. My hair is a simple light brown, but it hangs neatly today, swooping just slightly over my left eye. It just skims the back of my neck, and I tuck it behind my ears. Normally, in this case, I'd FaceTime Jessie and get her straight-girl opinion on my outfit. But for reasons I don't want to delve into right now, I don't want to involve anybody else. I don't want to explain what I'm doing or, worse, feel compelled to justify it. All I want to do is take my dog and enjoy an evening with Marina.

If we end up doing a little more making out, so be it.

Marina texted me her address, and when I plug it into my GPS, it tells me she's about seventeen minutes away.

"Ready, Reg?" I ask my dog, and he jumps to his feet, as if he's known all along that he's coming. I cross to the bed before he can get down and grab his little face in my hands. "Now, listen, sir. We're going to somebody's house that you've never been to, and I need you on your best behavior. All right? No chewing things that aren't yours. No lifting your leg on stuff to make them yours. Understood?"

He swipes his tongue across my chin before I can dodge it, but it makes me laugh. I've already packed up some dinner for him, and to that tote bag, I add a pair of flip-flops, knowing I won't last long in these heels, however slight, and the bottle of wine and package of fresh cannoli I grabbed an hour ago.

I clip Reggie into his harness and leash and we head out to catch our Uber. The driver gives Reggie a look, and for a moment, I think he might turn us away, but he waves us in. He's already got Marina's address, so we settle in, and I keep Reggie on my lap so the driver won't worry about his seats. Of course, I didn't think it through when I stepped into white pants, and I sigh as I think about how they'll be covered in brown fur when we get out. Ah, well. Life with a dog and all that.

Waze was correct, and the Uber pulls to a stop outside a large building in under twenty minutes. I recognized when we drove over the River Tiber and remembered Marina saying she lives here. This is Trastevere again, and it's hopping. I thank the driver, and Reggie and I exit. Again, the vibe is different, more boho, more relaxed, but just as busy as the city center, where I'm staying. I take a moment to simply look around—and to let Reggie pee on a small tree—before I turn to the building looking for the front door.

I find it, and it's not locked, which surprises me. But inside is a small foyer with a bank of mailboxes on one side, a row of buzzer buttons on the other, and another set of doors that is locked. Marina is on the fifth floor, and I push the button with her number next to it.

"*Ciao*. Lily?" Why is it that even hearing this version of her voice that sounds like she's standing in a tin can still does things to me?

"*Sì*," I say, hoping to impress her with my nonexistent bilingual talent. The buzzer sounds, and I pull the door open, and Reggie and I are in.

The silence descends immediately, and I chuckle internally because I'm at the age where the first thing I think is how well-insulated the building must be. I push the button to call the elevator and scoop Reggie up, knowing he won't step into it on his own. When the door opens on the fifth floor, Marina is right there, standing in her doorway to the left, her smile huge. Something inside me clicks, like I'm a puzzle piece that just snapped into the right spot. It's weird and wonderful at the same time.

"*Ciao, bella*," she says, and her happiness to see me is so crystal clear on her face, I can feel it settle in and warm me from the inside. She wraps me in a hug, and I breathe her in, that inviting apple pie scent filling me. She kisses me softly on the mouth, like it's the most natural thing in the world—and it feels like it is—then she takes Reggie's leash from my hand and steps aside so we can enter. My eyes roam over her quickly, so as not to be caught staring, and I swallow hard. She's in jeans and a drapey black tank top, her bronzed arms toned, her hair down, her feet bare. I remind myself to breathe.

I kick off my shoes and enter. Her flat is lovely, and very much Marina. It's modest, small, but smells like her and is decorated in lots of earth colors, which is exactly what I'd expect from her. From the deep chocolate brown of her sofa to the mustard yellow chair in the corner, from the creamy tan walls to the moody painting of what looks like a Roman street at nighttime, it all fits perfectly with the warm comfort I feel around Marina.

"This is nice," I say to her. "I love it."

She scoffs, but with a smile, and bends to unclip Reggie from his leash. He immediately begins to wander, and I feel a small zap of worry. Reggie's a good boy ninety percent of the time. The other ten? He's been known to pee on a random garbage bag or the corner of a bedspread. That's all I'm saying. Marina must see my expression because she waves it away with a fluttering hand.

"He's fine," she says. "Not to worry." We stand side by side, watching him wander and sniff, for a long moment before she turns to me. "Wine?"

I nod, and she runs her hand along my shoulders as she passes me. A pleasant shiver falls down my spine. It's in that very second I realize exactly where this night is headed. And I accept it. And I welcome it.

Reggie takes his time sniffing every single piece of furniture, plant, and even Marina's shoes on the mat by the door, and I watch him until I'm satisfied he's no danger. Marina appears with two glasses of a gorgeously crimson wine, and that's when I take a sniff of the air.

"Oh my God, what's that smell?"

"Dinner," she says with a coy smile.

"Duh." I do my best Chloe impression. "What is it, though?"

"I kept it simple. Cacio e pepe."

"I mean, I don't consider any kind of meal you say in Italian simple, but also won't be turning it down, so…" I hold up my glass. *"Cin cin."*

She touches hers to mine while her dark eyes capture my gaze and keep it prisoner for what feels like a long time. I couldn't look away if I wanted to. Which I don't.

"Come." She jerks her head toward the kitchen, and I follow. "The sauce is on, but I need to cook the pasta."

Her kitchen is a small galley type, and feels both snug and roomy—I'm not sure how. There is one pot on the stove, and before I can glean anything else about it, Marina slowly moves into my space until my back is against the counter and her nose is nearly touching mine. She leans in and kisses me softly, and when they say things like *the room fades away*, they're not kidding, because I swear to God, it does. There is nothing but me and Marina and her mouth on mine. The kiss is tender and wonderful and over before I can fully sink into it. But then she sets our wine glasses down, grasps my hips, and gives me a playful look.

"Jump up," she says, and I do, and then I'm sitting on her counter. "I want to talk to you and look at you while I cook."

Jesus, this woman.

"You'll get no argument from me," I say, doing my best to inject a bit of flirtatiousness into my tone, despite being woefully out of practice. "I'm happy to watch you while you cook."

Her grin is sultry, so I'm giving myself a point in the W column.

"So, tell me about this cachi-ohde—" I attempt, fully aware that I'm slaughtering the Italian language.

"Cacio de pepe," she says again, and how I manage not to swoon at her accent every time she speaks, I have no idea. "Cheese and pepper. It's a classic Roman dish, but so simple, I'm guessing you haven't ordered it yet. Most people come to Rome and want to try all the fancy pasta dishes. This one is deceptive in its simplicity, because it's *delizioso*. And my favorite."

"That right there sells me."

The pot on the stove is filled with nothing more than boiling water and the generous amount of salt Marina tosses in. She doesn't have a salt shaker, she has a little wooden box, and she grabs the salt with her fingers and sprinkles it into the water. Next is the pasta. She gives it a stir, then moves to the block of cheese on the counter. She slices a piece off and hands it to me, then takes one herself. It's heavenly. Creamy and firm with a slight tang.

"Pecorino Romano. From sheep's milk. Also a Roman staple."

She begins gathering items for salad, and I love watching her hands. The way she moves them—chopping, sorting, mixing—the way they are the perfect combination of strong and feminine. And yes, I start to picture them on me, doing things to me, driving my body to new heights.

"You okay?" Her voice yanks me out of my little fantasy world, and I clear my throat.

"Yeah. Yeah, I'm good." I clear it again, and she gives me a look that makes me think she probably knows exactly what was going on in my head.

"This dish is all right with you?"

"One hundred percent. Pasta and cheese? I could live on that."

Marina nods with relief, and I have a zap of guilt for making her doubt, but it's gone quickly when she looks up at me and sips her wine and the hunger in her eyes is as clear as a foghorn blowing in a library. She seems to take a moment, then turns back to the pasta and gives it a stir. "How did your work go today?"

Those six words open up a floodgate in me somehow, and suddenly, I'm gushing. "Oh my God, Marina, it's been going so well. Like, I'm kinda shocked. I've been so stuck recently." I let my head fall back against her cupboard door with a light thump. "But there's just something about Rome. The food, the art, the architecture, the people…" My sigh is dreamy, I admit it, but then I stop. My lips clamp shut on their own, and I barely notice. A beat goes by. Two.

Marina looks up from the pasta. "What just happened?"

I swallow. "What do you mean?"

"I mean you stopped talking. You were all excited and then," she slices her hand through the air, "done."

I blink at her.

She drains the pasta, then stops working to come and stand between my knees, a hand on each one.

"*Bella*, what is it?" Her entire focus is on me. The warmth of her hands, the steadiness of her gaze, the sincerity in her tone—the combination nearly brings tears to my eyes.

I take a deep breath before I speak. "The last person I dated—and this was years ago—told me I talked too much about my writing. She thought I was overshadowing her work by bragging about my own."

Marina's dark eyebrows meet in a V above her nose. "But I asked you about it."

I give a sarcastic laugh. "Yeah, so did she."

Marina narrows her eyes. "So, she asked you how your work was going, but then got angry when you talked about it?"

"Yeah, that's pretty accurate."

She tips her head. "Tell me you hear how ridiculous that is."

"I mean, I do. I do. But when you're in the midst of it and trying to maybe build a relationship of some sort, you tend to take that stuff to heart, you know? Like, *oh, she thinks I'm talking too much about my work, she must be right! Let me curb that behavior.* And pretty soon, you have nothing to say."

She strokes a fingertip along my cheek. "That makes me sad for you."

I pair a shrug with my frown.

"Just know that if I ask you? I want to know. Yes?"

"Okay," I say, and then she's wrapping me in her arms, and as I sit there with my chin on her shoulder and revel in the warmth and safety I feel with her, I think about what an easy discussion that was, and how I was never able to have it with the last woman. My stomach chooses that moment to rumble, and as if they timed it together, Reggie barks at us from the floor, and it's all perfect. We both start to laugh.

"Your stomach and your dog would like me to take a hint, I think." She takes my face in both hands, tips my head forward, and kisses my forehead gently. Then she refills my wine glass, lightly kisses my mouth, and begins to work on the pasta. Butter, freshly ground pepper, and hand-grated cheese go into the pan she has on the stove. She adds a little water she saved from the pasta, and she swirls it until it's all melty. That's it. The pasta goes in, she uses tongs to mix it up, then to deposit a generous helping onto each plate. More pepper and cheese on top, and she meets my gaze.

"I feel like I'm watching an artist at work," I say, and I mean it.

She blushes, and it's beautiful. "Looks aren't everything. It might taste terrible."

I scoff and slide off the counter. "Butter and cheese and pepper? Doubtful."

Together, we bring everything to the table. She lights two candles, and it's automatically romantic. Not that this whole evening hasn't been already, but the candles up the romance factor, and even though I knew this was a date, now it's a *date*.

Reggie must have changed his mind. He'd found himself a corner on Marina's chair, and he's relaxing, his big eyes getting heavy. I can see him from my seat, and I'm kind of amazed at how comfortable he is here. Marina doesn't seem to mind him on the furniture either. It's a bit early for him to have dinner, but I've got a baggie of his food in my tote bag. For now, I'm glad he's napping. It allows me to put my focus on my dinner date.

We sit. The table is small, for two, and we're across from each other. I dig in.

Humming in delight seems to be the only sound I can make for a good five or ten minutes, the pasta is that good. I don't know what it is about Italian food in Rome—well, that's silly, I do know; it's *in Rome*—but it's about seven levels above even the best Italian restaurants in New York City that I've ever eaten at.

"This is incredible," I finally manage to say.

Marina lifts one shoulder in a half shrug, but her facial expression says she's pleased with my approval. "It's very simple."

"Well, I could eat it every day." There's salad and fresh bread on the table as well, and I help myself to a hunk of Italian bread, slathering it with butter. "So, what did you do today?" I ask. "Did you have a tour to give?"

Marina shakes her head. "Not to give, no. But I created two new ones."

I tip my head. "Created? What do you mean?"

"It's my favorite part of my job, next to actually giving the tours. I like to do different themes. For example, today, I was working on setting up some holiday tours. You know, going to restaurants and cafés that have seasonal dishes that focus on the holidays."

"Oh, wow."

"Yeah, I've done other seasonal ones. Summer fare, seasonal veggies, garden tours, religious ones. There's really a food or wine for almost every occasion. I like to group them."

"So, what do you do? Search for local places and then call and see if they want to be on the tour?"

She nods as she chews, then takes a sip of wine. "I've developed some great relationships with owners, chefs, bartenders. They don't make a ton of money on the tours, but they know that if they make a good impression, they could get separate business. Word of mouth is everything in this industry."

I'm so impressed with her right now, as I think about how creative what she does is. "You must have to visit a lot of businesses."

"Wherever I am, I wander around the neighborhood and take in all the food and drink establishments. My head is always creating new tours."

"So, what's your long-term goal? Would you want your own business instead of working for somebody else?"

Her sigh is wistful. "I would, yes. The food tour industry is quite saturated here in Rome, though."

I nod thoughtfully. "Would you leave Rome?"

"Maybe. I might leave Italy if the right opportunity came up."

"Oh, wow."

"Yeah, my parents would—how do you say? Lose their minds?"

I laugh through my nose. "Yes. Exactly that."

"It would be hard on them not to have me nearby."

"And you? Would it be hard on you?"

She seems to give that some genuine thought before finally answering. "It would be difficult, yes. I've never been all that far away." She pauses. "But I think it would be good for me, too. To be on my own. To do something I'm proud of without worrying about what my family is feeling about it or how they're thinking I should be with them. It's..." She gazes off toward the small windows in her living room. "Something I think about."

We finish our dinner as the sun begins to set. I help clear the table, but Marina won't hear of me doing the dishes. She waves me away, telling me to feed my boy, so I do that. He gets his kibble with some Pecorino Romano grated on top, and you'd think I gave him a Porterhouse. He finishes in about 3.5 seconds, and Marina waves me to take him outside while she finishes cleaning up.

"I will have wine poured and ready for you when you get back," she tells me with that sexy smile of hers.

There are as many people out and about here in Trastevere as there usually are in my little slice of Rome, but they're different here. The feel, the attitude, it's all much more casual, which I didn't think was possible. Slower. More relaxed. People aren't in a hurry in my neighborhood, but they're even less so here. They smile and nod and bid me *ciao*. Reggie, God bless him, does his business in less than ten minutes, and I promise him extra treats later. He seems to get it and doesn't fight me when I turn us back to Marina's building.

At the front door, I stop.

I know what's going to happen tonight. I know it. I'm going to sleep with Marina. There's not a doubt in my mind. She's too beautiful, and our chemistry is too thick, hanging in the air like fog. It's impossible not to notice it.

Part of me wonders if we've been building to this night since the moment we met. Another part of me thinks that's just silly. We like each other. We're attracted to each other. We live on different continents, but we're allowed to have fun if and when we want. It doesn't have to mean anything more than that. Right?

I try not to calculate how long it's been since I had sex. Hell, since I wanted to have sex. And I shake my head, literally, before I can reach an accurate number of months, years, whatever, however long it's been because the bottom line is: I want this. I want Marina, and I want her now.

Deep breath in. Slow breath out.

I reach for the door handle.

CHAPTER TWELVE

Marina looks different when Reggie and I get back.

I mean, not *different* different. She's still Marina. Still tall and sexy and gorgeous. But there's something in her face, in her expression, that's changed ever so slightly.

"Everything go okay?" she asks as she carries two glasses of wine into the living room. Dusk continues to fall, and the room is dimming by the minute. She's lit a couple of candles, and the atmosphere is warm and inviting. And romantic.

My lower body starts to throb, just to let me know I'm alive.

I unclip Reggie from his leash, and he heads right back to the chair. I glance at Marina, and she smiles and shrugs. "He's fine."

My relief is palpable. I know my dog is well-behaved, and it's why I take him so many places with me, but I also know not everybody is a dog person. Marina seems to be, though, and that's yet another tick in the Win column.

She gives Reggie a scratch as she passes the chair and moves to the couch, sits, and looks my way with an expectant arch of a dark eyebrow.

I sit next to her, and she hands me my wine.

"To our first meal together not at a restaurant," she says and holds up her glass.

"And what a meal it was." I touch my glass to hers. "You have ruined me for all pasta."

"My plan all along." She sits back and stretches her legs out, crosses them at the ankle on the coffee table. Then she raises her arm, making a cozy spot for me.

I snuggle against her warmth, her softness, and it feels like it's exactly where I'm supposed to be. A long breath releases from my lungs, clearly conveying my comfort. "This is nice," I say quietly.

"Yeah?"

"Definitely." I take a moment to look around her flat once again. "I really like your place. How long have you been here?"

She scrunches up her perfect nose. "Three years? They finally put in dryers this year."

I remember the story Serena told me about how Italians have always hung their wet clothes outside, and I fill Marina in. "Still not sure I believe it," I say with a laugh.

"I swear to you, she was telling you the truth. Now dryers are selling like—what's the phrase?—hot cake?"

"Hotcakes."

"What are hotcakes?"

I pause for a moment, then shake my head. "Pancakes? I'm honestly not sure."

"Why would something sell like pancakes?"

We're both laughing now, and I say, "Listen, the English language is ridiculous. Things don't make sense. The same combination of letters makes seven different sounds. I don't know how anybody learns it." I meet her gaze. "Your English is excellent, though."

"We are required to learn at least a little, and we can go on if we choose."

"And you chose."

"Yes. I thought it would serve me well."

"And has it?"

She tightens her arm around me. "It has allowed me to talk to you, hasn't it?"

Our gazes hold, and we're so close, the tips of our noses are nearly touching. Which means it only takes the slightest tip of my head, and my lips meet Marina's.

This kiss starts off slow and soft but doesn't stay that way. I'm not sure if it's because we feel we've waited so long or what, but a mere instant passes before we are full-on making out. Marina's arm is tight around my shoulders, and I have my hand gripping the side of her head, pulling her in closer, even if she's as close as she can be. I want more, and she must realize it, because she presses her tongue into my mouth, and I moan.

Kissing Marina is like…God, I don't even have a proper description. Probably because it feels like my brain is short-circuiting, cutting off the power to rational thought in order to focus on the physical pleasure of it all. And pleasure it is. Marina kisses me like we've been kissing for years, and she knows just what I like. It's the push and pull, the hard and soft, the giving and demanding. It's the dichotomy that turns me on, and Marina seems to have a master's degree in it. She lulls me into sensuous relaxation with the softness of her mouth, the pliability of her lips, and just when I'm about to melt, she shifts things. Increases pressure, swirls her tongue, tugs my hair.

I'm nearly on my back on her sofa, though I barely remember getting that way. Having Marina's gorgeous body on me is a turn-on all on its own, and I halt our kissing just so I can look at her, above me, her face flushed, her lips glistening and full, her hair hanging down like an elegant sexy curtain enclosing us. I push it out of the way so I can see her more clearly.

"You're so fucking beautiful," I whisper.

She responds by crushing her mouth to mine, and I am lost once again.

While part of me feels like I could make out with Marina just like this, on her sofa, another—more insistent—part of me wants more. So much more. I wrench my mouth away and wait until she looks me in the eye.

"You got a bedroom in this place?" I ask, surprised by how breathless I am.

She doesn't even use words, just nods vehemently and pushes herself off me. Once on her feet, she holds out a hand. I grasp it and am pulled to my feet by one of the sexiest women I have ever had the pleasure of laying eyes on.

"Come with me," she says, her voice husky.

In that moment, I'd follow her anywhere.

The level of comfort I feel with Marina is completely disproportionate to, well, me. Sex always makes me the slightest bit self-conscious, no matter how well I know my partner, but it's somehow different with her. I don't feel self-conscious at all as she slides her hand under my shirt while we're kissing. The feeling of her palm on the bare skin of my stomach is something I can't describe—which says a lot, given my career—but only because my brain is on sensory overload. We're standing in her bedroom at the foot of her bed, our mouths fused together, kissing hungrily, and all I can focus on is *sensation*. I don't hear anything. I don't say anything. I don't think anything. All I can do is *feel*.

And what I feel is simply…glorious. I don't have a better word. Marina is taller than me, fitter than me, stronger than me, and all those things come into play as she backs me into her bed. The mattress hits the backs of my knees, and I sit, then crab-crawl backward until I'm in the middle of the bed. She stands there for a moment, just looking at me, and there's so much in those dark eyes of hers that a lump forms in my throat.

I clear it and crook a finger at her. "Come here."

"Yes, ma'am," she says with a sexy grin, and crawls on all fours until she's above me once again and her mouth is on mine.

Sex with Marina is…God. It's hard to know where to begin because, for the first time since I can remember—no, for the first time *in my life*—I turn off my brain and just let myself feel. People who know me understand just how hard it is for me to do that; I'm all about the overthinking. My anxiety and me? Super tight. So the fact that I feel totally, utterly relaxed with her is a little bit mind-boggling. But I go with it.

Kissing slides to touching, hands everywhere, clothes removed a little at a time. Undressing Marina is like unwrapping the most erotic of gifts, baring a limb here, a swath of olive skin there. She's soft and smooth and hot—hot in more ways than one, and I absently think, of every woman I've been with in my life, I've never been so attracted. Not like this. Everything about Marina is sexy. Everything. The way she feels, the way she smells, the way she kisses, the way she sounds. God. It's all I can do to keep this slow pace. Because I want to take my time. I want to savor and remember every tiny second of this experience.

I also want to rip her clothes off with my teeth, flip her onto her back, and have my way with her.

It's a conundrum.

But I push through, and I do manage to turn us so I'm on top, and

I focus on removing her clothes, because all I want is to see her naked body in all its glory.

Turns out, glory isn't even a strong enough word.

Marina is perfect. I take a moment to simply look at her, to let my eyes roam over her body. She's confident and sexy and she tucks her hands behind her head, completely content to let me ogle her nakedness. She smiles at me without worry or self-consciousness, and it's fucking beautiful. And so incredibly sexy.

I give myself another couple of seconds to gape before I'm on her with my mouth, tasting every inch of her. I'm vaguely aware of her hands in my hair, on my shoulders, her fingers digging deliciously into my skin, but I'm much more focused on her. The smell of her—that warm, inviting apple scent. The look of her skin—olive and bronze, tanned from the summer, but also part of her heritage. The sound of her—she's not loud, but there are small moans and little whimpers that let me know I'm doing everything right. I want to spend hours here. Days. Weeks, even. But my own body and my own arousal threatens to swamp me entirely if I don't take what I want, so I work my way down her body using my lips, my tongue, until I'm settled between her legs. A glance up her torso gives me a sexy shot of Marina biting her bottom lip in anticipation, and I wait until she raises her head and meets my gaze. I keep my eyes on her as I take my first taste, and I listen to the breath leave her body and watch her head fall back onto the pillows with an incredibly sensual moan of pleasure.

Christ, she's beautiful.

I focus on my movements, my rhythm, listening for clues and matching what I do to how she sounds. More pressure when she's louder, a swirl of the tongue when she whimpers, and it's not long before I feel her fingers gripping the hair on the back of my head. Her hand tightens, pulling me more firmly against her, and I grip her hips because I know it's coming, she's coming. And then her hips raise up, and a cry emanates from her throat, and I hold on to keep my place. I dig my fingertips into her hips as they lift and roll and finally lower slowly back down to the mattress. My mouth is still pressed against her, and I can feel her pulsing against me. When I finally feel her fingers loosen in my hair, I lift my head to look at her. Her eyes are squeezed closed and she's whispering something in Italian, so I wait with my cheek against her warm thigh, the taste and smell of her still on my lips.

Several moments pass by before she takes a deep breath and finally looks at me. The things I see on her face, the emotions, are many, and they're gorgeous. She's glowing, so there's that. She's smiling, also an amazing thing. She looks a bit sheepish, which is super cute. She crooks a finger at me, summoning me to her, and because I'm not a stupid woman, I oblige, slowly crawling up her body, kissing different parts as I go and loving how she gently twitches as I do so, clearly still very sensitive. Finally, I settle next to her, my head pillowed on her shoulder.

"Wow," she says. "That was…" She shakes her head, as if she has no words, and you know what? I will take that. All day long.

"Yeah?"

She nods.

"Well, that was pretty amazing for me, too." I run my fingertip across her collarbone. "You were gorgeous to watch." She covers her eyes with her hand, grinning and sheepish again. I pull her hand away. "I mean it," I say softly when she looks at me.

She pulls me in and kisses me gently…but gentle doesn't last, and in the next moment, she's rolling us so she's on top. This gloriously beautiful woman with the lustrous hair and the sexy accent holds herself above me and gives me the most erotic look I've ever had aimed at me as she says simply, "My turn."

"I need some water." Marina's voice is quiet as we lie wrapped around each other like two vines that have entwined. "You?"

"Yes, please."

She presses a kiss to my forehead, then slides out of the bed. I roll onto my stomach and marvel at her body as she walks naked out of the room. The swell of her hips, the length of her legs, her tousled raven hair falling down her back, and her glorious skin. I immediately feel a wave of loss, of longing, and I want her to come back. Like, now.

The water runs in the kitchen as I hunker down into the bedding, inhaling the scents it holds. Marina, fabric softener, me, Marina's perfume, us. An intoxicating blend, to say the least. Marina returns with two glasses of water and sets them both on her nightstand, then slides back under the covers.

"Reggie is still on the chair and is snoring like a freight train," she says with a gentle laugh. She sits with her back against the headboard and lifts one arm so I can scoot up against her. It's hard to believe I haven't been snuggled up in this spot my entire life because it feels like exactly where I'm supposed to be. She hands me my water and I drink like I haven't had any liquid in days.

I hand it back to her, nearly empty, and she laughs.

"Listen, you dehydrated me," I say in defense.

She laughs softly, kisses my forehead, inhales deeply, and my body rises with hers. Her exhale is complete contentment. Don't ask me how I know that, but I do. I'm sure of it as she squeezes me more tightly to her.

"We were pretty incredible together," she says, almost in wonder.

"You'll get no argument from me," I say. "I made sounds I've never made before."

She laughs again. "Tell me about your worst sexual experience."

"Worst?"

A nod. "And we don't count. Just in case it was terrible and you're lying to me." The twinkle in her eye—that I can see even in the growing darkness—tells me she's kidding, that she knows just how mind-blowing we were.

"Hmm…" I purse my lips in thought. "I think I'd have to go with my very first girlfriend."

"Really? Your first time was your worst?"

"Well, let me elaborate. I saw her for, I don't know, less than a year. Ten months? Young love, you're all in, nothing can compare, all that. Right?" Marina nods and I go on. "She broke up with me for one of our older, mutual friends. Because of course she did. She was my first. I was not her first. And I think she got bored with me fawning all over her."

"Fawning?"

"Yeah. It means, like, gushing? Being mushy?"

Marina nods her understanding.

"I was kind of weak and timid, but I was in love. And hello? My first lesbian relationship. I had no idea what I was doing. But whatever. She breaks up with me. I'm devastated, like any twenty-year-old after her first lover dumps her for somebody else. And my biggest concern was not only that I'd never love somebody like that again, but that I'd never find anybody who was *that good in bed* again." I roll my eyes at myself. "Like, what do I know about good sex at twenty, right?"

Marina laughs softly and pulls me closer. "Aw, poor little freshly out Lily."

"Yeah, well, the next woman I slept with blew the top of my head off in bed, so I learned pretty quickly that my first girlfriend wasn't all that." I look up at her face, marveling at her profile—straight nose, sexy chin. "What about you?"

She narrows her eyes and seems to take a minute to think about it. When it comes to her, she drops her head against the headboard with a *thunk* and groans.

"Oh, I can't wait to hear this," I say with a grin.

"Okay." She sits up a little straighter and meets my eyes. "So, I need to start by saying that the sex wasn't all that bad. Truly. The bad part was…" She searches for the right word—the right *English* word. I've been around her long enough now to recognize her face when she's doing that, and it gives me a little thrill that I know her that well. "Her response?" It's a question because she's clearly not sure that's the word she wants, but she launches in.

"This was a few years ago. I met her at a food show in one of the big hotels in the city center. One of my restaurant friends took me so we could see what kind of stuff was out there, what kind of new methods were showing up, that kind of thing. And this woman was there, too. We hit it off, we all went out for drinks at the hotel bar after the show, and one by one, people left, until it was just her and me."

"Ooh, this is like a movie," I say, giving a happy little full-body wiggle.

She chuckles. "Well, we both realize we're attracted to each other. She was not my usual type, but she was intriguing, and I liked her. I don't do one-night stands very often, but I'm not against them. So, we decide to get a hotel room."

I nod. I'm not against them either, but I've never had one.

"Things start off great. We're kissing, it's nice. We undress. She seems to like control, so I let her have that. For a while." She shoots me a grin that has me instantly wet again, and I poke her.

"Stop that. Story."

"Right, right. Sorry. So, she—er—takes care of me first and it's nice. Doesn't change my life, but it's nice. I begin to reciprocate and, Lily, when I say she was loud, I do not exaggerate."

I snort out a laugh. "What?"

She sits up straighter, like she's preparing to plead her case. "Look, I love some noise. I love knowing what I'm doing is working, yeah? You, my love, were perfect and sexy." She gives me a quick kiss on the lips. "But this woman? Jesus, Mary, and Joseph"—she crosses herself—"she was *so loud*. Before I even did anything! I touched her breast and—" Marina moans, and her volume is comical.

I laugh.

"I run my hand over her hip and—" She does it again, louder this time, and I laugh harder. "I even tried to make it a game." She lowers her voice to just above a whisper. "'It's late and there are other people in the building, so you have to be quiet.'" My laughter dies in my throat and Jesus Christ, I can feel the warm wetness between my legs just from the sexy pitch of her voice.

I swallow hard. "Yeah, um, that would've worked on me. Uh-huh."

"Right?" She's back to normal volume. "She said she'd try. Spoiler alert."

"She didn't try."

"*She did not try.* All I kept thinking was, does the entire hotel need to know we're having sex? I couldn't wait to be done and get out of there."

We're both laughing now. "Wow," I say. "That sounds…"

"Awful? Horrendous? Sad? Yes, it was all of those things. I was mortified." She meets my eyes. "Is that the right word?"

I nod. "Absolutely the right word. You poor thing. Did you wear a hoodie when you left and pull the hood up?"

"I wanted to!" She's cracking up now. "I was sure everybody would know." She points and stage whispers, "'There's the woman who was so loud last night. Does she look satisfied?' I wanted to tell everybody that it wasn't me."

"I guess the takeaway would be that one of you was loud and one of you was *really good in bed*."

"But which one is which?"

"That's the downside."

"I am not okay with that downside."

We're cracking up, both of us, naked in Marina's bed and laughing our asses off at stories of our past couplings, and it's…it's so crazily comfortable that I almost can't believe it's real. I don't know that I've ever felt this content this quickly with anybody in my life, and I don't know what to do with that, what to think. But it's the best I've felt in a very, very long time. Not sure what to do with that either.

"I want gelato," I blurt.

Marina blinks at me for a second. "Now?"

I sigh. "Yeah, it's a thing. Sex makes me hungry."

And Marina, God love her, doesn't miss a beat. She slides out of bed and holds out her hand. "Then let's get you some gelato."

CHAPTER THIRTEEN

Marina treats me like a queen.

She's been polite since I met her, that's true. She has manners, and she's kind. But since we had sex, she's become downright chivalrous.

I'm not mad about it.

I can't remember the last time somebody put my needs before theirs, but that's exactly what she's done.

I'm lying in her bed now in those lovely, quiet moments just before dawn. Reggie is snoring in a soft pile of blankets on the floor, having gotten tired of our moving and turning and noise-making last night. Marina is sleeping soundly beside me, her breathing deep and even, her chest gently rising and falling. I'm on my side, my head pillowed on her shoulder, my hand resting on her breastbone, and I resist stroking her velvet skin with my fingertips, wanting to let her sleep. I'm replaying the previous night because it's easily one of the best in my entire life, and I'm pushing fifty and have had a pretty great existence, so that's saying something.

Last night, we threw our clothes back on, leashed up Reggie, and went out for gelato. We strolled the neighborhood, which was bustling in a chill and relaxed way, which I'm learning is how it is in Trastevere. We held hands again, something I haven't done in ages before Marina, and it made me feel like a lovestruck teenager in the best of ways. Marina bought me gelato—pistachio—sorry, "pis-tahk-io." And then she helped me eat it, and I'm not even a little bit embarrassed to say that watching her lick my cone—not a euphemism—had me dragging her back to her flat so I could tear her clothes off and have my way with her well into the night. She was sweet and let me have the upper hand for a while before she took it back.

I feel worshipped.

That's a pretty bold statement coming from me, and I know it. But it's the truth. I felt it a little when I got here, but I definitely felt it in bed. I've never felt so sexy or so beautiful or so *desired* as I do with Marina Troiani, and that both lifts me up and terrifies me. I vow that when the sun comes up, we'll have a talk about what exactly it is that we're doing, what we expect, stuff like that. It's necessary.

I must doze off, because the next time I open my eyes, Marina is smiling at me, those dark eyes sparkling in the soft light of almost dawn.

"*Buongiorno, bella*," she says softly, and will I ever get used to the sheer sexiness of an Italian accent? I don't think so.

"Hi," I whisper, and I can feel my smile bloom on my face all on its own.

"I like this. Waking up with you in my bed."

"Me too," I say, and it's the truth. Despite whatever this is—a fling, casual sex, two people having their needs met—I could definitely get used to this type of morning. I also don't want to get out of bed, and so we don't. We snuggle for a few moments before hands start to wander and lips meet, and pretty soon, Marina's head is between my legs and her mouth and tongue are doing unspeakably sexy things to me, and I have to pull a pillow over my face because the last thing I want to do is reenact Marina's worst sex date ever.

As my breathing slowly returns to normal and Marina crawls back up my body, stopping here and there to kiss or lightly nip different parts of me, I start to softly laugh.

She arches a dark brow at me. "Laughter is not exactly the result I shoot for when it comes to lovemaking." She says it playfully, but there's a quick shadow that zips across her face, and it makes me grab her and pull her up so we're eye to eye.

"Oh, honey," I say. "You have nothing at all to worry about. I'm laughing because I was afraid of becoming another Unattractively Loud bed partner." I jerk a thumb to my right. "Thus the pillow."

She barks a laugh. "Oh, thank God." After a moment, she kisses me softly and says, "There is nothing unattractive about you. At all. Trust me."

And I do.

It's weird and wonderful and terrifying to realize it, but I trust Marina implicitly.

Scary.

We lounge for a while longer, alternating between dozing, making love, and chatting, until I know I need to get poor Reggie outside. "He's been so good," I say. "But he also has a tiny bladder."

"I'll take him." Marina sits up, the sheet falling off her upper body, revealing her gorgeous breasts, her dark nipples still swollen from all the attention I've lavished on them. I reach out and stroke a fingertip across one. She gives me a sexy grin and grabs my hand to stop further exploration. "Save it. I'll take Reggie out. And then we have to get moving, I'm sorry to say." She's up and then pulls a pair of joggers out of a drawer.

She's right. She has a tour to give, and work beckons, but I sigh and pout a little anyway. "Fine. You okay if I jump in the shower first?"

"Of course. Towels are in the closet." She pulls on a T-shirt and leans forward to kiss me lightly. "Be back in a bit. *Ciao*."

"*Ciao*," I say as she calls Reggie to follow her out of the bedroom. He glances at me for a split second and then is off, the traitor. I can't stay mad at him, though. I'd follow her, too.

All of Marina's toiletry products are labeled in Italian, because of course they are, but her shampoo bottle shows a picture of an apple orchard, so I now understand why she smells like apple pie, and I love it. I lather up my hair, loving the fact that I'll be able to smell her even after I leave. I towel off and am applying some lotion to my legs when I hear her return.

I also smell baked goods.

She knocks on the bathroom door—which I've left ajar—before she enters carrying a cup. "For you," she says and waves her hand with a flourish.

"Bless you," I say and take the coffee from her, bring it to my nose. "Italians know how to do coffee," I say. "Did you get some?"

"I had a cappuccino with Reggie."

"Just what Reggie needs," I joke.

"I got some breakfast. Come out when you're done." She leans in and kisses me, then disappears back out the door.

It's all so incredibly domestic that it freezes me in place for a moment. But I shake it off, finish getting dressed, dry my hair, and then follow my nose out into the flat, where a plate of baked goods sits all perfectly arranged on the table. They look like croissants but aren't.

"Ooh, what are these?" I ask, picking one up. It's made of flaky layers of pastry, and it's still warm.

"Sfogliatella," Marina says.

"Bless you," I reply, but her brow furrows because she doesn't get dumb American humor. "Sorry." I wave my hand. "Ignore me."

"Two of them have ricotta filling and two have chocolate custard."

I waste no more time because I don't care which one I get. I bite in and it's ricotta, and I'm humming my delight. Also delighted is Marina, judging from the smile on her face.

"I love watching you try new things," she says. "I love watching you doing anything, though."

I get that little flutter in my belly, because how sweet is that? Remember when I said I felt worshipped? Yeah, prime example right there. Nobody's ever told me they like watching me doing whatever it is I'm doing in the moment. Can't say I hate it.

After we eat, finish our coffee, and do some serious kissing in the doorway of Marina's flat, Reggie and I head back to our hotel, and it almost feels like going home. I've lost count of how many weeks I've been here, but it's starting to feel like I live here now. I miss New York, I do, both my upstate house and my Manhattan apartment. But with every day that goes by here in Rome, I am more and more comfortable, something I never expected to feel.

I'm very aware that I'm wearing last night's clothes, not that anybody saw me then, but I also want to make sure Reggie gets some exercise. I don't know how far he and Marina walked earlier, so once our Uber drops us off, I stroll along our street with him for a bit, and again, I'm hit with the feeling of *this is my neighborhood*. I have grown to know these shops and the habits of the shopkeepers. When they open, how they sweep their entry area, which ones know each other and stop to chat. It's like I'm in a Broadway musical—or better yet, a Disney movie—about a quaint little street where everybody knows everybody. I'm reminded of the Disney movie *Beauty and the Beast*—the animated one from the nineties—where all the villagers know each other and Belle, and they sing to one another as she walks past their shops. Corny,

I know, but it's making me smile as Reggie trots along beside me as if he's feeling the same way. We feel at home here, like we belong.

When in Rome, right?

❖

I have blazed out nearly three full chapters when my phone dings a notification from my mom. She wants to call, but she'd rather warn me and have me tell her I'm busy than call and have me not answer. I've learned this over the years. It's been a few days, and my eyes are burning from staring at my laptop screen, so I decide to give myself a break, and I call her.

"How's Italy?" she asks, clearly thrilled that I called.

"Italy is amazing. The food is unbelievable. You and Dad would love it. You should come here."

"Well, you'd have to find me a tranquilizer gun and help me shoot him to get him on a plane, but yeah, I'd love to go." We both laugh, but I file away that if my mom is ever going to make it to Europe, it'll have to be me or my brother bringing her. My dad has a lot of talents and hobbies, but adventure isn't one of them. "Is Reggie doing okay?"

"He's loving it. He makes friends wherever we go."

"That's my boy. And what about you?"

"What about me?"

"Are *you* making any friends? You've been there for quite some time now." You have to know my mom to become fluent in her tone, or Barbara Speak, as my brother AJ and I have called it for years, but I'm a pro. So that means I know she's both asking me if I'm okay—she really does want to know if I've made friends—while at the same time chiding me for being away for so long.

"I've made a few," I say. Not a lie, right? "But I'm here to work, remember?"

She pauses for a moment before dropping "And your niece can't keep a secret to save her own life, *remember*?" on me. There's a definite tint of satisfaction in her voice. Yeah, she knows about Marina.

Well, shit.

I make a mental note to text Chloe about how she's getting no Christmas gifts from me this year. It's not that I'm embarrassed. I'm not. There's nothing wrong with some casual sex. Or a little fling while away from home. I have needs, don't I? Nothing wrong with taking care of those, is there?

But this is my *mom*, and as liberated as she is, I don't really love the idea of her knowing all about my sex life.

"Fine," I sigh. "I have met a woman. Her name is Marina and we've been…hanging out a bit."

"Hanging out. Is that code for something?"

"Your delight in this is kind of obvious, Mom."

"Can I help it if you've been single way too long?"

"Gee, thanks."

She laughs, then gets somewhat serious. "Honey. I just want you to be happy. Is that so wrong?"

"No, Mom. It's not. I appreciate that. I just…" My thoughts drift, and I inhale a deep breath and let it out slowly. "She's just keeping me company. That's all." My stomach does an uncomfortable flip right then, as if I've betrayed something. The truth? Marina? I don't know. I somehow manage to steer the conversation to other things, and my mother reluctantly follows, finally realizing she'll get no more from me. But even after we hang up, I feel weird.

Marina and I never had "the talk" about what we're doing, what we are exactly. But…do we need to? Maybe we don't after all. I mean, we both know this is just a temporary thing, don't we? We live on separate continents, our age difference is significant, the logistics are just impossible for anything beyond a fun and casual fling. Right? I know it, and I have to assume Marina knows it.

With a literal shake of my head, I try to get rid of the confusing train of thought and refocus my attention on my pastry chefs. They're having a lot of sex, I have to say. More than my usual books. I refuse to wonder about the correlations between my fiction and my life, but I can feel a soft smile playing on my own lips, and I have no control over it.

❖

I take Reggie out for a quick zip around the neighborhood—which has finally cooled off to a pleasant seventy-eight degrees. Once we get back to the suite, I sit down to work some more and whip out another chapter. I never write this much in one day. Never. This Italian inspiration I'm suddenly immersed in has triggered my creative energy in a big way. A very big way, and I absently wonder what I can do to keep it going. I'm contemplating another love scene between my characters when there's a soft, rapid tapping on my door.

I squint at my screen, make sure to save—I'm a little paranoid about that since my computer crashed three years ago and lost a full twenty-five pages of a screenplay I'd been writing—and cross the room. My door has no peephole, so I pull it open and there she is.

Marina looks like she just stepped out of a European travel magazine, with her linen pants, cropped T-shirt, and large sunglasses. Her lips glisten with gloss and she's smiling.

I don't even have time to register my surprise because she steps into the suite, directly into my space, and kisses me soundly, slamming the door shut with her foot.

My body responds immediately, and I marvel at that even as I kiss her back. She backs me into the room until my legs hit the couch and we fall down onto it, our lips fused the entire time. My blood is rushing, hot and fast. My underwear is instantly wet, my body preparing itself for her. It's shocking to me, how in tune we are this way. Sexually. Sensually. Erotically. Three minutes ago, I was working diligently, and now I'm on my back on a couch and actively undressing the beautiful woman above me.

We never reach fully naked. We reach naked enough to reach important things. Breasts and nipples. Hot, bare skin. Wet centers. How is it we know each other's bodies so well after just one night together? This question only has time to bounce around in my head for a couple seconds before her fingers have worked their magic, and my orgasm blasts through my body. All my muscles strain, and I grind my head back into a throw pillow as Marina slides her fingers into me and I contract against them.

I come down slowly, and when I finally open my eyes, she's looking down at me with that sexy smile and a satisfied twinkle in her dark eyes. "Hi," she says softly.

"Do I know you?" I joke.

"You do," she says, but she seems much more serious than me. Pressing a kiss to my forehead, she pushes herself up. "I have a tour in fifteen minutes, but I had to touch you."

I push myself to sitting, still breathing a bit raggedly, and I reach for her. She lets me latch on but also grasps my hands, I presume to keep them from wandering. "But I want you," I say, hoping I sound sexy.

She grins, and her cheeks flush pink, so I think I succeeded. She lifts my hand and brushes her lips across my knuckles. "No time, *bella*."

"Later?"

"I have another tour tonight." At least she looks as bummed about it as I do. "Tomorrow?"

That's better. "Definitely."

"Good." She gives me a quick kiss, then pushes to her feet and rights all her clothing. I lie back, still half-undressed, and watch. It's a pretty awesome view. When she's all fixed and has run to my bathroom to wash up, she gives me a look.

"Thanks for stopping by," I say. "You can pop in any time you want."

"I shall make a note." She bends to me, gives me what I think is meant to be a quick kiss, but I grab her head with both hands and deepen it. She lets me and moans into my open mouth before wrenching herself away. She points at me with a grin. "You are trouble."

"You love it."

"I do. One hundred percent." She's at the door now, her hand on the knob. "Text you later."

I nod and watch the door close behind her, and then I continue to lie there on the couch, my shirt up to my chin, my bra unfastened and my breasts spilling out, my joggers halfway down my thighs, my underwear soaked. I don't move. Instead, I close my eyes and replay the last several minutes. Pretty sure there's a stupid grin on my face, and when I hear the clickety-click of nails on the floor, I turn my head to see Reggie staring at me from the bedroom doorway.

"Hey, don't you judge me. Do you know how long it's been since a woman popped in just because she wanted my body? Do you?" He clearly does not, so I go on. "Like, a decade. Two, maybe. I think. If ever. And you know what? I deserve it. I deserve it!"

He stares for a moment longer, then the little bastard has the audacity to yawn at me just before he turns and goes back into the bedroom.

"I said don't judge me," I shout after him.

I had to touch you.

Had to touch me. That's what she said. Aaand the stupid grin is back.

I lie there for a little while longer, just floating in that lovely, cottony aftermath of sex, when your limbs are like jelly and you can feel your own pulse against your skin. The sun coming through the window above me is warm, and before long, my eyes close and I can feel myself about to drift off. And then my phone chimes from the desk, and I sigh, reminded that I'm in the real world and have a real job and real people trying to get hold of me.

"Ah, well," I say as I push to my feet and fix all my clothing.

The chime was a text from Serena.

Busy tonight?

As I'm standing there, I lean backward, stretching the muscles in my back that I only just now realize are kind of achy. I remember Marina saying she has a tour tonight, which means I'm free.

Nope, I type back.

Come over. I miss Reggie. That's followed by a smiling emoji and a wink.

We settle on a time, and I find myself relieved to have something to do other than sit around my suite drinking wine and wishing Marina wasn't occupied by other people.

Oh. I'm getting possessive.

Not sure what to do with that.

"I feel like I haven't seen you in ages!" Serena wraps me in a hug, the scent of her sandalwood perfume enveloping me, her blond hair tickling my nose. It feels good, knowing someone cares about you. And I missed her, too.

"I know. What *is* that?"

She takes Reggie's leash from my hand and bends down to give him some scratches, then unclip him. He's free but doesn't leave her side, instead standing up on his hind legs for more attention, which she gives him by swooping him up into her arms. He clearly loves it, the look of satisfaction and importance on his furry face super clear to me, and I just shake my head.

"It's Italy," she says. "Rome in particular. Time feels like it's going so fast when it's hardly moving. I have no idea why." She leads us out into the courtyard. "Thank God the heatwave broke, right? We can sit out here and not swelter. Finally." She tells Ria to bring us wine and nibbles, and we sit.

"So, what's new?" I ask her, and it really does feel like we haven't seen each other in weeks and weeks, when it's really only been a handful of days. "Any more out-of-town guests coming?"

"Next month," Serena says. "A couple that were good friends of Tony and me."

"Well, that sounds fun."

"It will be. I'm always happy to get a little blast of home, you know?"

"I do," I say as Ria hands me a glass of chilled white that makes my mouth water just from looking at it. She sets a charcuterie board filled with goodies, smiles at me, and disappears back into the kitchen, or wherever it is that she goes. "I love it here, but I've felt a tiny bit homesick recently, especially after talking to my mother today."

"I understand that. Kind of inevitable when you're away for a long stretch."

I nod and sip. The wine is crisp and acidic with just a touch of fruitiness. Perfect.

"How's the book coming along?" Serena watches my face as she sips.

"It's been great recently," I say, and I don't know if there's something in my expression or the tone of my voice or what, but suddenly, Serena is looking at me with a knowing grin. "What?"

"Sounds like the inspiration experiment paid off."

"The inspiration experiment?"

She gives me a little *pfft*. "Please. You know what I mean. Marina."

Of course I know what she means. But I'm trying to be more subtle about it. "Yeah, I know what you mean."

"And?" Serena gives her hand a roll as if to spur me on. "Details!"

I inhale a deep breath and let it out. On the one hand, I don't want to talk about me and Marina. It's private, and I'm not a gossip. On the other hand, though, I'm so freaking giddy at the thought of her, and I can't keep from smiling.

Serena points directly at my face. "I knew it. I knew you two would be good together."

I hold up a hand. "Okay, slow your roll, ma'am."

"I want to hear all about it," she says, as if she's been waiting for this exact story all day. "What have you done? Where have you gone? How does it feel?"

"That's a lot of questions," I say with a laugh. "But…it's nice. She's great. We're having a lot of fun."

She narrows her eyes at me. "Sweetie. Those are not details." She takes a sip of her wine, then asks, "How's the sex?"

I am mid-sip, which I nearly choke on at her words. Serena laughs and laughs as I cough through my shock. Once I manage to find my breath again, I meet her gaze, ready to remind her how private that question is, and I wonder, do I even want her to know that we've slept together? But one look at her face and I give up. "It's fucking fantastic."

Serena gives a whoop of joy, coupled with another *I knew it*, which makes me laugh.

"Wow. I don't think anybody's ever been so happy about my sex life. Including me."

She pulls herself together and reaches for a bite of cheese from the charcuterie board. "I just love it when a match I knew would work out works out. Thrills me no end."

"Well." I shrug and help myself to a dolma from the board. "It's not anything serious. We're just enjoying ourselves." As I chew, she nods and seems, I don't know. Pensive? "What?" I ask.

She shakes her head. "Nothing."

But I feel like I've grown to know her pretty well. "Bullshit." I say it with a grin to let her know I'm teasing.

A shrug. "I just don't want either of you to get hurt is all."

I frown. "We're fine. No need to worry. We both know what's what."

"Okay. Good." She nods and sips her wine and doesn't look convinced, but she lets it go. I wish I could, but it sits in the back of my head for the rest of the evening. When we leave, it's gorgeous out, and Reggie and I go for a stroll up and down the street before heading back to the hotel. As usual, shops are open and people are happily milling around, drinking Apérol spritzes and eating pasta well into the night, and it feels a bit like Manhattan, which I love so much. As we walk, I think back on my very first visit to New York City. I was in my twenties, and my girlfriend at the time was a bit older than me, settled into a well-paying job, and took me to the city for a long weekend getaway. Neither of us had been before, but she got us a nice hotel room in the Theater District so we could catch a Broadway show. We got back to our hotel after ten that night and were starving, so asked the concierge where we could get some food. He gave us directions to a restaurant, the name of which I can no longer remember, and off we went. It was late, and we were not terribly optimistic when we arrived at the small Italian restaurant, but the place was utterly packed. Every table full. People laughing and joking and eating plates of spaghetti and drinking wine, and it was almost eleven at night. We sat at the bar and drank wine and ate pasta, and I'll never forget it. It made me fall in love with Manhattan, and maybe that's why I love Rome so much now—because it feels so much like Manhattan to me, though with a slower pace.

As Reggie and I make our way back into the hotel, my phone buzzes with a text notification. I pull it out and grin: Marina.

Ciao, bella! Still awake? Just wanted to say hello.

I get us into the room and lock the door behind me before responding. *Hi there! Just getting in. Reggie and I were at Serena's. She says hi and she misses you.*

The gray dots bounce to tell me Marina's typing. I kick off my shoes and head to the little kitchen area where there's a bottle of red wine I opened a day or two ago. *I owe her a visit.*

I pour myself half a glass and take a seat on the sofa where I can look out the window at the lights and the nightlife. I have a sudden flash of earlier today on this same sofa, and a tingle runs through me. *How was the tour?*

She sends an eye roll emoji and says, *Mostly fine. One stronzo who thinks he knows Italian food better than his guide. American. Sorry, bella.*

I don't know the proper translation for the word *stronzo*, but I can take a guess. *Of course he was American. Don't apologize. We are a country full of arrogant people.*

The dots bounce. *Have a good time with Serena?*

I did. I nod, even though she can't see it. *Hey, can I ask you something?*

Her answer comes in seconds. *Always.*

I type and send before I can change my mind. *We're casual, right? This thing we're doing?*

The dots bounce. Then they stop and go away. I wait, and they come back, but then disappear again. Uh-oh. I nibble on the inside of my bottom lip until the dots show up again, then words.

Oh, assolutamente! I can only assume that means absolutely, and it's followed up by two smiling emoji, one laughing, and two more smiling. I double-check Google Translate to be sure of my own interpretation. I am right and relieved, but when I look at her text again, *Lotta smiles*, is what I think. Another text comes. *It's the only thing that makes sense, no?*

I stare at that line for a moment, wondering why I feel slightly ill reading it. I'm also not as relieved as I thought I'd be at her agreement, but I don't want to examine that. Not tonight.

Okay, I type. *Just wanted to check. You free tomorrow?*

There's a pause. No bouncing dots or anything. Just a pause with nothing. Just when I think something happened and she's maybe not coming back at all, the dots appear. Then, *I am. Want to come here again?*

I don't wait at all. *Love to*, I send back, adding a string of my own smiling emoji.

I'm off to bed. Sleep well, she says next, and while it seems a bit abrupt, I also remind myself that she gave two tours today. That's a lot of talking and a lot of being "on," and when you have to deal with an asshole in the process, like the guy she described, I imagine it takes an even bigger toll. So I say good night, send her a kiss emoji, and set my phone aside.

The wine is lovely. Peppery and rich and deep, and with each sip, I feel relaxed, happy. I had no idea I'd feel so comfortable here. In a foreign country, away from the things I'm used to, my things. Having Reggie here with me definitely helps, but I realize, despite my conversation with Serena earlier, I am surprisingly less homesick than I thought I'd be at this point. If I'm being completely honest, I predicted I'd have headed home by now.

Of course, I also predicted I'd have headed home empty-handed by now, with no novel, no plot outline, barely an *idea* of where my book should go. And look how that's turned out.

Life, am I right?

I stay there in the dark and finish my wine, just letting my mind wander and my muscles relax, until I finally decide to push to my feet and wander the few feet to the bedroom where Reggie is already sound asleep and snoring.

I undress, brush my teeth, wash my face, and crawl into bed to play big spoon to my tiny dog. My body is tired, but my brain is still rolling, replaying conversations between me and Serena, me and my mother, me and Marina, around and around until I decide to use the exercise I got from a yoga teacher once. I focus on my breath. It sounds silly and it's damn hard to get good at, especially for somebody like me whose brain has a hard time shutting the fuck up. I close my eyes and inhale through my nose, deeply and slowly, trying to focus on nothing but my breath, the air filling my lungs, my lungs expanding in my chest, then I let it out slowly through my mouth. As I do this a few times, I can feel my body start to relax and my brain's whirring slow to a more acceptable speed. And in my mind's eye—which I'm supposed to keep blank for this exercise—I see Marina's beautiful face smiling at me, her dark eyes crinkled at the corners, her high cheekbones rosy. She reaches for me.

Yeah, there's really no better way to fall asleep.

CHAPTER FOURTEEN

I spend another three weeks in very near bliss.

Not gonna lie, it's pretty awesome.

I'm blowing through this book as if the words are literally flowing from my fingertips onto the screen. Every day feels better than the last. My characters feel real, three-dimensional, realistic, and likable. Hell, *I'm* rooting for them, and I already know they're going to end up together. I've never written this quickly. Never.

Scott is flabbergasted when I tell him I'm almost done. I can tell by his stuttering and how long it takes him to formulate a complete sentence, and there's a part of me that's mildly insulted, but I let it go. He finally figures out how to speak coherently, and then his joy is apparent. He says he'll send my news through the proper channels, and by the time we hang up, he's almost giddy. So am I.

My mother is ready for me to come home, and I'm not surprised. This is the longest I've ever been away, and she's feeling it. I am, too, if I'm being honest, but Rome has started to feel almost like a second home to me, and I'm not sure what to do with that feeling. But I miss my family. I miss my friends. I miss my house and my yard and my stuff and the rest of my wardrobe.

But then there's Marina.

We've spent time together almost every day over the past three weeks and change, and it feels like life now, if that makes sense. We talk every day. We go out. We also stay in. I've had more sex this month than I think I've ever had in my life. I've learned her neighborhood and could probably find my way around with no issues at all. I keep a toothbrush in her bathroom, and she bought my favorite body wash online and surprised me with it one morning when I stepped into her shower and there it was. I have a side of the bed and a drawer, and a couple of her T-shirts that I've taken over as my new pj's.

It's all very domestic.

It also scares the shit out of me.

Maybe that's why I say what I say tonight when we're cuddled on her couch watching a movie. Marina is super tired, having given two tours today and sat in a very long meeting with the owners of the company she works for. We spent dinner talking about that meeting, what was said, how much she disagrees with it and how badly she wants to be the one in charge of the tours. I let her vent, because I got the sense that she didn't want help with a solution, she just wanted to be mad for a while and have somebody else nod along, so I did that. Now we're watching a rom-com on my Netflix account. We have the subtitles on in Italian, which tells me that she's very tired and doesn't have the bandwidth to translate in her head right now. She's lying in my arms, and we're cuddled up all sweet and snug and comfortable.

My timing couldn't be worse.

"So, I think I'm going to head home soon." I say it quietly, matter-of-factly. Reggie sighs from his spot on the chair, as if annoyed with me. I shoot him a look.

"Oh, okay. I thought you'd stay over tonight."

Oh. She thinks I mean home to the hotel. Crap. I clear my throat. "No, I mean home home. To the States home."

If she hadn't been lying in my arms, I probably wouldn't have noticed her stiffen, but I can feel it. Her entire body goes very subtly rigid for a split second and then relaxes again.

"Ah, I see." She swallows audibly, and then she's silent.

I wait her out for what feels like hours, even though I know it's only a minute or two. "You okay?"

"Mm-hmm."

I shift so I can look at her face, and her gaze is riveted on the TV, so I pick up the remote and pause it. "What's going on?"

I see the muscle in her jaw tighten, so I know she's clenching her teeth. She doesn't look at me. "Nothing."

"Marina."

She sighs. "Is it so bad that I don't want you to go?"

"Of course not, but you didn't think I'd stay forever, did you?" I don't mean it to sound callous or unfeeling or abrupt, but I'm afraid it may have come out as all three when I see the hurt that crawls into her eyes and makes itself at home there.

"No." She looks like she's got more to say but seems to press her lips firmly closed.

"Sweetie," I say, softening my voice. "I have to go back. You know this."

"I know," she says, and her voice is barely a whisper. Finally, she looks at me, and her eyes are wet. "I will miss you."

The combination of her tears and the slight break in her voice tries hard to undo me. It very nearly succeeds, and I pull her in close and hold her tightly. "I'll miss you, too," I manage.

Our lovemaking tonight feels different. And I know how corny and cheesy and romance-novel-hokey that sounds, but it's true. We feel urgent, almost desperate. It's more than the act itself—which is always amazing with Marina. God, I've never been with a woman so focused on my pleasure. But tonight, it's more than physical. It's emotional. And I'm not gonna lie, it's been sliding toward emotional for a while now. But this? This is…it's heavy. And erotic. And deep.

When we first start, she doesn't look at me, won't meet my gaze. But after a few moments pass, and she looks me in the eye, it's as if she can't look away. I know I can't. We kiss passionately and deeply and thoroughly. I feel her hand between my legs, pulling my underwear down my thighs, then sinking into my wetness, which is copious right now. Her fingers slide through my folds, touching every nerve ending and sending my arousal higher and higher.

But it's when she pushes inside me, when she sets up a rhythm of in and out, slowly at first, then a little faster, a little harder, and I'm gripping her shoulder with one hand and her forearm with the other, it's then she looks into my eyes, and—I swear to God—into my very soul. She drives into me, and I rock my hips to her pace, and I stare back into those dark, dark, loving eyes of hers. What I see there is enough to bring tears to my own eyes, except my orgasm hits at that moment, and I explode. My hips raise up off the bed as Marina adjusts to stay with me, her thumb massaging the outside of my center while her fingers push inside over and over, in and out, taking me higher, drawing it out to impossibly endless joy.

My God. Oh my God.

Did she whisper *I love you*? I thought I heard it, but honestly, with my own blood rushing in my ears and the strain of all my muscles, I can't be sure, and I don't have the energy to devote to wondering. I push it away and colors blossom behind my eyelids like my body's own personal fireworks. I've never felt like this. Ever. And I'm having a hard time with coherent thought.

When I finally begin to come down, my hips settling back to the mattress, the steely grip of my fingers easing up, having left marks in Marina's skin, I open my eyes to meet her face, looking down at me. There are tears in her eyes and the expression on her face is filled with so many things—wonder, joy, sensuality, arousal, and yes, that one other thing I don't want to deal with, because I have no idea how.

I swallow hard.

We don't say anything as we shift positions so I'm on top. We don't say anything as I undress her the rest of the way and run my hands across her olive skin, marveling, as usual, over the smooth softness of it. We don't say anything as I slide my fingers into her wetness and take a nipple into my mouth. I move down her body with my tongue, stopping here and there to kiss a particular favorite spot or two, before settling between her legs.

I feel the grip of her hands in my hair, and it doesn't take long to bring her to the edge. She's incredibly responsive to me normally—something I find endlessly arousing about her—but even more so tonight, it seems. I keep her there for long moments before finally tipping her over. A cry I haven't heard before comes from deep within her as her muscles spasm and she lets go with one hand so she can grab a pillow and hold it over her face.

I ride it out with her, listening to the sounds she's making as I pay attention to the contractions in her center. I love it so much, this exact moment. It's so erotic, so sensual, so intimate. She comes down slowly, and I lay my cheek against her thigh as I wait for her to collect herself.

That's when I hear it.

It's quiet and soft, but there's no mistaking it.

Marina is crying.

"Oh, baby." I quickly crawl up her body, and I'm gentle when I pull the pillow away from her face. Her cheeks are wet, and her eyes are a bit red, and she sniffles and turns away from me.

"I'm sorry," she says, her voice quiet.

"No, no. Don't be." It's like I can actually feel my heart squeeze in my chest at the sight of her crying. It's awful, and I want to do anything I can to make her feel better…except I don't know what that is.

"No." She reaches for a tissue from the box on the nightstand and blows her nose, wipes her face. Gently moving me off her, she pushes herself to sitting. "No, I *am* sorry." She doesn't look at me as she speaks, just rolls the tissue in her hands, toying with it. "We said this was casual. Well, *you* said this was casual, but I went along, so I don't get to be upset now. Forgive me." She takes a deep breath, then another, and it seems to calm her. She finally meets my gaze, but there's something different, like she's shuttered somehow. "Sorry about that."

"No, not at all," I say, and honestly, I'm a little taken aback by the change. I'm floundering a bit here with what to say next.

Before I can come up with anything, Marina slides out of bed and starts to get dressed. I frown. A glance at her clock tells me it's after nine, and Marina sleeps naked, so I'm not sure what she's doing. I follow her into the kitchen without putting my own clothes on. There, she opens the fridge and grabs herself a bottle of water, cracks it open, and takes a long pull from it. She's beautiful, standing there bathed in the fridge light, wearing joggers and a T-shirt, her hair tousled. She takes another long sip, wipes her mouth with the back of her hand, and turns to me.

"You should probably go." Her voice is quiet, and while I try to hide my surprise at her words, I do a crappy job of it.

"Oh." I stand there, naked, unable to move my feet.

She lifts one shoulder in a half shrug and doesn't look at me as she says, "It only makes sense. Why prolong the inevitable, right?" Even her lovely accent doesn't help to soften her words.

"I…oh. Um, okay." And now I feel stupid. Foolish. I stand there for a minute longer, not sure what to do. Then I turn and head back to the bedroom in search of clothes. Hot tears burn behind my eyes. I didn't expect her to toss me out. I mean, I don't know what I expected, but it wasn't this. It wasn't dismissal.

I fumble in the dark for my clothes. I should just turn the lights on, but I'm too embarrassed. I don't want Marina to see my shame. Reggie has hopped off the chair and is following me around, clearly confused, as I dress quickly, run my fingers through my hair, and tuck it behind my ears. I pick up my dog and go back out to the living room where

Marina is now standing in the dark, looking out the window. It feels so weird and wrong to leave like this, and I tell her so.

"Can't we talk a bit?" I ask. "Or, I don't know, just enjoy what time we've got left? I mean, I'm not leaving tomorrow."

Her shoulders are stiff. In fact, her whole body is rigid, and the fact that I can tell those things just by looking at her silhouette from the back tells me how well I actually know her. "I don't think that's a good idea." Her voice is quiet. Monotone.

"But why not?"

She turns to me, and she's backlit by the window, so I can't quite make out the expression on her face. I should go to her, but I feel weird. Ashamed and uncertain. "I think you know the answer to that," she says, still very quiet. "And if you don't, then that's all the more reason you should go."

My brain isn't working. I'm a smart woman, but things are not firing as they should be because her words don't compute, and all I want right now is to escape to something familiar. It feels heavy in the flat. Hard to breathe. Reggie starts to pant in my arms, and I wonder if my emotions emit actual heat, enough to warm him. I open my mouth to say words, but none of them will come. I close it and open it twice more before I exhale in frustration, slide my phone into my bag, and sling it over my shoulder.

Maybe she just needs a little time. That's reasonable, right?

"Okay. I'll text you tomorrow," I say.

Marina is looking out the window again, and she doesn't turn around. With a quiet sigh, I leave the flat, closing the door behind me with a quiet, anticlimactic click.

On the street, I stand there. I've put Reggie on his leash and he doesn't pull or try to go anywhere. He simply looks up at me while I stare off into space. I'll need to get an Uber or a cab to take us back to the hotel, but I keep standing there doing nothing. When I finally risk a glance up at the window I know is Marina's, she's not there.

I look down at Reggie. He's looking up at me, God bless him. He is easily enamored with other people, but he is ultimately my boy, and he knows when I'm hurting. He looks worried, the concern clear in his big brown marble eyes.

"I'm okay, buddy," I say quietly to him, though I'm not sure that's true. "I'm okay."

We walk for a block or two because I can't just stand there under the window of Marina's flat. It feels weird, and I'm also starting to feel a little bubble of anger in my gut to go along with the hurt. What a fun combination.

When we've turned a corner and we're in a spot that can't be seen from her place, I call up my app and order myself an Uber. He arrives within a couple minutes, and soon Reggie is seated in my lap and we're driving away from Trastevere. As we cross over the River Tiber, I absently wonder if I'll ever see it again.

The tears choose that moment to spill over and leave salty, wet tracks down my face.

I have no idea what happens next.

CHAPTER FIFTEEN

I gave Marina twenty-four hours.

Twenty-four hours to not answer my texts, to not return my voicemail messages, to not stop by to see me.

Twenty-four hours.

It's now been thirty-six hours and change. It's after ten in the morning, more than a full day later. And I've heard nothing.

Listen, I haven't gone crazy with texts. I've been very cognizant about giving her some space or whatever it is she might be needing right now, and I just want to talk.

Clearly, Marina does not, and I'm not handling it all that well. Which is annoying me.

I get up from my desk, where I've been trying to work for the better part of two hours, and I carry my phone into the bedroom, leave it on the nightstand, and come back out, shutting the door behind me as if it might try to escape on its own. When I sit back down at the desk, I glance at the sofa, and Reggie is judging me. I'm sure of it.

"What? I can't be looking at it every ten seconds to see if she's texted me back, now can I? I'll never get anything done." I hold his gaze—or he holds mine, I'm not actually sure—for a long moment before he sighs and puts his head back down. Definite judgment there.

The fact that I'm in the last quarter of the book is a good thing, because my endings usually write themselves. I always know how it will end, so once I get past the climax and into the denouement of the story, things flow faster, and it takes less focus and creative energy from me. That's a good thing right now, because it allows me to work.

If I was in the middle of the book while dealing with all this stress and worry, I'd be in trouble.

I do my best to concentrate, and I end up getting to one scene before the end, but it takes me way longer than it should. I manage not to go check my phone, but I also find myself gazing out the window, trancelike, for ten, fifteen, twenty minutes at a time.

We said this was casual. Well, you *said this was casual, but I went along, so I don't get to be upset now.*

Marina's words cut through the silence in my head for the millionth time today. The way she stressed that *I* was the one who said we were casual…that has sat in the back of my mind since I left her place. But before I can grab onto it and turn it at different angles to examine, the chime for a FaceTime call goes off on my laptop. Of course my heart jumps, because for a split second, I think Marina is finally calling. Doesn't matter that she's never FaceTimed me, my heart is hopeful anyway. Idiot that it is.

It's Jessie, and I give my hair a quick finger comb and look at the picture on the screen to make sure my makeup isn't smeared. Finally, I hit the answer button, and Jessie's smiling face appears.

"How are all things Roman?" she asks with a grin. She's in the dark and it occurs to me that it's only, like, four in the morning or something godawful there.

"What are you doing up?" I ask. "I know you're a night owl, but taking things a bit far, aren't you?"

"Nope." She holds up a champagne flute of golden liquid. "Finished my book."

"What?" I clap my hands once. "Jess, that's fantastic! If it wasn't before noon, I'd have a glass of wine with you to celebrate."

Jessie pouts dramatically, and I take a quick second to recall the situation I'm in right now.

"You know what? Fuck it. Hang on." I go to the kitchen area, where I've left a bottle of Chianti I opened two days ago, and pour myself a small glass. Back at the desk, I hold it up so Jessie can see it. "*Cin cin,*" I say. "Way to go, my friend. Hope it's another bestseller." I touch my glass to the screen in an imitation of cheers, and we both sip.

"You didn't answer me," Jessie says after a few seconds of enjoying our drinks. "How's the hot Italian chick?"

I consider lying—or at least fibbing a little bit, but Jessie has only ever been good to me, and I owe her more than untruths. I sigh as I try to choose the right words.

"Uh-oh," Jessie says, leaning closer to the phone as if trying to see my face better. "That doesn't sound good. What's going on? Are you okay?"

"I think I'm ready to come home soon." I start there.

"Okay. Makes sense. You've been there for more than two months."

"I told her that."

"Didn't take it well?"

I shake my head and swallow hard, and the profound sadness over the situation that I've been keeping at bay for more than a day threatens to swamp me.

"You don't look so good, hon," she says quietly. That's when I realize that my eyes have welled up.

I clear my throat. "I mean, she didn't think I was going to stay forever, right?" I ask, but my voice cracks halfway through. "We said it was casual."

Jessie gives me a moment to collect myself before asking, "Was it?"

"Was it what?"

"Casual. Did it stay casual? Because I've known you for a long time, and your face tells me maybe it wasn't."

I groan at myself, wipe my face as if I'm trying to disprove what she's saying, and try to pull myself together. "There are so many reasons why it had to be," I explain. "The distance. The age difference. The places we are in life, in our careers. It would never have worked beyond just some fun. Never." I swallow down the tears that threaten while Jessie looks at me. I don't like it. I'm feeling scrutinized. She's right, she does know me well, and right now, I feel like an open book, exposed, laid bare.

"Are you trying to convince me or yourself?" she asks quietly, and it's the last thing I want to hear.

"I just want to go home," I say, my voice barely a whisper. "I really just want to go home."

And it's the truth. I'll feel better at home. But when I hang up with

Jess, I don't think about going to my home. Instead, I kiss Reggie on the head, lock my suite, and hurry down the stairs to call an Uber.

I'll go to Marina's home.

❖

I have no idea if this is a good thing to do or a stupid thing. What does it say about me? That I'm doing the right thing? That I'm taking the bull by the horns, so to speak? Because maybe she's too ashamed or frightened or angry to talk to me? Or does it say I'm some kind of creepy stalker, going to her house? She said it was over, that I should leave. Am I supposed to just leave it alone, after all the time we spent together? All the intimacy we had? All the things we said?

Maybe I am.

And this is the circular path my thoughts take for my entire Uber ride. Round and round, easing my stress, then sending me into a panic. I'm not sure how much more my stomach can take, but then the Uber coasts to a halt, and I get out. I watch him drive away, and I stand there. It's just me, no Reggie, no overnight supplies. Just my small crossbody purse slung over me.

The weather is pleasant today, comfortable, no humidity. I'm dressed in denim shorts and a simple T-shirt, but I've already broken out in a sweat just standing there doing nothing but being nervous. I stand there long enough to garner a strange look or two from others. A passerby looks back at me after she passes me. Then a shopkeeper off to my right is putting a sign in his window and gives me a furrowed brow, and it makes me force my feet to move, now that I've been standing in front of Marina's building for a year and a half.

I go to the front door, a place I feel like I've been about a million times now, and I pull it open, let myself into the little foyer with the mailboxes.

Where I stand some more.

"Jesus Christ," I mutter, and decide maybe I'll just read all the names on all the mailboxes first. "D'Angelo. Capuano. Manelli. Troiani-comma-M."

I had rehearsed what I would say to her, but standing here now, I realize it has all flown from my head. I drop my chin to my chest and remind myself that I'm being ridiculous. Before I can overthink anymore, I reach up and poke the button next to Marina's name.

And I wait.

Nothing.

Did I push the button hard enough? I mean, I was nervous, and I hit it quickly. Maybe it didn't register.

I push it again, firmly this time, and for a second or two longer than before.

I wait again.

Still, nothing.

"Okay," I whisper in the tiny box between doors. "Maybe she had a food tour or…something." Totally possible. Completely valid. I try once more, just in case.

Nope.

I take in a deep breath and blow it out slowly. So much for all my rehearsing. My nerves are frayed to nothing for no reason. Shaking my head, I push my way through the doors and back out onto the street. I wander slowly, phone in hand so I can call an Uber back again. I glance up and I swear there's a flash of movement in Marina's window.

Wasn't there?

I squint as I stand there, trying to focus, trying to see past the reflection of daylight on the glass, but to no avail. Maybe I imagined it. I hope so. Because imagining I saw her is far preferable to having actually seen her trying to avoid me.

I stare for a few moments longer before I get annoyed at myself. "It's fine," I mutter. "She clearly doesn't want to talk to you. If that was even her." I have enough wherewithal to glance around quickly and make sure nobody's noticed the weird American lady standing on the street talking to herself.

Maybe I didn't see her. Maybe my eyes were playing tricks on me. Or the light was. Or it was wishful thinking that she was looking, even if she didn't want to let me in.

"Okay." I give my head a gentle shake and order an Uber. "Enough."

It's clearly time to go now.

❖

The next night, I'm relaxing on Serena's love seat.

Well, relaxing might be pushing it a bit. I'm as relaxed as I can be for a woman who still hasn't heard from or seen the person she'd been kinda dating for a month, and also, a woman saying goodbye to somebody who's become a very dear friend. So, not really relaxing at all.

"When is your flight?" Serena asks, her voice as soft as I've ever heard it.

"Tomorrow afternoon," I say, and those words somehow make it all real. I am leaving Rome. Tomorrow.

"You're sure you have to go already?" Serena says, her voice tinted with sadness. Then she laughs softly. "I say already, but you've been her for what?"

"Nearly three months," I say. "I've just about finished my book, though, so I'll need to go meet with my publisher and my agent eventually and get things all squared away."

"That's in New York City?"

I nod and sip the excellent wine Ria's opened. "I'll be at my place there for a bit and then head upstate in time to spend Thanksgiving with my family."

We're both quiet for a beat or two before Serena meets my gaze. Hers is gentle, her eyes wet. "Well," she says softly, "I will certainly miss you, my friend. It's been a joy having you around." She turns to Reggie, who's all curled up next to her in her chair, as usual. "And I will absolutely miss this guy." She strokes his head, and he lets out a long, happy sigh, one of those sounds a dog makes when it's completely content.

The lump in my throat ignores my attempts to swallow it down, lodging itself solidly. My own eyes well up. "You have made my stay in an unfamiliar city so much more comfortable than it might have been. I don't know how to thank you."

We're both crying now, and we laugh when we realize it, each of us standing up and reaching for the other. We hug tightly for a long moment, until Serena lets go and waves her hands in the air. "Okay. Enough of that."

We sit back down and both reach for our wine. Something to do with our hands while we collect ourselves. It takes a few minutes, and it's nice to be around somebody who gets it. She doesn't rush me, and

I don't rush her. She beats me to feeling normal again, so she's the first one to speak.

"What about Marina?"

"What about her?" I ask. It doesn't come out snarky, but it's maybe a little chillier than I intended.

Serena tips her head to one side as she regards me. "Ouch."

I frown and shake my head. "She is clearly not interested in talking."

"What do you mean?"

The expression on Serena's face tells me she doesn't know any of this, has no idea that Marina has been avoiding me for two solid days now. I sigh my frustration. "She won't talk to me. We were together two nights ago. That's when I told her I was ready to head home." I take a sip of wine because just telling the story makes my heart squeeze in my chest. "She basically sent me home. Right then. I mean, she didn't throw me out, but it was pretty damn close to it. She said that I'm the one who said it was just casual, and I should go. I've been texting her and calling her for three days. I've been to her flat twice now. She refuses to talk to me." It's when I stop to take a breath that the depth of my hurt around the whole situation rears its ugly head, and my eyes well up again. "It's been really hard to have her just shut me out like this."

Serena is genuinely surprised. Her raised eyebrows and slightly widened eyes tell me so. "That's very unlike her." She says it quietly, almost to herself, like she's thinking out loud. When she looks up at me, her eyes are clear and a little sad. "Maybe it wasn't so casual for her after all." She sips her wine, and her eyes never leave mine.

"I mean—" I cut myself off with a dismissive wave of my hand, but I'm pretty sure my own emotions mirror Serena's. I don't even know what to say at this point, because maybe things weren't so casual for me either. But admitting that would take things to a whole new level of complicated, a level I just don't think I'm ready for. I flick my hand once more and try to cover myself with a sip of wine.

"She can be very stubborn," Serena says, and the fondness in her voice is unmistakable. "Just ask her mother."

I grin. I can't help it. Her words about Marina don't surprise me at all. "I'm sure."

Serena sighs heavily and looks off into the night sky for a moment before returning her gaze to me. For a second or two, I think she's about to say something profound to me, but instead, she simply smiles and says one more time, "I'm going to miss you, my friend."

The tears make a return appearance.

❖

I can change my flight.

I could, right? It would make sense to do so. It feels crazy to leave like this, with Marina refusing to see me or talk to me or even answer my texts. Yes, I'm annoyed that she's being this childish, but I also woke up this morning feeling like I had a boulder sitting on my chest. I'm not sure I've taken a full breath in almost four days.

I get up and shower, giving myself a bit of time to think about it. I'm pretty well packed up, but I could find one more outfit if I needed to. I'll just bump the flight a day. Two at the most.

I dress, dry my hair, and sit down at my computer when my phone pings a text. As has been the case for seventy-two hours now, my heart skips a beat on the off chance it's finally Marina.

It's not. Of course.

It's Scott.

Got everything set for tomorrow. He names two of the biggest bigwigs at my publisher, people I know don't have time in their super busy schedules to turn themselves into pretzels trying to jibe with *my* timeline. He goes on to tell me he's sending a car to pick me and Reggie up from the airport when we land, that he'll have us taken to my apartment so I can get a few hours' sleep, and that the biggest of bigwigs are so looking forward to meeting with me to go over the book. In an unprecedented move, I was sending the book to Scott as I wrote it. It's not my usual process—I don't normally let anybody see my work until it's completely edited—but I was so far behind, and I knew Scott was beginning to panic, so sending him chapters as I went, even before edits, was the best way to calm him down. He's seen everything except the last two chapters, and the fact that these people want to meet is huge. And that only means one thing.

I can't change my flight.

I can't be all, "Gee, sorry, Scott, but this girl I like is ignoring me and I can't leave Italy until I go stand outside her house with a boom box blasting Peter Gabriel." Yeah, okay, I'm fully admitting to being middle-aged, but still, you get my point.

"So, that's it then."

I whisper the words as I drop down onto the bed and just sit there, staring off into space, seeing nothing and feeling everything. Reggie gives my arm a nudge with his nose, something he does when he's worried about me. I pick him up and hold him close. "I'm okay, sweetie," I say softly.

But am I?

I don't feel okay. I feel so many things—sad, angry, stressed, incredulous, frustrated—but okay isn't one of them. I pull out my phone.

Hi. I wish you'd talk to me. I don't understand. I wanted to change my flight and stand in your lobby until you had to see me, but

I stop typing. Fuck it. I dial instead. As expected, it goes straight to voicemail. I clear my throat.

"It's me. Again." I take a deep breath and blow it out. "Look, I was going to change my flight, but I can't now. My publisher wants to meet with me tomorrow, and these are people I can't blow off, but I want you to know I was all set to change my flight." I stop. Ugh. This is coming out all wrong. Accusatory. I steady myself and try again. "I'm so sad you're shutting me out. I didn't want to leave like this." I pause again. "Okay, well, you have my number. I really hope to hear from you." One more pause, because this time, that lump is back in my throat. I try to clear it, but my voice is husky and breaks slightly when I say, "I'll miss you, Marina." I don't say goodbye, I simply hang up.

I sit there, looking down at my hand holding the phone. I feel disbelief, but also numb and empty. Of all the ways I saw things going, this was not one of them. Maybe that makes me naive. Maybe I'm just stupid. Or maybe I'm being selfish. Marina isn't wrong: I *did* suggest we were casual, and I meant it. For my protection and for hers.

So why does the idea of leaving her feel so awful in my heart?

CHAPTER SIXTEEN

I love New York City in the spring.

Not that March is technically spring, but it's when things start to turn. Winter loosens its grip and eventually gives up the fight, letting flowers and warmer breezes enter the chat. All the snow finally melts away, pops of yellow from early-blooming daffodils taking its place in the parks. Brown and muddy gradually dries up, making room for newly green grass that will be lush and bright in the next eight weeks. And now that it's late March, rather than early, I feel like I can wander Manhattan without needing boots or some kind of rain gear just to keep my shoes and pant legs from being spattered with dirty wet from the sidewalks.

In fact, today is gorgeous. High fifties, sunny, electric blue skies. Definite signs of spring. I'm meeting Jessie for lunch, as she's in town to see her publisher, and whenever we're both in the city, we try to meet up.

There's a small, unobtrusive bar and restaurant in the Theater District called Mandy's. It's off the beaten path and kind of hard to find, which is what I like about it. It's not touristy at all, and if you don't live here—not just in New York, but in this area of several blocks—you probably have no idea it exists. I had my apartment here for nearly two years before a friend clued me in on Mandy's.

It's small and dim inside—hard to tell what time of day it is when you have a table at Mandy's place—and I have to stand inside the door for a moment so my eyes can adjust. When they do, I spy Jessie at the corner of the bar waving her arm in the air.

I head her way, a smile on my face. "I take it we're eating at the bar?" It's her favorite.

"Listen, I even commandeered the corner so you can look at my gorgeous face while we chat." That's always my complaint: that sitting side by side at the bar means I can't see her face without turning my head the entire time.

She slides off her stool to give me a hug, wraps me up tight. Jessie gives the best hugs.

We sit back down, and she's right—the corner really does take care of my one complaint about eating at the bar. "Whatcha drinkin'?" I ask, glancing at her martini glass.

"This one's a lemon drop, but I'm gonna move on to either a chocolate or an espresso one next."

"I haven't had a martini in forever," I say, then order one, telling the bartender to make it as dirty as he can. A few minutes later, he slides me a glass of the cloudy deliciousness, a stick with three stuffed olives sunk diagonally into it. "To friends," I say, holding my glass up. Jessie touches hers to it and we sip. I hum my approval, because damn. This is a good martini.

"So?" Jessie says. "What's new? Got sick of being upstate?"

"I did a little, yeah. Spent the holidays with my family, got some work done, did a couple interviews, tossed around some ideas, and got bored." I chuckle. "I felt like I needed some hustle and bustle and to see a few new shows." Jessie is not a Broadway girl, so we don't dive into which shows I have tickets for or am trying to get tickets for. She just nods in understanding because she knows me.

"And how is Reginald Aloixious Chambers, my favorite dog in the whole wide world?"

I laugh at the name she christened my dog with, totally without my permission. Nobody calls him that but Jessie. "He's great. We took a long walk around Bryant Park today, so he's crashed out on the couch."

"You'd think a dog that small would hate the streets of Manhattan. It's gotta just be a sea of legs for him."

"I know, right? Nope, he loves it here."

We both sip, and my martini is deliciously strong. We decide to order some food to keep us from becoming schnockered too quickly.

"So," Jessie says, and draws the word out. "How long are you staying down here?"

"In the city? I don't know. A few weeks, probs. Maybe a month. Maybe more." I shrug. Kinda playing it fast and loose lately, but I don't say that.

She nods, finishes off her lemon drop, and signals the bartender. Once she's ordered her chocolate martini, she returns her focus to me. "I'll be back in two weeks. Riker wants to meet up again." John Riker is Jessie's agent. He's based out of Manhattan and works for a very large, very well-known agency. Jessie is a big deal. You'd never know it talking to her because she's so normal and down-to-earth, but she's pretty huge in the field of horror lit. Not Stephen King huge, but she's not far off. She's in New York City quite often.

"That's great," I say. "New project?" I lift my glass in salute.

"Who knows with him," she says with a soft laugh. Riker drives her a little nuts sometimes. "But I'd like to get together with you again."

"Absolutely. Just let me know when."

"I have someone I want you to meet."

Ah, there it is. I stifle a sigh because I know she means well.

"I don't know, Jess…"

Jessie grabs my forearm. "No, she's great. I promise. She works with Riker, and I've known her for quite a while. I've actually been kind of scoping her out for you since, well"—she lifts one shoulder—"since Italy."

Italy has become the code name for Marina. We never say her name. It started as "Heard from Italy?" And it's moved on to "Fuck Italy. Italy sucks." Jessie has even offered to put "Italy" in one of her books and then kill her off in spectacularly horrifying fashion. I declined.

"I don't suppose anything's changed." It's Jessie's way of asking if I've heard from Marina.

I haven't. At all. I've been back in the States for four months. For a while, I texted her every day. Then it tapered to every week. I called. I left messages. I might as well have been shouting into the void. I heard nothing but the echo of my own voice. "No." I say it quietly and try to hide the little wave of shame that washes over me. I was going to delete her contact information from my phone to help curb the temptation to reach out. I told Jessie I was going to. I didn't. In fact, I sent a text last week. But I don't tell her that.

"You've gotta get back out there, Lil," Jessie says, and her voice has a firmer tone to it than usual, probably thanks to the alcohol. "You deserve someone who adores you. *Adores you.* Treats you like a queen. And you certainly deserve better than someone who ghosts you like a teenager instead of having an adult conversation." I love how irritated she is for me, and she's not wrong. Marina's way of going about... whatever it was she hoped to accomplish...was mean and hurtful, and if I dwell too long on how I'm still hanging on with the tips of my fingers instead of simply letting go, that shame will well up again and swamp me like it has so many times in the past sixteen weeks.

"I know." I nod and gaze into my glass. "I know." And I do. But knowing and accepting are two very different things, it turns out.

"I assume there's been nothing?"

I shake my head.

"Ugh. Fuck that bitch."

I can't help but laugh, even as some small part of me wants to defend Marina, because Jessie never was a person to mince words. She blurts. I can't tell you how many times we've been in some kind of group or public situation and whatever inappropriate comment was rolling around in my head came right out of Jessie's mouth.

"At least tell me something like, *we'll see.* Then I can pretend you're thinking about it. I'll call you when I'm back in two weeks and we can talk about it then."

I'm quiet for a moment, but finally say, "We'll see." It's partly just to steer Jessie off the topic, but it's also because there's a little smidgen of me that *does* think *We'll see. Maybe. Possibly. Who knows?* A very little smidgen. Like, microscopic.

"That's my girl," Jessie says, and pulls me halfway off my stool in an awkward one-armed hug.

"That was such a guy hug," I tease her, and that makes her bark out a loud laugh that has a couple other bar patrons looking our way.

My time with Jessie is always well spent. We settle back into our visit, sharing food and drinks and stories. It's nice to have a friend who does what I do and gets all the inner workings and ins and outs of publishing. Jessie's people are working on a movie deal for her. Mine are looking into another Netflix series. If Harlan Coben can do it, why can't I?

The whole time we're chatting, though, there's a face hovering in the back of my mind. A smiling one with a tender smile and kind, gentle eyes, all framed by waves of soft, dark hair. I don't want to think about why it's been so hard to simply let her go, how I've been hanging on to her in my head and in my heart four times longer than I spent with her. It makes no sense to me, but it also makes all the sense.

Jessie's talking, and I spin my ring on my finger, noticing how much easier it is to do. I've lost weight recently. Turns out I don't like to eat when I'm sad. Or when somebody I'm in love with ghosts me.

Yeah. I said "in love with." I've known for a while, probably since the day Marina tossed me out of her flat. I know I should tell her, but that's not something I want to say to a woman in a text or over the phone. That's an in-person discussion, and Marina clearly never wants to be in the same room with me again.

I swallow my sigh because Jessie's in the midst of a story about her very strange doom prepping neighbor, and I don't want her to think I'm bored. I'm not. Just caught up in my own thoughts. My own crappy, self-sabotaging thoughts. As usual.

They say when you break up with somebody, you need one month for every year you were together. So, if you were together for ten years, you need a good, solid ten months of recovery.

Marina and I were together for, like, a month. I should've been over her in what? About a day?

But I'm not.

"You know what?" I say to Jessie suddenly, totally interrupting her. "Set it up. Do it."

"Set what up?"

"The date with your friend at the agency."

The way her entire face lights up like she's a little kid and I just told her she could choose any toy she wants from the toy store is almost comical, and I can't help but grin. Her story totally left behind us in a cloud of dust in the middle of the road as we drive on to something else, she asks, "Seriously? You're in?"

"I'm in."

"Amazing! She's gonna be so psyched."

We talk about the date—two weeks from now—and I put it in my calendar. This time, she gets off her stool and gives me a real hug, using both arms and squeezing me tight.

"I'm so proud of you, Lils," she whispers in my ear.

"I'm proud of me, too, a little bit," I say, as she climbs back onto her stool. And I am. I just have to do that one teeny, tiny other thing that I haven't been able to yet.

I have to let Marina go.

Completely.

❖

I shouldn't be this nervous. Should I?

"It's just a date," I whisper to my reflection. "Just a date. Nothing more. You're not going home with her. You're not proposing. *She's* not proposing. It's just a date."

Her name is Kya, and like Jessie told me a couple weeks ago, she works for Jessie's agent as his assistant. She's from North Carolina, lives in Brooklyn, has two cats, and loves to cook. Jessie texted me a photo, and Kya is quite attractive. Jessie used the word *hot*, and her dark eyes, mahogany skin, and seemingly confident posture in the photo seem to support Jessie's words, but I'm reserving that assessment for when I meet her in person.

There's an emotional war going on in my head that's pissing me off. Part of me is very much looking forward to this date, and despite my nerves, I'm excited. The other part of me?

Yeah.

The other part of me feels like I'm cheating on Marina. Which is absolutely fucking ridiculous, and I know it. I promise you, I know it. But knowing it and being able to crawl out from under it are two very different things.

I give my head a hard shake. "Stop it."

I breathe in slowly through my nose, let it out through my mouth, and take in my reflection. I tried to walk the line between casually comfortable and comfortably dressed up. I toyed with the idea of a dress, but it's a bit chilly, so pants it is. Black ones with a light blue sweater that buttons in the front and leaves quite a bit of skin showing. It's not scandalous, but it's awfully sexy. I bought it a couple weeks ago when I was trying to cheer myself up, and the salesgirl said it made the blue of my eyes pop. I was sure she was just trying to make a sale, but damn if she wasn't right. I don't wear a ton of makeup, but the dark mascara with my blue eyes and sweater looks damn good, if I do say so myself. And a little blast of confidence is exactly what I need right now.

My phone rings, and it's my mom. I answer it on the way to the kitchen. "Hi, Mom. Putting you on speaker. I've gotta feed Reggie."

"Are you ready for your big date?"

I grin and shake my head, glad she can't see me roll my eyes. I think she's more excited about tonight than I am. "Just about."

"What did you decide to wear?"

"Black pants. Blue sweater. Low heels." I scoop Reggie's kibble into his dish, then pull out the shredded chicken I made for him last night. "And no, I'm not sending you a picture."

"I wasn't going to ask you to."

"You lie," I say with a laugh. "I've met you."

She laughs, too, caught. "Fine. I wanted to see. But I can use my imagination." She pauses, and her tone slides back into a more serious version. "Are you nervous?"

"Yup." I don't want to elaborate for fear I'll fall back down the panic spiral I just managed to avoid.

"Honey. It's gonna be great. You're wonderful, and maybe she is, too."

"Maybe."

"Just promise me you'll give her a chance. Okay?"

I'm trying hard not to get annoyed. I know she means well, and she only wants what's best for me. But I'm almost fifty and don't need a pep talk from my mommy.

And yet.

"I promise. I'm actually looking forward to meeting her." I mix up Reggie's food and then set it on his place mat, where he descends on it like a shark on a seal.

"Great. That's what I want to hear." My mother is clearly relieved, and it's kind of sweet. "Well, make sure you report back and let me know how it went."

We talk about a few mundane things—my dad's latest project and how much space it's taking up in the basement, my brother's promotion, which I already knew about but let her gush over, the political thriller she started last week—before I have to remind her I need to take Reggie out to do his business before I leave for dinner. She wishes me well one more time, and I finally get her off the phone.

"Your grandma is a chatterbox," I tell my dog as I leash him up. We head out to the elevator.

Having a dog in Manhattan is interesting, to say the least. There's very little grass, and the trees are planted directly into the sidewalks. At my house upstate, I have a large, fenced-in yard, so it took Reggie a bit of time to figure things out here. But he has a favorite fire hydrant for his number ones and a favorite tree for his number twos, and it's almost as if he knows I've got plans tonight because he doesn't drag his paws. Trust me, he can get on a sniffing spree that lasts for hours. Not tonight, though, thank God.

"You're the best boy, Reg," I say to him as he finishes up and turns us back to our street. We stop for a moment to chat and sniff when we see Mrs. Haversham and Ralphie, her miniature schnauzer, out for their own walk, but after that, we walk one more block and we're at our building. I have my hand on the door handle when I think I hear my name.

I turn to my left, then hear it again coming from my right, and suddenly every nerve in my body is standing at attention because it instantly recognizes that voice. I swallow hard and turn to meet dark, dark eyes and a very hesitant smile.

It's Marina.

CHAPTER SEVENTEEN

It is so good to see you, *bella*" are the first words out of her mouth after my name. She has stepped close but wisely hasn't touched me, which tells me she must have at least some inkling of how awful she's made me feel for the past four months.

That being said, God help me, it's good to see her, too, though I manage to keep that thought to myself. She doesn't *look* different—she's still remarkably beautiful, still with those smiling eyes and the endless waves of midnight hair—but there's definitely something different *about* her. She seems...lighter somehow. Breezier. Happy.

Apparently, I've completely forgotten the entire English language, because words won't leave my mouth, and I'm pretty sure I'm just gaping at her as I stand unmoving. Reggie isn't suffering the same issues, and he jumps at her leg, tail wagging, clearly thrilled to see her.

She doesn't ignore him. She squats down to give him pets and love, but her eyes never leave my face.

I have so many fucking questions.

Mainly what is she doing here, and how did she find me? Why did she let me leave without answering any of my texts or calls? Oh, and of course, the biggest one of all: *What the actual fuck is happening?*

As I stand there, doing my best impression of a fish—opening and closing my mouth but making no sound—Marina stands back up. Goddamn it, she looks incredible, and I can smell her without getting any closer, that inviting apple scent of hers tickling my nostrils and bringing feelings of comfort and warmth rushing into my system, despite how I've felt the complete opposite for a third of a year.

"I was hoping we could talk," she says then, and I blink at her. Because what?

"You were..." Okay. Two words. Half a sentence. I guess that's better than guppy silence.

"I know," she says, lowering her voice. "I have some explaining to do. And some apologizing." Her smile then is sheepish. "A lot of apologizing."

There's so much bubbling up in me right now. Things have gone from a calm simmer to a rolling boil as I continue to blink at her, unable to believe she's actually standing in front of me, unable to believe she can so easily tell me she wants to talk.

"You want to talk." It's not a question. It's a statement because I don't even have the ability to bring the tone of the end of my sentence up so it sounds like a question. My anger won't let me. I try again. "You want to talk...*now*?"

Her smile finally falters just slightly, and she nods and holds her hands out in a placating gesture. "I know. I know. It's a lot. I'm asking a lot of you. I understand that." Her damn accent is making her words flow like cream, and they coat my anger just enough to cool it a bit. "I have so much to explain to you and so much to say."

"You know I texted and called you endlessly before I left Rome, right?" It's a rhetorical question. Of course she knows, but I'm starting to gear up now, my anger returning to a bubble. "Endlessly."

Her smile falters a bit more, and I'd say chagrined is the best way to describe her expression now.

"I even stopped by your flat. Twice." I hold up two fingers in a peace sign to punctuate my point. "And I'm pretty sure you were home and just chose to leave me standing in your foyer like a pathetic idiot."

The smile slides the rest of the way off her face, and I see her throat move in a nervous swallow.

I jerk a thumb over my shoulder at my building. "I texted and called from here, too. For weeks. *Weeks*, Marina."

"I know." Her voice is barely a whisper. "I—"

But I don't let her finish. Oh, no, I'm on a roll now, and the words just pour out of me. "Do you know how confused I was? How sad? How fucking hurt? Maybe it *was* just casual, but I thought we were at least friends. I guess I was wrong. The friends I know don't do that to each other. They don't leave each other hanging like so much damp laundry for months and then just show back up wanting to talk. No. That's not okay."

She looks stricken now, like I've slapped her. The blood has drained from her face, leaving her white as the whipped cream on my latte this morning, and I finally stop, feeling a little bloom of guilt in the center of my chest. It's not huge because I don't have anything to feel guilty about, but it's enough to stop my verbal rampage.

"I'm sorry," she says quietly. "I shouldn't have shown up like this. I shouldn't have surprised you."

"No. You shouldn't have."

She swallows again, and I almost feel sorry for her. Almost. When she finally meets my gaze, her eyes are wet as she asks, "May I text you? And maybe, when—or if—you're ready, we can talk?" She has gone from super confident and smiling to incredibly hesitant and blinking a lot, and I *do* feel guilty about that. But I'm still mad.

I sigh. Loudly. And I make a show of looking around, up and down the street before I return my gaze to her hopeful one. "Sure, Marina. Text me. Maybe I'll answer." I bend down and scoop up Reggie. "Now, if you'll excuse me, I have a date."

With that parting shot, I turn on my heel and head into my building, hurrying past Teddy, my doorman, and into an open elevator waiting for me. I manage to keep it together until the doors slide shut and I'm sure it's just me and Reggie in there.

I intend to simply blow out a breath, relieved to be out of that situation, but with the air comes a sob, and it surprises both me and Reggie, who turns his head in my arms to look at my face. I close my eyes and the tears slip out from under my eyelids.

Back in my apartment, I hit the bathroom to fix my makeup. I only have a tiny inkling of *maybe I'll skip tonight* before I shake my head hard and say *no* out loud to my reflection.

"You will not let this ruin your night. You're going." I point at the reflection, lest she chose not to listen, and fix myself up. I give Reggie a kiss on his head and leave him a couple of treats. I don't want to run into Marina again, so I leave out the back door of the building and grab a cab, and by the time I'm getting out of it in front of the restaurant, I feel a little better.

"Lily!"

I hear Jessie calling me from up the street, and she picks up her pace as I wait for her. "I forgot your place was nearby," I say as I hug her.

She holds me at arm's length and studies me, and I do my best not to squirm or look away. "What's wrong?" she asks. "Cold feet?"

"No." I blow out a breath. "I'll give you three guesses who showed up out of the blue at the front door of my building forty-five minutes ago. And the first two don't count."

Jessie squints at my face, and I can almost hear the wheels turning in her head. I know exactly when she comes to the answer because her eyes go hilariously wide and she gasps, "No! Italy?"

"Italy," I say with a nod.

"What the actual fuck?"

"Exactly my question."

"Gotta say, Italy showing up in New York unannounced was not on my bingo card."

"Same, my friend. Same."

We stand there, shaking our heads in wonder for a moment before Jessie turns serious. "Do you need to bow out?"

There's no accusation in her voice, and I know that if I *did* need to bow out, Jessie would cover for me. "No. No, I'm good. I want to meet Kya. I've been looking forward to this."

Jessie's face lights back up, and I know she's thrilled with my decision. "Excellent. Let's head in, then. They're already here." But then, before we can move toward the door, she stops me with a hand on my arm. "If you start to feel like you need to bail, just say so, okay?"

I nod, surprised and touched by her sensitivity and not understanding how much I needed it from her until I heard it. Because the truth is, I am not myself right now. Emotions I have worked tirelessly for months to keep tamped down or boxed and put away have spilled all over the inside of my head, making a mess I'm not sure how to clean up. And now I need to be "on," so to speak, while I meet somebody new. Somebody who's heard about me and wanted to spend an evening and a meal with me. Somebody who is not Marina.

I plaster a smile on my face and follow Jessie into the restaurant, the heavy scent of steak seasonings like garlic and onion hanging in the air, and there's only one question echoing through my mind.

How the hell am I going to do this?

"There they are," Jessie says, pointing to a back corner.

I swallow hard and follow her into the dimly lit dining area.

❖

It turns out, Kya is lovely.

She's beautiful, funny, and kind. I've only known her for a couple hours, but I like her a lot.

Also at the table, besides Jessie, are Davis and Guy, a gay couple Jessie's known forever, and her sister Celia with her husband, Jeffrey. Jessie is the only one without a date, but that's typical of her. I actually don't know a ton about her love life, and while I've never really thought of it as odd, looking around the table now, it kind of is.

"Does she ever date?" Kya whispers the question to me as I'm watching Jessie laugh with her sister. "I've known her for years and have never seen her with another person."

"I've known her for years, too, and she's never even talked about another person," I whisper back.

Kya picks up her water. Her fingers are long, her nails polished a deep purple. "Sometimes it makes me sad, and other times, I wonder if she has the right idea."

"About?"

"About staying single. Love is hard."

I raise my wine glass to her water. "Amen to that." We both sip, smiling. "Been hard on you?" I ask, setting my glass down. The others are having a conversation amongst themselves, so Kya and I are free to talk to each other without extra ears.

She gives me a sad smile. "Very. In fact, I'm still in the midst of getting over my last girlfriend. Just when I think I'm about to step completely out of the mire, something grabs me by the ankle and drags me back in."

I blow out a breath and nod my understanding. "I get that, totally."

"I'm sorry," she says, grasping my forearm in her warm hand. "I shouldn't be talking about that when I'm on a date with you."

"Listen, you have no need to apologize. I'm in a similar boat."

Her grip tightens. "Oh, God, tell me so I don't feel quite so alone."

"I'll share if you will."

"Deal."

I let her go first, and she proceeds to tell me all about Deborah, her most recent girlfriend. It seems Deborah had both a jealous streak and an assumption that once they became official, Kya's job would magically stop taking so many hours in her day.

"I did my best to curb my time at the office," Kya tells me. "But it's hard in my line of work. John's got a lot of clients, and they're demanding. Things need to be done when they need to be done. So not doing as much in the office sometimes meant answering calls and emails from home."

"Which Deborah didn't handle well," I surmise.

"Which Deborah didn't handle well." Kya sighs and switches from her water to her cabernet. "She was wonderful in many ways. But the job thing became a constant source of angst for us."

"Oh, I understand that," I say. "I dated a woman once who said I talked too much about my writing, which I then internalized until I didn't talk about it at all, and she never asked about it. Took me longer than it should have to realize what a narcissist she was. Everything was about her. If I didn't bring something up that related to me, nothing about me was ever discussed. But when I did bring it up something personal, I was made to feel self-centered. I spent much of the relationship utterly confused. Once I figured it all out, it just made me so sad."

"Ugh. That's hard. Is that the one you're getting over now?" Kya asks, her voice gentle.

"No." I shake my head and sip my wine and find that I am surprisingly not hesitant to talk about Marina to Kya. "No, she's more recent and has just reappeared after about four months to talk." I widen my eyes for a second—because even just saying it out loud sounds nuts—and have another sip.

"What?" Kya is understandably confused, and before I even realize it, I'm telling her the entire story of me and Marina. Every last detail. How we met, how it started, how amazing it was, how it was casual, but also not, how it became almost domestic in its comfort and warmth, how it ended, the subsequent months since, and her showing up out of the blue to chat. "My God, your head must be spinning," she says when I finish, and laughs a soft laugh. "Mine is."

"Understatement of the year, right there," I say with a slightly bitter laugh.

"What will you do?" Kya's dark eyes are wide, and she's leaned in slightly, clearly invested.

"I am honestly at such a loss right now," I say, and it's me being completely open and honest. With her and with myself.

"I can imagine." She studies me over the rim of her glass as she sips.

"What?" I ask, after a moment of her simply looking at me.

"I think you should hear her out."

I tip my head, more than surprised by her words. "You do?"

A nod. "Just from your story, it sounds to me like you two really had something, and I'm wondering if it was something she'd never felt before, and therefore didn't know how to handle."

I press my lips together as I absorb her words.

"Which is not an excuse for her shitty behavior," she adds. "Don't get me wrong." She looks into her glass for a moment before meeting my eyes. "Your face lit up when you talked about her and your time together. Like, I don't know you well, but I could tell your feelings for her run deep."

I'm glad for the dim lighting of the restaurant because I'm pretty sure I'm blushing right now.

"Seems to me like it'd be a mistake not to at least listen to what she has to say." She lifts one shoulder in a half shrug. "Just my observations."

And just like that, I learn two facts. One: Kya is going to end up being my friend, no matter what happens down the road. And two: Kya is right. No matter how upset, angry, or bitter I am about the way things ended and the way they've gone for the past four months, I'd like to hear what Marina has to say. As I sit there at the dinner table and Jessie meets my eye across it and winks, I know without a doubt that I will be reaching out to Marina. Hopefully, I'll be able to wait and not do it tonight when I get home. Because if nothing else, she deserves to sit and wonder for a bit. But I think Kya is right. I think maybe I should at least listen to what Marina has to say.

When I pull myself out of my head and return to the dinner, Kya is grinning at me. "Just hear her out. That's all I'm saying."

I touch my glass to hers. "You are a truly nice person, Kya."

She sighs wistfully. "I know. That's always been my problem."

We return to dinner, and the rest of the evening is a lot of fun. I feel a kinship with Kya that I didn't expect, and while we both know we're not going to end up dating, we will end up hanging. Jessie is disappointed but seems to accept it as we all say our goodbyes outside the restaurant.

Davis and Guy grab a cab and wave through the window as they pull away. Celia and Jeffrey decide to take the subway home and begin walking. Kya hugs me as her Uber arrives.

"You have my number," she says quietly in my ear. "Let me know how it goes."

"I will," I promise. She gets into the car and I shut the door after her and watch as she pulls away.

"No go, huh?" Jessie stands next to me and bumps me with her hip.

"Oh, she was wonderful," I say. "Truly a great person."

"But you're still in Italy." There's no sadness or accusation in her voice. Only fact—and possibly a trace of understanding?

"I am," I say with a nod, and for the first time in four months, I feel like I can see the path ahead of me. "But it's okay."

"It is?"

"Yeah. It is." I hail a cab, then turn to hug Jessie. "Thank you for tonight. I had a great time." I jerk a thumb at my cab. "Wanna share?"

Jessie squeezes my hand. "Nah. I'm going the other way." She holds my gaze for a beat, then taps her finger on my chest over my heart. "Take care of this first, okay? It's important to me."

I hug her again, suddenly filled with gratitude for her friendship. "I will. Promise."

I climb into the cab. Jessie shuts the door and steps back with a wave. I blow out a breath and somehow feel...I don't know how to describe it accurately. Easier? Lighter? Relieved? Determined? All of those things?

Yeah. Maybe all.

I watch the city go by as we drive...this city I love so much. A few of the longer Broadway shows are just letting out and the atmosphere is jovial, as it so often is here in this part of town. And in that moment, I think about taking Marina to her first Broadway show, what she'd think. Would she love it? Would she be bored? I feel like these are things I suddenly have to know. Have to.

But I also want to wait.

Once I'm home, I leash up Reggie and zip my phone into my pocket so I'm not tempted to send any certain Italian women texts. We walk, Reggie does his business, and we head back inside.

While I perform my evening routine, I purposely leave my phone charging in the kitchen instead of the bedroom. It's not that far away, but it's far enough. I brush my teeth, wash my face, use the facilities, and change into my pj's. Leaving my phone in the kitchen is harder than I expect, and for a moment or two, I wonder if I feel at all like an addict going through withdrawal, picturing the phone, wanting it, having to consciously keep myself in bed. But I turn on the television and find an episode of *Dateline* I haven't seen, and once I'm sucked in, the phone fades away.

Reggie lets out one of those deep, grumbling sighs that dogs make as they're settling down for sleep, and I lay my hand on his warm body. As Keith Morrison's soothing voice lulls me to sleep, I dream of random texts, letters floating through my mind. Looking for the perfect words is part of life for me, so instead of stressing me out, this dream calms me.

I'm asleep before Keith tells me whodunit.

CHAPTER EIGHTEEN

I spend the next morning vacillating between "puttering" around the house, as my dad would call it—the whole time trying desperately to ignore my phone, still sitting on the counter—and rolling different versions of what I will text to Marina around in my head.

It's fucking exhausting. My God.

Finally, after washing the stovetop, rearranging my kitchen cabinets, vacuuming the living room, and cleaning the bathroom until it sparkles like a gemstone, I let myself unplug my phone and take a look. A missed call from my mother, a few photos from Chloe of a new pair of shoes she bought, and a text from Kya that simply says, *You got this!* with a smiling emoji.

"I got this," I whisper into my empty kitchen. Then I walk into the living room and stand at the large bank of windows. Looks like a nice day, sunny with a bright blue sky—the sliver of it I can see, anyway— and my weather app tells me it's already fifty-eight degrees.

Quickly, I open up a new text and address it to Marina, then I type before I can second-guess myself.

Hi. Gonna walk Reggie in Bryant Park off 6th Ave. in an hour. If you still want to talk, I'll be near the Wafels & Dinges stand.

"This way, if she doesn't show, I can at least have a waffle," I reason out loud to nobody. The text is a little bit cool and a lot impersonal, but I send it before I can get myself lost in editing it, which I know could easily happen. I tuck my phone away, change into some comfortable walking clothes and my trainers, then leash up Reggie. We'll wander the neighborhood before we head to the park. We need to take advantage of this spring-like weather while we can. It's early

April, and in this part of the country, we could still get a snowstorm. Like, tomorrow. You never know.

I love New York City. Have I mentioned that? Don't get me wrong, it can get overwhelming, especially if you're a person who, like me, grew up in a small city suburb where it was fairly quiet and uneventful. They don't call New York the city that never sleeps for no reason. It. Never. Sleeps. It's always bustling, always loud, and there are always people. A lot of folks say things like "it's nice to visit, but I wouldn't want to live there." And I get that. I am lucky. I have the money to say, "I can live there part-time but need to get away every so often." Which is exactly what I do.

The fall and the winter in New York are my favorites, because there's nothing like New York City at Christmastime. The first time I brought Chloe to Rockefeller Plaza in December? I don't think her mouth closed once the whole time. She just walked around slack-jawed at all the lights and decorations. I still do that.

But spring in New York isn't bad, especially today, and once Reggie and I have wandered a bit, we make our way to Sixth Avenue. Walking between buildings tends to block out much of the sun in Manhattan, but Sixth is more open, and the sun is higher now and has a clearer shot to warm us as we walk. Reggie has done a lot of sniffing and got all his business finished, so he moves at an easier pace now, next to me rather than dragging me down the street.

I'm aware of my heart rate as we close in on Bryant Park. I don't feel like it beats faster, but it definitely beats harder. We get to Wafels & Dinges, and there isn't much of a line. I glance around but don't see Marina, and I force myself not to have any kind of reaction, positive or negative. It's not easy.

I order my waffle, then take it to a table near the Ping-Pong section. Chloe would scold me and correct me, reminding me that the proper name is table tennis, but it'll always be Ping-Pong to me. I tie Reggie's leash to my belt loop and take a seat, and he immediately lies down at my feet. I cut a bite of my waffle—which is covered with chocolate sauce and walnuts—and eat it as I watch the games going on and listen to the happy, clicky-tappy sound of bouncing Ping-Pong balls.

Reggie seems to love the games. He doesn't bark. He doesn't try to chase the wayward balls that inevitably roll off the courts and into the paved path through the park where walkers hurry by. He just watches, his little canine head moving from one side to the other like a spectator at a tennis match. I think it relaxes him somehow, which makes little sense, I know. Pretty soon, both of us are absorbed in the two matches going on. I don't notice right away when somebody takes the seat across the small round table from me.

And then I feel her presence.

It's weird, but true. I *feel* that Marina is here before I ever lay eyes on her. So when I do turn to meet her gaze, I'm not even a little bit surprised.

"*Ciao, bella*," she says softly, and then a quick flash zips across her face, and I wonder if she's chiding herself for still using that pet name. The truth, though, is that I don't mind even a little bit. Just like I don't mind when Reggie gets up and moves toward her, his tail going a mile a minute. Marina's wearing jeans and a black fleece, and her dark hair is loose and wavy around her shoulders. She's stunningly gorgeous, and a small part of me is annoyed by that. But it's very small, because mostly, I'm just happy to have her sitting across from me.

"Hi," I say, and my smile is genuine. Seeing her warms me. Still. Even after everything.

"How are you?" She looks up from petting Reggie.

"I'm okay," I say with a nod. "You?"

"I am in New York City and sitting in a park with you. How bad can I be?"

All right, that was pretty charming, and that damn accent still works on me, but I quickly remind myself of how the last sixteen weeks have felt, and I simply look at her and wait.

She gives a slow nod, as if realizing that this is not the time for flattery, it's the time for explanation. She continues to nod slowly, as if the rhythm of it calms her. She spreads both hands out on the tabletop and takes a breath. When she looks at me, I can feel all her emotion; I can feel her anxiety as well as her hope and her fear. It's weird and not like anything I've ever experienced before. I swallow.

"First and most important," she begins, "I am sorry. I am so, so very sorry for the way I handled things, and mostly, I'm so sorry for cutting off all contact. I had my reasons at the time, but I know now that it was selfish, and it was hurtful. I apologize."

"Okay," I say. "I accept your apology." I have questions and comments, but I also get the feeling she's not done yet, so I wait.

"Second," she says, then swallows and clears her throat twice and looks off at the Ping-Pong players. She's nervous. That much is obvious to me. I wait her out, which isn't easy. She's clearly struggling with words, and I want to help her, but I also know this is her show, so I force myself to sit quietly. When she finally turns so those dark eyes are locked on me, they're filled with so much, and again, I see it all. I feel it all. Worry, fear, hope, desire, they all collide in that rich dark brown. "Second, I'd like us to try."

I give her another moment, but that's all she says. I swallow and wet my lips. "Try what?"

"Try again. Being together." She holds up a hand as though I'm interrupting her, even though I've said nothing. "Yes, it's a little crazy, but there are some things you should know first."

"Okay."

"So, I'm not just here on vacation. I'm here on a work visa."

Well, that's a surprise. "Seriously?"

She nods, and her smile is wide and genuine. She's proud of herself, and she should be.

"Marina, that's great. Wow."

Her smile grows, and that little flutter I used to get whenever she lit up is back, flitting around low in my body. "It was something I have been working on for a while but never told you because I wasn't sure it would come through. But it did, and I came here to work for a food tour company here in the Big Apple." Spoken like a true tourist, and I smile at her. "I'm not designing the tours—yet—but my boss is very open to my ideas, and he lets me be creative, so it's working out really well. At least I think so. I hope he does, too." At that, she makes a face with her teeth clenched, and it makes me laugh.

"I'm sure it's just a matter of time before he has you making up the tours."

She lifts one shoulder in a modest half shrug. "Maybe. But anyway, I'm here for a while, and I'd like to take you out. If you'll let me."

God help me, I can't seem to find my anger. I mean, it's there, don't think it's not, but in all my fantasies about the possibility of seeing Marina again, I unload on her. I unleash all the hurt and pain she caused. I let her have it. But that's not happening now, because goddamn it, I'm just so glad to see her. I'm not sure what to do about that.

"Take me out, huh?" I nibble on the inside of my cheek as she slowly lets herself smile.

"Yes. I have learned of some really great places. I knew New York was a"—she snaps her fingers, looking for the word—"heaven?"

"Haven."

"Haven! That's it. I knew it was a haven for amazing food from all cultures, but it's even more than I ever could have imagined." She seems to realize her excitement is running away with her, and she takes a moment to calm herself. When her voice is back to a normal register, she says, "I spend two days a week just wandering around, stopping into little places that might fly under the radar and tasting their food." She gives a small, self-deprecating chuckle. "If I wasn't walking so much, I'd have to be careful of how much weight I could gain here."

"You have nothing to worry about. You're still gorgeous." I was only thinking it, so I'm as surprised as her when the words leave my mouth. She flushes a pretty pink on top of the olive tint of her skin.

"I'm so happy to see you, Lily." She says it so softly, I almost don't hear her, but her eyes are wet, and when she reaches her hand across the table to me, there's no way I'm not going to take it.

"Can we go back to something you said earlier?" I ask it quietly because I feel like I need to step carefully here. I don't want to chase her off, but I need some clarification.

She nods, slightly wide-eyed, like she's nervous about what I might say next.

"You said you had reasons for cutting off contact in Rome. Can you tell me what they were?"

She presses her full lips together and looks off to her right for what feels like a long time but probably isn't really. Then she swallows, something I see and hear and says, "I knew—" She stops and clears her throat, then looks down at our hands while she tries again. "I already had feelings for you. Pretty early. Even when you asked me about us being casual and I agreed." She swallows again. "I maybe should not have."

"Oh," I say softly, drawing the word out as I take in what she's said, roll it around in my head.

We sit there, looking at each other silently for a long while. The ball is in my court now, she knows it, and I know it. The Ping-Pong games go on. Reggie sits looking up at us both as if waiting for what will happen next.

"I'm so sorry," Marina whispers. "I've missed you so much." With those words, I think her nerves can't take anymore. The tears spill over and track down her beautiful face, and I can't stand it.

"Okay." It's just one word, but it's as if it has power, and it blows the clouds away.

"Okay?" Her eyes go wide, and I think she can't quite believe it.

I say it again, and punctuate it with a nod. "Okay. Take me out."

And before I realize it, she's pulled me to my feet and has me in her arms, hugging me tightly. God, she smells amazing, and the feel of her, of being this close to her, sends so much emotion rushing through me that I feel my own eyes well up.

We're not okay. We're not magically better. I know this. But for right now? For right now, I'm happier than I've been in four months.

I am more nervous right now than I was the first time I went on an actual date with Marina. Like, a hundred times more. It's ridiculous. I am ridiculous.

I am also giddy. Just absolutely fucking giddy.

Yeah, I've got to reel that in.

I remember Jessie telling me to protect my heart, and it was excellent and wise advice. I need to focus on that today because all I want to do is go have the best time ever with Marina. And possibly kiss her face off.

I didn't call Jessie. I didn't call anyone.

I didn't want to be talked out of this date.

As I check out my reflection in the mirror, I know that may come back to bite me in the ass, but right now? I don't care. It's been three days since Marina met me in the park, apologized, and told me she wanted us to try. We've texted fairly regularly since then. I've had three days to decide this is a bad idea, or to change my mind, but if I'm being honest, backing out was never even a glimmer of a possibility, and I feel like I knew that the second I said yes to her.

I don't know where she's taking me, and that's okay. If there's only one thing to trust about Marina Troiani, it's that she knows food. I've enjoyed thinking about her wandering the city, ducking into little holes in the wall to discover delicious foods. It's her passion, and she followed it here. To me. That says something.

I check my look in the mirror. Simple black pants and a powder blue long-sleeve top with small silver buttons. A slight heel, because I don't know how much walking tonight will entail. I check my makeup, add a little gloss to my lips, tuck my hair behind my ears. I tip my head as I scrutinize myself, then unfasten one more button—a little something to distract Marina a bit. I grin at my reflection. Okay. Not bad, if I do say so.

"What do you think?" I ask Reggie, who is in his usual spot of observation from my bed. He gives me a little snorfle sound that I take as approval. "Okay. Good." I'm kissing his nose when my intercom buzzes. My doorman.

"Hey, Teddy," I say into the speaker.

"Good evening, Miss Chambers. I believe your date is here to pick you up."

Huh. Well, that's interesting. Usually, Teddy will just say I have a visitor or I have a package or whatever.

"I'll be right down," I tell him. I look back at Reggie, who has followed me out of the bedroom. "My date is here." He gives his tail a wag, then heads for his bed in the corner. "Don't wait up, okay?" I gather up my purse and a coat, as it's cooler today than it was a few days ago, lock the apartment behind me, and head for the elevator.

The entire elevator is mirrored, and it's annoying me because I was confident three minutes ago in my own bedroom. Now? In this tiny box with the horrendously unflattering lighting? Ugh. Everywhere I look, there's my reflection waiting for criticism.

I stare at my feet. The ride down to the lobby never felt so long.

Finally—*finally*—the elevator comes to a stop and the doors slide open. I step out and to my right toward the lobby where Teddy greets me from behind his desk. He grins at me—is his grin larger than normal?—and leads me to the front doors, which he pushes through, then holds open for me.

I thank him, look up at the street in front of me, and stop dead in my tracks.

Oh my God.

CHAPTER NINETEEN

Marina is an absolute vision.

A gorgeous, sexy, fantastical vision in a black one-piece jumpsuit that makes her look even taller, even more sensual than she already is. Her hair is swept up, leaving her long neck exposed. Thin silver hoops sparkle in her ears, and some sexy locks of hair escaping from the updo corkscrew along her neck.

She's standing next to a long, black limousine and talking to someone I assume is the driver, judging by his black suit and hat.

She glances over and catches sight of me, and I swear to God, her entire face lights up. It's an amazing feeling, and I can't remember the last time somebody looked that happy to see me.

"*Bella*," she says in that accent, and she reaches out her hands to me. "You look stunning."

"I look underdressed," I say with a chuckle. "Because oh my God, look at you. *Look at you.*"

She blushes prettily, but her hands tighten on mine. "Nonsense. You're dressed perfectly." She bends to lightly kiss my cheek, then leads me by the hand to the limo. "This is Jacob, our driver for tonight."

Jacob gives a nod, then opens the door for us and we climb in. It's roomy and wonderful and there's a bottle of Champagne chilling in an ice bucket. Jacob shuts us in, and Marina pours two glasses as he gets into the driver's seat.

"Marina," I say, waiting until I have her attention. "What is all this?"

She shrugs, and for the first time since I laid eyes on her seems to falter for just a second. "I wanted to take you to dinner in style."

I don't want to embarrass her, so I don't ask her how expensive a limo in Manhattan must be, and she seems to read my mind.

"Jacob is a friend and is doing me a favor," she says with a grin. "Stop worrying." She hands me a flute of golden bubbly Champagne, then touches hers to it, and it makes a lovely pinging sound. "To being with you," she says simply, and it's that simplicity that makes it so touching to me.

"You look beautiful," I say to her, my voice soft.

"Thank you." She's just as quiet, and our eye contact is so hot right now, the inside of the limo feels electrically charged. I think we both notice it at the same time because we both grin, and then Marina leans in and kisses me softly on the mouth.

It's been a little over four months since we've kissed, but it honestly feels like no time has passed at all. I'm right back there, in that place where I'm trying hard to make myself believe there's nothing solid here, it's just fun, just a fling, something to occupy my time. And just like before, I'm not truly convinced.

She sits back next to me and puts her hand casually on my thigh, as though we sit this way all the time. And it *feels* like we sit this way all the time.

"I've missed you," she says, then nibbles on her bottom lip.

I nod slowly.

"I know." Her sigh is soft as she glances down at her drink. "It would have been nice for you to know that."

"Not gonna lie," I say. "It would've."

"I know. Of course. I'm so sorry."

I don't want her to spend our entire evening apologizing, but I have to admit, it's nice to know she's so contrite. "So, where are we having dinner?"

At the change in subject, she perks up. "It's a small, out-of-the-way place called Antonio's. Very, very authentic Roman food. The best I've had here." She arches a dark brow. "So far."

When we pull to a stop, I realize she isn't kidding. We get out, and I have to search for the door to the restaurant—which makes me wonder why they don't have better signage.

"I don't see it, but I can certainly smell it." I sniff the air like a bloodhound, and the scents of tomato sauce and basil and oregano instantly propel me back to my suite in Hotel Cavatassi. "If I close my eyes, I feel like I'm back standing at my open window in my hotel in Rome," I say quietly. When I open my eyes again, Marina is smiling at me.

"Good. I was hoping so." She holds out her hand to me, and I take it. Hers is warm, soft, and strong as it closes around mine, and she leads me to a door that I didn't realize was there.

Marina greets the host like they're old friends, hugs and smiles and laughter. I take the opportunity to look around. It's a bit bigger than I expected from the outside. Maybe fifteen or twenty tables, nearly all of them occupied. The lighting is typically dim, and there's a small bar to the right. The quiet hum of hushed conversation serves as background music, and I'm instantly comfortable here. The host—I wonder if it's Antonio himself—leads us to a cozy table for two in a back corner, and it's perfect. Removed from the bustle, but we can still see everything.

We sit. "I might want to live here," I say, and Marina laughs as a server fills our water glasses.

"I had a feeling you'd like it."

"Seriously. If the food is half as good as the atmosphere, I might move in."

"You'd better start packing your things, then."

When our waiter arrives, he has an accent similar to Marina's and soon, they're bantering in Italian. She catches my eye. "Do you mind?"

"Not at all," I say, and it's true. I love, love, love listening to her speak in her native language.

"I will translate for you."

I wave her off. "No need. Just order me something delicious. I trust you."

She holds my gaze for a moment as if my words hit her especially hard, but in a good way. Then she smiles and returns her attention to the waiter. They continue to banter, then he gives me a nod and takes his leave.

"He's bringing us a Chianti. Also, what I like most about this place is their simple, traditional dishes. You don't have to go fancy or complicated to have amazing food. So, I ordered us the lasagna, the penne with vodka sauce, and a side of their homemade meatballs, which are fantastic. Also, salad and bread, of course."

I'm just looking at her, staring really. I can't help it, she's so goddamn beautiful.

She shakes her head with a grimace. "Is that not okay?"

"It's perfect," I say and reach across the table to grasp her hand in reassurance. She squeezes mine and doesn't let go until the server brings a basket of warm bread and a saucer, into which he pours olive oil. We tear off bread, dip it in the oil, and holy mother of God, it's delicious.

"Thank you for coming out with me." Marina chews her bread. Her face has grown serious.

"You don't have to thank me. I'm glad to be here."

She holds my gaze for a moment before saying very quietly, "You must have been so angry with me."

And here we go.

I take a moment, let myself settle, because the mention of the past four months has the effect of lighting up everything in my body, and not in a good way. I inhale slowly through my nose and wait for my nervous system to calm before I speak. "I was angry, yes. But more than that, I was hurt, and I was confused."

She nods and rolls her lips in to bite down on them.

"I wanted us to talk, to figure out how and if we could find…" I sigh. "I don't know what. Something. Anything. But when you agreed that we were casual, I started to accept maybe that's what you wanted."

"No, that's what *you* wanted." She's not loud, but she's firm when she says it. She glances at the table closest to us, surmises that the couple there is paying no attention to us, and repeats, "It's what *you* wanted."

She's not wrong. "I know. It was. I insisted on that, but…" I lift one shoulder and pick up my wine. I look away from her. Her dark eyes are too intense right now.

She lets things sit for a moment, and the waiter arrives with our salads. She seems to study hers for a moment or two before glancing back up at me. Her eyes are wet, which makes my heart squeeze in my chest. "It wasn't." Two words. Two simple words that lodge a lump in my throat.

"Wasn't what?" Yeah, I'm gonna make her spell it out. It's the least she owes me.

"Casual. It wasn't casual for me. It's *not* casual for me." She picks up her wine, and her eyes don't leave my face. I can feel her gaze, even as I look everywhere but at her. "Was it for you? Tell me the truth.

Be honest with me and I will accept whatever you say. I promise." Her words are firm, but when I return my gaze to her face, she looks terrified. If it wasn't such a serious moment, I might laugh.

Tell me the truth.

She's not asking a lot, wanting the truth. Of course she isn't. And I owe her nothing less than that, right? My heart is hammering in my chest now, I can feel it in my head. I clear my throat and glance down at my untouched salad for a beat before I whisper, "No."

"No, it wasn't casual or no, you won't tell me the truth?"

I lift my gaze, wondering if she's toying with me, but her face is open. "No, it wasn't casual." I clear my throat again, because what the hell with the lump that won't go away? "It started out that way. It was my intention. It was what I wanted. Something fun. Something not serious. And it started out that way."

Marina nods and sips, and the terror is gone from her expression now, replaced with something I can't quite put my finger on.

"I honestly don't know exactly when it changed for me, but it did. I didn't even realize the extent until after I was home and had time to mull it all over, to replay everything in my mind."

"And what was it that you realized? After the replaying?"

Goddamn, her questions are poignant.

I sit for a moment, not sure if admitting my true feelings will help or hurt. Will it mean happiness or disappointment? Why is being true to myself—out loud—so fucking daunting?

While I'm stuck in my own confusing head, the waiter arrives with our lasagna and penne and a plate of the largest meatballs I've ever seen, and I take the opportunity to breathe, to think, to glance across the table at Marina, who's trying to help him make room, since neither of us have touched our salads yet. Before he leaves, he tops off our wine, and then I'm looking across a feast to meet dark, sparkling, loving eyes.

"I was in love with you." I just blurt it out, and I'm not even surprised. There it is, hovering in the air between us.

"Was?" she asks, raising her dark brows.

"Am," I clarify. "I *am* in love with you."

"Well, thank fucking Christ," she says as she blows out a breath and it ends up a snort-laugh. And the F-word in her accent is…

"Wait. You're happy about this?"

"Of course I am. Shouldn't I be?" She's laughing outright now as she puts down her fork and leans toward me. She lowers her voice and says, "I'm in love with you, too, *sciocco*."

I have no idea what that means, but her smile is radiant, and I let myself bask in it for a moment or two. I smile back. Maybe not as hugely as her, but I do. I can't look at her face and not. "Now what?" I finally ask.

She cuts a meatball in half, then in half again, stabs a bite, and pops it into her mouth. She gazes at me as she chews. "Well," she says after what feels like an hour of staring at me, "we can't not try to make this work, right? We are in love."

"Are you going to grin like a goof every time you say that?" I ask softly.

"Probably. Because we're in love." And the goofy grin remains.

I shake my head and cut myself a bite of lasagna and look at her, wide-eyed as I chew. "Oh my God."

"Told you."

There seems to be an unspoken agreement that we table the conversation while we enjoy our amazing food. Our words have changed to hums and moans of approval, and at one point, our eyes meet across the table and we both burst into laughter.

It's a most enjoyable dinner, and I'm sad when we're finished. At the same time, I'm glad, because I'm ready to be alone with Marina.

We're outside, standing on the sidewalk and waiting for Jacob to pick us up when I say four words that I know are going to alter everything going forward.

"Come home with me."

Marina holds my gaze for a split second before she nods. Just one nod. Then she holds out her hand and I take it.

"This is all yours?" Marina wanders my apartment, wide-eyed, mouth agape. She stops at the bank of windows in the living room and gazes out.

"It is." I move to stand next to her. "This view has given me much peace over the past couple of years I've had the place. I love to stand here without any lights on and just look." The buildings are a combination of offices and apartments, various squares lit up.

Sometimes I can see people, sometimes not. "It's a little voyeuristic, but also kind of entertaining."

Marina wraps an arm around me and pulls me in tightly. "You're cold," she says, pressing her lips to my forehead.

I've just walked Reggie. "Then warm me up."

She takes that for the gentle command that it is and lowers her mouth to mine, and it's like no time at all has passed since the last time she kissed me. We've kissed, what? A hundred times? Two hundred? It doesn't feel at all like I've been deprived of these lips for more than a quarter of a year. Rather, it's so achingly, lovingly familiar that it feels like the last time was yesterday. I pull back and turn in her arms so we're face-to-face. She's looking down at me with such love in her eyes, I can't understand how I didn't see it before. It's so clear. I reach up and stroke her cheek. "I love you," I whisper, and there's no fear, no worry. Only certainty.

"I love you, too," she whispers back, and she kisses me again.

We make our way to my bedroom. We move almost as one, kissing as we go, slowly backstepping, sidestepping, dancing our way there. Reggie seems to get it, because instead of hopping up onto the bed, he makes himself comfortable on his own little donut bed in the corner.

It's different tonight—it seems so clichéd to say it, but it is. We don't have sex, we make love. Every move is slower, more intentional, at least I know it is for me. I don't just want to rip Marina's clothes off, I want her to know that it's about love tonight. I want to see her naked body, I want to touch it, because I want her to feel how much I love her. And I don't know for sure, but I think she's having similar feelings. She undresses me slowly, taking the time to look at me, her eyes moving over my skin so hungrily that I can almost feel them.

She's above me on my bed, and as she meets my gaze in the dark, she says, "I've never wanted someone so badly in my entire life, Lily, the way I want you right now."

A surge of warmth runs through me, and if my underwear wasn't already soaked, that would have done it. I swallow hard, grab her face in both my hands, and kiss her as thoroughly as I have ever kissed any woman. I want her to know. I *need* her to know how I feel.

Clothes are removed, and hands explore and mouths crash together and tongues come into play to stroke sensitive skin, and when Marina finally slides her fingers inside me, the cry that is ripped from my throat is so foreign, there's a split second when I wonder where it came from. And then I'm taken to heights I've never seen. Marina pushes me to the edge, then backs off. Again and again, she gets me so close, and then she stops, teasing me mercilessly until I'm practically begging for release.

"Look at me," she says, and the words don't compute for me the first time. "Lily."

God, I love the way she says my name.

"Look at me."

I meet those rich brown eyes, sparkling even in the dark of the night. I can see them, see the love radiating from them. I've never seen anything like it before. I've never been so sure of anything before.

"I love you," she whispers as she holds my gaze, and my eyes grow wet.

"I love you, too."

And she tips me over into the abyss. Down I go, but I only fall for a short time and then I'm flying, tethered to the earth by her fingers as they slide in and out of me, and we rock together in a rhythm we both feel, we've both created. My hips are up off the bed, but she's holding me, and I know I'm safe as I cry out, my hands gripping her body like I may never let go.

We are awake on and off all night. We make love, take forty-five minutes here or twenty minutes there to doze, and then we are on each other again. I've never wanted another person so badly in my life, and while I have been ridiculously attracted to Marina since pretty much the moment I laid eyes on her, this goes beyond. Way beyond. At one point, I start to chuckle as she's kissing down my body, and she stops to shoot me a look of confusion.

"Sorry," I say, still laughing softly. "I'm just wondering how long I can keep up this level of desire before I simply burst into flames and turn into a pile of ash in this bed."

Her confused face morphs into a very satisfied grin. "Let's find out," she says, before lowering her mouth to my center and taking me even higher than the last three times.

I do not burst into flames.

It's almost dawn as we lie tangled up in each other like two vines of ivy grown inextricably wrapped together. The world outside the window has gone from midnight to deep purple to light pink as I lay here with my cheek on Marina's chest. Her fingers play in my hair, and I feel her press a kiss to the top of my head.

"I love you, *bella*," she says softly.

"I love you, too," I whisper back and tighten my arm around her middle. She sighs in what sounds like great contentment, and before long, her breathing becomes deep and even, and she's finally asleep.

I stay awake for a bit longer, wanting to remember this day, this moment. Because I feel different. It's so hard to explain, and as a writer, that's a little frustrating for me, but it doesn't make it less true. I feel different, and it's because I know we're going to make this work. Fourteen years and an ocean separate us, but Marina is here now. I don't know yet what her plans are, but I do know I want to be a part of them. All of them. I won't let her run from me or shut me out when there's a problem. I will chase her down if I have to.

I push myself up onto an elbow and just watch her sleeping face. Her smooth skin and long, dark lashes, and full lips, her face framed by all that hair. She's stunning to look at, there's no arguing that. And she loves me.

She loves me.

I lie back down and snuggle in. It's my turn to inhale deeply and let it out as my body finally settles into relaxation. I'm going to be sore in muscles I didn't know I have tomorrow, and the thought brings a smile to my face. I burrow into Marina's neck, inhaling her apple pie scent.

"I love you," I whisper, knowing she's asleep but wanting to put the words out into the universe anyway.

This is where I belong.

EPILOGUE

Fourteen months later

Marina is nervous.

I can tell by how many times she's smoothed her hands down her sides. I've been working at my desk for an hour now while she gets ready, and she's walked past my doorway about a dozen times so far.

"Baby, you ready?" I call out.

A beat or two goes by before she appears in the doorway. "I think so? How do I look?"

She's not dressed up, but her look has changed. The food tour business doesn't require her to wear a suit or dress if she doesn't want to, but she's starting a new position today, and she wants to impress. So she's wearing her dark jeans, but also a white blouse and a herringbone blazer that looks fabulous on her, makes her look like a sexy college professor. I'm not sure how she'll feel about that comparison, though, so I keep it to myself.

"You look amazing. Professional."

She blows out a breath. "Okay. Good."

I get up and cross the room to take her hands in mine. They're clammy. "Babe. You're gonna be great. Chuck already thinks you're the best thing that's ever happened to his business." Chuck owns Big Apple Food Tours, and he's said a hundred times over the past year or so that he doesn't know what he'd do without Marina. She practically runs the place already. And today is her first day as Tour Coordinator. "How many restaurants do you visit today?" Asking her to spout facts, I have found, helps her to relax.

"Six," she says, then pulls out the little notebook I gave her back in Rome because I finally talked her into actually using it, flips through a couple pages, and relays them to me. By the time she gets to number six, she's much calmer. She takes a deep breath and lets it out, then jerks her chin toward my desk. "How's the writing?"

"It's coming along." I'm about halfway into a new script I'm working on, and not being able to write hasn't been a thing—not even a blip—for over a year now. "Got a meeting with Scott next week."

"And dinner with Serena at seven, yes?"

I nod. "I'll grab us some wine and cheese from that place down the street. We'll head out as soon as you get home."

She nods, then glances at her watch. "Okay. Gotta run." Her colloquial English has greatly improved in the time she's worked here, but her accent is still my favorite thing. She leans in and kisses me. "Love you."

"Love you. You're gonna have a great day." I kiss her again and follow her out to the living room where she stops to kiss Reggie on his furry head. She waves at me one more time and is out the door.

My phone rings before I have a chance to do much else.

"Hey, Jess," I say, happy to hear from my friend, who is arriving in town this week to meet with her publisher. "Flight okay?"

"Yup. Just checking to see if we're still on for lunch tomorrow."

"We absolutely are," I say, looking around my living room.

"You good? You sound…wistful. In a good way, I mean."

It amuses me that she can pick up such things just from a few words. "I am. Marina just left for work and Reggie is watching me from his chair in the living room, waiting for our morning walk, and I'm just…thinking about how different my life is from this time even a year ago."

"You've had some changes, that's for sure."

I grin as I slowly wander. "I mean, there's art on the walls now that Marina helped me pick out. Her shoes are next to mine near the door. Her jacket is draped over a dining room chair. My guest room closet is hers now."

"It's good, though, right? I mean, she needs a room."

I snort a laugh. "Oh, no, she doesn't have a room. *We* have a room. My room is her room, and the guest room is the guest room. She just needed extra closet space. She has a ridiculous amount of clothing!"

Jessie laughs along with me, then says, "Something else that's changed? You."

"Have I?" I'm both surprised and not to hear her say that, which makes no sense, I know. "For the better?"

"Oh, honey, very much for the better. I've never seen you this happy. Makes me a little ill." I laugh, and she goes on. "I admit, when you told me a few months ago that you were going to have her move in, and even stay in your place when you went back upstate, I was a little worried."

"Did you have visions of me returning to an empty apartment, having been robbed blind by a hot Italian woman?"

"Yes!" She says it adamantly.

I can't help but laugh. "I very much appreciate your worry. I have yet to be robbed of anything."

"Except your heart," she says, and she's teasing, but also not.

"Except my heart."

"You sound great, Lil. Truly. I can't wait to see you."

"Same."

We sign off, and I'm left to think about the call as well as the past year or so. I pick Reggie up and sit down with him on my lap. Looking around my Manhattan apartment—something I was so proud of when I bought it—I can't imagine Marina not being here. Like, it won't compute. My brain won't accept it.

"This is it, Reg," I say softly to my dog as I kiss his head. "This is where we're supposed to be."

My phone pings a text notification, and I glance at it, then hold it up for Reggie to see. It's a text from Marina.

Just texting to say my home is with you and Reggie.

I love you both so much.

Can't wait to come home to you tonight.

The lump lodges solidly in my throat, and it takes me a couple of tries to swallow it down. I kiss Reggie's head again as I feel the most wonderful calm settle over me.

"This is where we're supposed to be."

About the Author

Two-time Lambda Award–winning author Georgia Beers has written more than forty novels of sapphic romance. She resides in upstate New York, where she was born and raised. She strongly believes in the beauty of an excellent glass of wine, a good scary movie, and the unconditional love of a dog. Fall is her very favorite season.

She is currently hard at work on her next book. You can visit her and find out more at www.georgiabeers.com or search her on Patreon.

Books Available From Bold Strokes Books

An Extraordinary Passion by Kit Meredith. An autistic podcaster must decide whether to take a chance on her polyamorous guest and indulge their shared passion, despite her history. (978-1-63679-679-6)

Heart's Appraisal by Jo Hemmingwood. Andy and Hazel can't deny their attraction, but they'll never agree on the place they call home. (978-1-63679-856-1)

That's Amore by Georgia Beers. The romantic city of Rome should inspire Lily's passion for writing, if she can look away from Marina Troiani, her witty, smart, and unassumingly beautiful Italian tour guide. (978-1-63679-841-7)

Through Sky and Stars by Tessa Croft. Can Val and Nicole's love cross space and time to change the fate of humanity? (978-1-63679-862-2)

Uncomplicate It by Kel McCord. When an office attraction threatens her career, Hollis Reed's carefully laid plans demand revision. (978-1-63679-864-6)

The Unexpected Heiress by Cassidy Crane. When a cynical opportunist meets a shy but spirited heiress, the last thing she plans is for her heart to get involved. (978-1-63679-833-2)

Vanguard by Gun Brooke. Beth Wild, Subterranean freedom fighter, is in the crosshairs when she fights for her people and risks her heart for loving the exacting Celestial dissident leader, LaSierra Delmonte. (978-1-63679-818-9)

Wild Night Rising by Barbara Ann Wright. Riding Harleys instead of horses, the Wild Hunt of myth is once again unleashed upon the world. Their ousted leader and a fey cop must join forces to rein in the ride of terror. (978-1-63679-749-6)

A Thousand Tiny Promises by Morgan Lee Miller. When estranged childhood friends Audrey and Reid reunite to fulfill their best friend's dying wish, the last thing they expect is a journey toward healing their broken friendship and discovering a newfound love for each other. (978-1-63679-630-7)

Behold My Heart by Ronica Black. Alora Anders is a highly successful artist who's losing her vision. Devastated, she hires Bodie Banks, a young struggling sculptor, as a live-in assistant. Can Alora open her mind and her heart to accept Bodie into her life? (978-1-63679-810-3)

Fearless Hearts by Radclyffe. One wounded woman, one determined to protect her—and a summertime of risk, danger, and desire. (978-1-63679-837-0)

Stranger in the Sand by Renee Roman. Grace Langley is haunted by guilt. Fagan Shaw wishes she could remember her past. Will finding each other bring the closure they're looking for in order to have a brighter future? (978-1-63679-802-8)

The Nursing Home Hoax by Shelley Thrasher and Ann Faulkner. In this fresh take for grown-ups on the classic Nancy Drew series, crime-solving duo Taylor and Marilee investigate suspicious activity at a small East Texas nursing home. (978-1-63679-806-6)

The Rise and Fall of Conner Cody by Chelsey Lynford. A successful yet lonely Hollywood starlet must decide if she can let go of old wounds and accept a chance at family, friendship, and the love of a lifetime. (978-1-63679-739-7)

A Conflict of Interest by Morgan Adams. Tensions rise when a one-night stand becomes a major conflict of interest between an up-and-coming senior associate and a dedicated cardiac surgeon. (978-1-63679-870-7)

A Magnificent Disturbance by Lee Lynch. These everyday dykes and their friends will stop at nothing to see the women's clinic thrive and, in the process, their ideals, their wounds, and a steadfast allegiance to one another make them heroes. (978-1-63679-031-2)

Big Corpse on Campus by Karis Walsh. When University Police Officer Cappy Flannery investigates what looks like a clear-cut suicide, she discovers that the case—and her feelings for librarian Jazz—are more complicated than she expected. (978-1-63679-852-3)